BURLINGAME PUBLIC LIBRARY
480 PRIMROSE ROAD
BURLINGAME, CA 94

P9-CNA-966

SLICKROCK

Also by Laura Crum

Roped
Roughstock
Hoofprints
Cutter

SLICKROCK

LAURA CRUM

THOMAS DUNNE BOOKS
ST. MARTIN'S MINOTAUR
NEW YORK

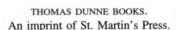

THOMAS DUNNE BOOKS.
An imprint of St. Martin's Press.

SLICKROCK. Copyright © 1999 by Laura Crum. All rights reserved. Printed in the United States of America. No part of this
book may be used or reproduced in any manner whatsoever
without written permission except in the case of brief quotations
embodied in critical articles or reviews. For information, address
St. Martin's Press, 175 Fifth Avenue, New York, N.Y. 10010.

"Ramblin' Jack & Mahan." Words and music by Guy Clark
and Richard Leigh. Copyright © 1992 EMI April Music Inc.,
GSC Music, Lion-Hearted Music. All rights controlled and ad-
ministered by EMI April Music Inc. All rights reserved. Inter-
national copyright secured. Used by permission.

Library of Congress Cataloging-in-Publication Data

Crum, Laura.
    Slickrock : a Gail McCarthy mystery / Laura Crum.—1st
St. Martin's Minotaur ed.
        p.   cm.
    "Thomas Dunne Books."
    ISBN 0-312-20910-X
    I. Title
PS3553.R76S55   1999
813'.54—dc21   99-15948
                                                        CIP

First Edition: November 1999

10   9   8   7   6   5   4   3   2   1

For Andy Snow, allways.

Thanks to Wally Evans, Carl Dobler, and Bill Crum, who helped organize many mountain pack trips, and to Willie Ritts, Matt Bloom, and all the crew at Kennedy Meadows—a constant inspiration.

Thanks also to Dr. Craig Evans, D.V.M.

And especially, thanks to my mother, Joan Awbrey Brown, who encouraged me to write this story.

AUTHOR'S NOTE

The Sierra Nevada Mountains of California are very real, as are the lakes, rivers, and peaks of the area around Sonora Pass, where this book is set. I have visited most of the places described in the story, but they have been rearranged and sometimes changed to fit the purposes of the plot, and the descriptions and locations of various lakes and passes, etc., are not always accurate. Though the pack station described in this book may resemble a real pack station in many respects, it—and its crew and visitors—is entirely a figment of my imagination. Happy trails!

"Jack, as far as I can see
mistakes are only horses in disguise
ain't no need to ride 'em over
'cause we could not ride them different if we tried."

> —Guy Clark, quoting bronc rider Larry Mahan,
> in the song "Ramblin' Jack & Mahan"

SLICKROCK

PROLOGUE

It all started with the dead man in Deadman Meadow. Not the original dead man, of course. An unfortunate emigrant who came west in the 1800s, the first victim met his unspecified end in one particular meadow along Crazy Horse Creek in the Sierra Nevada Mountains of California. The place thereafter recalled his fate; I always wondered if the naming of the creek and the meadow were related.

But it was the second dead man who changed my world. Or rather, the events that followed in his wake. Until I came upon him, I thought I knew the direction my life would take; afterwards, I found that the only thing I knew was that I did not know. Knowing is much more comfortable than not knowing, and I can't exactly say I'm happy about that eventful summer and the upheaval it caused. Yet I can't really regret it either. Who would not move closer to the truth?

ONE

The roan colt rocketed around the bullpen, making every jump high, wide, and handsome. Stirrups swung wildly, latigos popped and slapped, leather squeaked with strain. The colt grunted, head down between his knees, and put all his effort into stiffening his front legs and kicking his back feet as high as possible. I stood outside the bullpen and watched Ted Reiter watch the colt.

Ted was in the middle of the pen, a short, stocky figure wearing dirty jeans and a white straw cowboy hat. He watched the colt buck with the empty saddle on his back and spat out some tobacco juice. Ted didn't look like the boss of a big outfit; he looked like another dirt-poor ranch cowboy. But appearances were misleading in his case.

The colt was getting mad. He was determined to rid himself of the saddle that had been cinched so uncomfortably around his belly, he had made every effort to do so, and the saddle was still there. He bucked harder and began to squeal—grunting squeals, like a pig. His eyes had a blind look. Ted dodged out of the horse's way when the roan bucked in his direction.

Not exactly an easygoing colt, was my thought. Oh well, he wasn't my business. My business was finding a vodka tonic. I'd had a long day, and I was ready for a drink. I waved a casual hand at Ted and headed down the hill toward the bar.

It was six o'clock on a July evening in the Sierra Nevada Mountains of California. This time of year Deadman Meadow was brilliantly green. It stretched out in front of the Crazy Horse Creek Pack Station like a patch of the Emerald Isle itself. The little bar sat facing the meadow, a small shack of a place with a porch all along the front. I pushed open the door and went inside.

Six o'clock on a Friday evening in July meant the Crazy Horse Creek Bar was fairly crowded. I found a gap and ordered my drink from the bartender.

Talk rose around me like bubbles through tonic.

"Did you see the bay son of a bitch Charley was riding?"

"I swear to God he caught a fifteen-inch brookie out of Kennedy Lake."

Horse talk, fisherman talk. I sipped slowly and let the talk and laughter swirl and fizz around me. Like Ted's roan colt, it wasn't my business.

This turned out to be a mistake. When you're sitting in a bar full of drunks it pays to stay alert. But I was absorbed in my own thoughts and didn't see it coming.

The first clue I got was when the stranger on my left pushed me hard against the bar and shoved his body in front of me. My angry "What the hell" was swallowed up in a jolt of surprise as I felt the secondhand impact of the drunk on my right, who catapulted into my benefactor (as I now realized), who in turn launched the drunk into the open area in the middle of the bar. Scuffling and shouting rattled around me.

In a minute I pieced it together. Two of the fairly drunken fishermen in the group to my right had gotten in an argument and were now engaged in the sort of shoving match of a fight that drunks usually pursue. The original attack had thrown the one guy in my direction, and the solitary man on my left had seen him coming and fended him off. At this point my rescuer stepped away from me and resumed his place at the bar; the fight, if you wanted to call it that, was moving out into the parking lot.

"Thanks," I said, looking up at him.

"No problem. I didn't want to see you get run over."

This man was big. I'm five-foot-seven and he looked to be about a foot taller. Wide shoulders, too, although he was fairly lean. I could see why he wouldn't have a problem defending strange women from drunks. Some sort of further politeness seemed to be called for.

"I'm Gail McCarthy." I held out my hand.

"Blue. Blue Winter," he said, a little sheepishly. His hand felt surprisingly fine-boned and slender.

"Do you know those guys?" I asked, gesturing in the direction of the shoving group at the doorway.

"No."

Polite conversation was proving difficult. Blue Winter (could that possibly be his real name?) stared at his drink. Not only was he roughly six-and-a-half feet tall, he had red hair and wore a gray felt hat somewhere between a cowboy hat and a fedora. Regulation Wrangler jeans, a faded denim shirt, and cowboy boots completed the effect. He looked exactly like the "tall red-headed stranger" in Willie Nelson's song.

I tried again. "Are you here for a pack trip?"

"Yes, I am."

"The pack station taking you in?" I asked.

"No, I'm packing myself."

My ears pricked up. "So am I."

He looked directly at me for the first time. "Are you with a group?"

"No, I'm going alone."

"So am I."

We looked at each other with mutual curiosity. The bar fight still seemed to be going full swing in the parking lot; at least, there was a fair amount of shouting outside. The bar, however, was relatively empty, most everyone having dashed out the door, either to participate or to spectate. Blue Winter and I were surrounded by vacant bar stools.

"So have you packed in the mountains much?" Blue Winter's shyness or reticence or whatever it was seemed to have been swallowed up by his curiosity. Gray eyes regarded me steadily from under the brim of his hat.

"Well, no, I haven't," I admitted. Knowing what was going through his mind, I added, "I'm pretty well prepared for this trip, though."

He watched me quietly, and I had the sense he was wondering what to say. I decided to help him. "Have you done a lot of packing?"

"Yes, ma'am."

"Any advice for a novice?"

He smiled. Immediately I liked him. He had crooked teeth and kind eyes, and when he smiled his somewhat somber expression became shy and friendly.

The smile receded and his face was once again reserved.

"Sometimes you need to doctor a horse," he said.

My turn to smile. "I'm a vet," I said.

As I expected, a brief flicker of surprise in his eyes. Women vets aren't uncommon anymore, but still, I often caught that look. "A horse vet," I added. "I'm from Santa Cruz."

At this, he looked startled. Then that charming, unaffected smile. "You must be Jim Leonard's lady vet."

"That's me," I agreed. Jim was my boss. "How did you know?"

"I'm from Watsonville."

Watsonville was maybe thirty minutes from Santa Cruz. The same neck of the woods, in other words.

"So if you're from Watsonville, and I take it you have horses, you must use Bob Barton."

"That's right."

"Bob's a good guy." This was professional courtesy; in my opinion Jim was a vastly superior horse vet. Bob Barton was mainly a small-animal practitioner who did horses on the side. He *was* a nice guy, though.

"So, what are you doing here at Crazy Horse Creek, about to take off in the mountains on your own?" It was the most forthcoming question Blue Winter had asked yet, and I couldn't think of a simple answer.

Crazy Horse Creek Pack Station was five hours from my home on the coast of California. I had never taken my two horses on a pack trip before, though I had done some solitary backpacking up in these mountains during my college years. However, I hadn't been camping in any way, shape, or form for many seasons; the three-week vacation I was currently indulging in was the first time off of any length I'd had since I started working as a veterinarian five years ago. So, what exactly was I doing here, preparing to take my two flatland horses over the granite of four High Sierra passes on a two-week expedition?

I decided to cut to the chase. "Well, the reason I'm here, specifically, is my boyfriend used to own this pack station, and the people who run it were willing to put me and my horses up for a few days while we got acclimated."

He took that in. "Your boyfriend must be Lonny Peterson."

"That's right."

"I know Lonny a little."

I changed the subject. "So, how about a few tips for a beginner."

He was quiet, considering. "Well, you obviously know how

to take care of your horses, and I guess you must have some idea about camping, or you wouldn't be going.''

I didn't respond to this, and I could sense him sizing me up, looking me over the way a man will size up a horse. I tried to imagine what he was seeing.

A tallish woman in her mid-thirties, with dark hair in a braid, olive skin, wide shoulders and hips, long legs. I wore a T-shirt, jeans and boots, hoop earrings in my ears, no other jewelry. I weigh about 140—not fat, but not thin either.

"You look strong enough," he said.

I laughed. "Why, thanks."

He smiled. "To deal with the packing. That's hard, when you're alone."

I nodded. "Uh-huh."

It had been my main problem. I was packing Plumber, my younger horse, and he and I had learned the routine of putting on the pack rig fairly easily. Plumber hadn't minded the back cinch, or the crupper under his tail, or the wooden forks straddling his back. But he hadn't been crazy about my lifting the heavily loaded panniers up onto him.

Docile as always, his only expression of objection had been to sidestep away, but since I had a hard time lifting the pack bags up at all, it had proven virtually impossible to get the straps over the forks that were to hold them unless Plumber stood perfectly still. Thus, we had practiced the routine of packing over and over again, with many reprimands for moving.

Plumber had learned. His name wasn't Plumb Smart for nothing.

"I had to work at that," I told Blue Winter. "My pack horse is only about fifteen hands," I added. "That helps."

"What kind of horses are you taking in?" he asked.

"Well, they're Quarter Horses."

He nodded. Many, if not most, western riding horses in California were American Quarter Horses.

"I've used the saddle horse as a team roping horse, mostly. The pack horse used to be a bridle horse, a show horse, before I got him."

Another abbreviated story. Gunner and Plumber, my two horses, with their complex histories and equally intricate personalities, had been a big part of what my life was about for many years.

"So, how about you?" I asked. "How do you come to be here?"

"Oh, I come here every year." His face looked withdrawn.

"You take your own horses?"

"Yes, ma'am." No further information forthcoming.

I half shrugged. If he didn't want to answer questions, that was no skin off my back. The conversation had gone on long enough for politeness. Trouble was, I was in this bar waiting for Lonny, and he still hadn't shown up. Oh well. I could look for him later.

"Speaking of horses, I guess I'll go check on mine." I held out my hand. "Nice to meet you."

Blue Winter took my hand in his oddly long, slender one. "Likewise," he said.

Nice man, I thought, as I left the bar. Quiet, though.

Stepping out the door I took a deep breath of the cold-water, pine-tree scent. It was a sunny summer evening, and I happen to think that such evenings in a Sierra meadow are perhaps the prettiest things on earth. I don't know what it is—the generous gold of the light, the contrast of soft green meadow grass against hard silver-gray granite ridges, the smell of the mountains, the lively voice of the creeks. It filled me right up with happiness, just being there.

Taking another deep breath, I strolled toward the horse corrals, reviewing with pleasure the proposed events of the next couple of weeks. I had arrived here this afternoon, horse trailer in tow, prepared to meet Lonny and spend the weekend with him here at the pack station. Tomorrow we had plans to take a short ride, Sunday I would rest, and on Monday ride in on my solitary two-week excursion. This trip was the result of a year of planning on my part, and I felt a deep sense of anticipation and excitement that it was happening at last.

As for where Lonny was at the moment—"out for a ride," the bartender had said. Ernie, the bartender, tended to use as few words as possible; I hadn't pressed him. Lonny and I had agreed to meet in the bar Friday evening before dinner—no doubt he would show up eventually.

A familiar nicker rang out as I neared the corrals. Plumber. My younger horse was a talker. He constantly nickered at me—when he was tied to the rail waiting, while I saddled him, whenever I approached his corral, even occasionally when he saw me in the midst of a group of people.

Walking toward him now, I smiled. His head was thrust out between the bars of the corral where I had put him and Gunner, his eyes bright and inquiring. "So there you are," he seemed to say. "What's up, what are we going to do?"

Gunner, in contrast, had his head down, munching on the hay I had put in the corral. He glanced up and over his shoulder at me, snorted softly, and went back to eating. I had been using Gunner as my main saddle horse for several years now, and he knew the score. We were here to work, no doubt in his mind. Best for him to eat while he could.

I leaned on the fence for a moment, watching them. Gunner, at 15.3 hands, was fairly tall and leggy for a Quarter Horse. He had a bright bay coat, three high white socks, a big blaze, and one blue eye. Plain-headed and big-boned, his friendly, clownish expression made him appealing.

Plumber, on the other hand, was almost cute. Smaller than Gunner, he was finer-boned, with rounder muscling, and he had a little breedy head. Cocoa-brown in color, with a small white spot right between his bright, mischievous eyes, and the sort

of personality that caused him to thrust his head into your lap—
Plumber was a real puppy dog of a horse.

I rubbed his forehead for a minute, told him to go back to
his dinner, and turned away. The horses were fine.

Next stop—the pickup. It was parked nearby, my brand new
acquisition—the very first new truck I'd ever purchased. A gray
Dodge, it had four-wheel drive, an automatic transmission
(good for hauling horses), and an extended cab (good for piling
junk in). It also had a camper on the bed. For Roey.

A short, excited yip emanated from the camper as I approached. I'd been spotted.

Sharply pricked red ears pointed at me through the screened
windows of the camper. Heavy-duty metal screen, I might add.
Roey had destroyed the light nylon screens that had come with
the shell months before.

I had hopes that at a year old my young dog's destructive
impulses were diminishing. It was debatable, though. I had
taken the pup last summer; she was a purebred Queensland
heeler, bred by a friend of mine. I liked both the parent dogs,
I missed my old dog, Blue, who was also a Queensland, and I
thought I was ready to raise a pup. I'd simply forgotten just
what that entailed.

Blue had died a couple of years ago at the age of fifteen, so
it had been many years indeed since I'd dealt with a puppy. I
was accustomed to a dog who understood what I was saying
to him, who knew my ways (and human ways in general),
and who obeyed me (albeit with a lot of grumbling). I was
now faced with a fluffy bundle of energy who had no clue
what I wanted in the way of behavior, and who had a strong
desire to tear things up with her teeth. Any things. Not to
mention, she saw no reason why she should not defecate
wherever the impulse took her, or why she should follow my
arbitrary orders. She was, like most Queenslands, smart, stubborn, and endearing.

I opened the door of the camper and rubbed the wide, wedge-shaped head that was thrust over the tailgate at me. Roey wagged her tail frantically and wiggled all over. I ran my hand down her back. Roey was a red heeler, like her mother, Rita, and with her small size and her pricked ears, I often thought she looked just like a little red fox.

She reminded me of my old dog, Blue, in being very intelligent and incredibly hard-headed, but unlike Blue, Roey was generally friendly. She liked people, and other dogs, and cats, and for that matter, the whole world, as far as I could tell. Lonny teased me that she'd never make a watchdog; she'd probably try to inveigle potential burglars into throwing a stick for her. This was true. After Blue's protective tendencies I found Roey's amiable nature somewhat of a relief. No more worrying that my dog would nip (and mortally offend) a client.

A few more pats, a check to see that her water and food bowls were full, and I shut Roey back in the camper. I'd taken her for a run when I first got here; she should be fine for the night.

So where the hell was Lonny? Out for a ride. But the sun was sitting right on top of the western ridge at this point, and nobody had come riding in down the trail for the last hour.

Lonny knew he was meeting me tonight. So why wasn't he here? Annoyance and worry struggled for dominance in my brain.

Well, neither of those emotions was going to help anything. I stared off across Deadman Meadow, already in shade. Crazy Horse Creek ran along its far side, as I knew. And right where the creek emerged from the canyon and rushed out into the meadow was a pretty little waterfall. I'd just walk quietly up and check out the waterfall. Spend a moment enjoying the mountains. If Lonny rode in, he'd know I was here—horses in the corral, rig parked nearby. We'd find each other.

Resolved, I headed off down the trail that crossed the

meadow, looking around with a deep sigh of relief. I was here, at last, about to achieve a goal I'd held all my life. I was going to spend a sizable chunk of time in these mountains all alone, with just my horses and my dog for company.

The farther I walked into Deadman Meadow, the more the busy bustle of the pack station receded and I could feel the presence of the mountains around me. Granite and pine tree–clad ridges rose up all about me; the meadow was springy under my feet. Ahead of me the chatter of Crazy Horse Creek grew louder. In another few strides the bright water was visible, jumping and chasing between boulders.

I followed a faint trail that led upstream, worn by the feet of many fishermen over many seasons. The creek got noisier and noisier as I neared the canyon from which it emerged.

It was dusk now. The air was soft and still and dim—with every moment that passed, the shapes around me dissolved further. I could see the lights of the pack station across the meadow. Wondered if Lonny had come in yet. Don't worry, I told myself, Lonny's had more experience in the mountains than anyone you know.

Still, I peered hopefully through the gathering darkness at the big barn, although it was impossible to see anything as small as an individual horse and rider from here. And even less possible along the unlighted main trail, though I traced its course along the far side of the meadow. I could see a white horse, maybe.

In point of fact, I saw nothing. I scanned the meadow one more time, started to turn away, and stopped. There was something out there. Something shiny. A car.

The car was behind a clump of willows that screened it completely from the pack station and the main trail. It was partially obscured, but visible from where I stood on the banks of the creek. Small and low and dark, some sort of sports car, it had only caught my eye due to the sheen of light reflecting off its metal surface. It was pretty damn well hidden.

This, I supposed, was because it shouldn't be there. The Forest Service did not allow cars to be driven out into the meadow. However, the big gate that blocked such vehicles from the main trail was often left open so that various ranger Jeeps, or pack station trucks, could go up to the ranger station at Bright Water Flat, a couple of miles up the trail. The gate had been open this afternoon, I recalled. But duly posted with many signs declaring it off-limits to cars.

Well, this car had clearly ignored them. I guessed it belonged to a particularly lazy fisherman, and wondered briefly if it was now stuck. The meadow was damp in spots and the car didn't look the sort to have four-wheel drive.

It was possible. And the light was dying fast. If I wanted to reach my destination, a mere hundred yards away up this canyon, I'd better go.

I turned and headed for the waterfall.

TWO

Twenty minutes later, when I got back to the meadow, it was almost dark and the car was still there. Knowing where to look was the only thing that made it visible.

I stopped and studied it in mild consternation. What in the world was it doing here? Was it, in fact, stuck?

I had a small penlight in my pocket (as well as a Swiss Army knife and a waterproof container of matches). Perhaps I should go and see.

Ten steps in the direction of the car and I stopped. Was this smart? I was a woman alone; I had no idea what the car was here for. On the other hand, I argued, I was perfectly safe skulking out here in the dark willows. No one who was in the car would be able to see me without a light.

Cautiously I approached the vehicle from the rear, out of headlight range, my hand on my own small flashlight. No humans seemed to be about; the car looked deserted. But it also looked too expensive to be cavalierly abandoned.

From twenty feet away, I stared. It was some kind of two-seater sports car; I couldn't put a name to it. No movement in it, or around it. My eyes tracked along the ground nearby. A patch of white. Not large. Bigger than a paper bag, smaller than a picnic blanket. Next to the car, about ten feet from the front bumper. I stared. The white thing didn't move.

Cautiously I brought the flashlight out of my pocket. Wiggling gently behind a sheltering screen of willow branches, I aimed it at the white shape and clicked it on.

For a second I still couldn't figure it out. White cloth, it looked like; I moved the light. And something darker. A face. Shit.

The white was a shirt, a shirt that was on a man lying flat on his back in the meadow.

I clicked the flashlight off. This was weird.

Peering through the near-dark, I ascertained that the man hadn't moved. I mentally replayed what I'd seen. A man lying flat on his back—I'd had a brief glimpse of his face, staring upward. No one I recognized.

Was he hurt? Dead? Asleep? Drunk?

I clicked the light on again. The grass and willow branches obscured him somewhat, but there was no doubt of what I was seeing.

Pointing the flashlight right at his face, I looked for signs of life. For a second, nothing. Then the face turned slowly toward my light. I couldn't read his expression.

I hesitated. Before I could make up my mind what to do, the man sat up.

Big, dark blotches all over the front of his white shirt. What? No. Yes. Blood. Dark red blotches. Blood, or something like it.

"Leave me alone," he said.

My mind spun.

He lay back down.

Now what the hell was I supposed to do? Could it really have been blood on his shirt front?

15

I kept the flashlight on his face. Thought about it. Then I shouted, "Do you need help?"

No response. And then, slowly, he sat up again, looking in my direction. "Leave me alone," he said again. And then quite distinctly, "I'm trying to kill myself."

Once again, he lay back. Shit, shit, shit. This time I was sure the dark red blotches were blood. "I'm trying to kill myself," he had said. I played the flashlight on the ground around him. In a moment, I caught the dull flash of reflected light off the blued barrel.

A gun. Lying on the ground near his right hand. Within reach of his hand. If I approached him, he could shoot at me.

I trained the flashlight back on his face. "I'll get help," I shouted.

This time he spoke without moving, and I had a harder time making out his words. "No, no help. Don't want help."

"Just hang in there," I said, using my strongest reassuring-veterinarian tone. "I'll help you."

"No. Leave me alone. No help. Let me die."

I tried to decide what to do. If I went near this guy, he could potentially shoot me, though he had made no move toward the gun so far. I had no idea if he was dying, or if there was anything I could do immediately that would help him. Get some help, I thought. Don't get yourself shot for no good reason.

"Listen," I yelled at him, "I'm going to get help. Just hang in there. You'll be okay."

"No, please." He didn't move; I thought his voice was weaker. "Don't try to help me. I'm dying. I want to die. Like the horses."

"Like the horses?" I repeated, startled.

"Dying." He stared straight up at the night sky. "Green fire in their bellies. I couldn't save them. Dying."

This made no sense to me. "I'll be back," I yelled. "Please. Just hang in there." Then I turned and ran.

Running through the dark, to the jouncy, jerking beam of the flashlight, running down the trail. I could see the pack station lights ahead of me, across the meadow; they seemed a long way away. I stuck to the trail; I could run faster on the trail than I could through the meadow.

All I could hear was the thump of my feet, the panting of my breath. Hurry, hurry.

The lights across the meadow flickered and bounced to the rhythm of my feet, the bob of my head. Faster, a little faster, I urged my body. I kept my eyes on the trail as it flared and faded before me in the flashlight's lurching beam.

Even as I ran, I planned. I would go straight to the bar; someone would be there, there was a phone there. God, what in hell was that man doing out in the meadow? Why shoot himself there, of all places?

Hurry, hurry. I was tiring; my breath came in gasps. Find the rhythm, keep breathing, keep running, I chanted to myself. Keep your eyes on the trail, keep moving, keep running.

I looked up. The pack station was closer. Eyes back on the trail, I forced myself to put one foot in front of the other in a steady rhythm.

A man with blood all over his shirt front, lying on his back in Deadman Meadow, wanting to die. Had he picked this spot to shoot himself because of the damn name?

Come on, Gail, I urged myself. Move it a little. Save this guy's life for him.

I could see the bar, with the long porch across the front of it. Not so far now. God, I was out of breath, though. I was really out of shape.

Closer, closer, almost there. The meadow was soggy, almost boggy, here; my feet squished and stuck a little. I could feel moisture seeping through my boots.

No matter. The lights were in front of me, the parking lot, the cars. Gasping for air, I pounded across the dark road—

17

empty of tourists, for once—up the wooden steps, across the porch, and through the open door of the bar.

Lights, noise, faces, confusion. My eyes struggled to adjust to the bright light; all faces looked my way. And then I saw Lonny.

Standing at the bar with Ted, I registered. Turning toward me with a look of welcome changing to concern.

"Gail, what's wrong?"

He took three fast steps toward me, put his hand on my arm.

"A man . . . shot himself . . . still alive . . . in the upper meadow." I said it between pants.

Lonny had never been slow. "Damn. Go get the Jeep," he ordered one of the boys. "Pick us up along the trail. Bring the first-aid kit. We're headed up there." He turned to Ted. "Better call the ambulance, and the sheriff."

"I think," I gasped, "he's going to need a chopper."

Ted nodded. "Okay." Then he headed for the phone.

"Come on, Gail, show me where." Lonny had hold of my arm.

"He's got a gun," I said.

"Ernie." Lonny held out his left hand.

Without a word Ernie produced a short shotgun from under the bar and handed it over the counter to Lonny.

"Okay. Let's go," Lonny said.

"Okay."

I started out of the bar, still panting, but a little better for the rest. I could keep going until the Jeep picked us up.

Lonny had the long stride of a six-foot-plus man, and despite the fact that he walked rather than ran across the parking lot and down the main trail, I had to jog every few steps to keep up.

Before he'd had time to ask me more than, "So just where is this guy?" we could hear the noise of the Jeep behind us. Headlight glow lit the trail as Jake, one of Ted's crew, pulled the vehicle up beside us.

18

As we climbed in, I told Lonny, "Behind some willows at the far end of the upper meadow. His car's out there. Some sort of black sports car."

I could barely see Lonny's face in the peripheral glow of the headlights; he looked strained and tired. And old, I thought.

Well, he was fifty-one. Considerably older than I was. But until recently I'd always thought he looked young for his age.

"So, did you recognize this guy?" he asked.

"No." I thought about it. "He had dark hair, sort of an aquiline nose. He'd be about your age."

We were bouncing along the trail now. Lonny asked Jake, "Did you bring the first-aid kit?"

"Yeah. And three flashlights." Jake was all of sixteen, but, like most of the crew, he had already picked up Ted's laconic way of speaking. He said nothing more, just kept manhandling the Jeep over and around boulders, jolting up the trail.

When I judged we'd gone far enough, I said, "Stop."

Jake stopped.

"See if you can get the headlights pointed out into the meadow."

Jake began jockeying the car; Lonny and I were already scanning with the flashlights.

In a second I saw the sharp reflected gleam. "There."

"Take it as far as you can without getting stuck," Lonny told Jake.

Then he was out of the Jeep, with me scrambling to follow him, and we were both half walking, half running through the meadow grass and low willow scrub toward the car.

"He has a gun," I reminded Lonny.

"Did he threaten you with it?"

"No, but that doesn't mean he won't."

Lonny grunted. We both kept moving. Until, about twenty feet from the car, he stopped. "You wait here," he told me.

"What are you talking about? I'm not going to stand back here watching while somebody shoots you."

"Gail, will you for once in your life do what you're told? Especially when it makes sense. Why should we both get shot? Now stay here." And he walked off.

I stayed. What the hell. He was right, more or less. I kept my flashlight on the car. From this angle I couldn't see the man, but I knew about where he was.

Lonny moved cautiously forward; I could see him sweeping the ground with his flashlight beam. In the other hand he held the shotgun loosely. He stepped quietly around the front of the car, stopped, stepped forward again, and stopped.

"My God," he said. "It's Bill."

THREE

D o you know him?''

"Yeah, yeah I do. It's Bill Evans. He was my vet."

"Your vet?" I walked toward Lonny.

He bent down; I saw him come up holding the pistol.

"While I was running this pack station; he's Ted's vet now. Or was."

Lonny handed the pistol and the shotgun to me and bent down again, pressing his fingers under the man's jaw. No response from the recumbent figure. He was either unconscious or dead.

"He's got a pulse," Lonny said.

We both stared at the big, dark blotches on the white shirt front, the still face. Bill Evans didn't appear to be bleeding heavily.

"Is there a blanket in the Jeep?" I asked.

"Should be."

I could hear Jake slowly piloting the Jeep toward us around scrub, boulders, and wet spots.

"I guess all I know to do is keep him warm, maybe try to put some pressure on the wound if it's still actively bleeding."

"Yeah." Lonny looked stunned; he stared down at the man as if he couldn't believe what he was seeing. "Jesus," he said quietly. "Bill."

"So why would try he to kill himself?" I asked.

"I don't know. But he has been acting real strange. He was up here last night, got drunk and obnoxious, and Ted threw him out of the bar. Jesus."

The Jeep was behind us now; Lonny yelled, "Bring a blanket."

In a minute Jake stood beside me, staring down at Bill Evans. I handed him the guns and took the wool blanket out of his hands. Jake didn't say a word. Bending down, I covered the man's legs with the blanket. Gingerly, I explored with my fingers the wet red spot in the center of the chest. Seeping. Not much of a hole. The pistol had been a .22, I recalled. The bullet appeared to have gone right into the sternum. Whether it had hit the heart or lungs I had no idea. Probably not the heart, or the guy would be dead by now.

"Get the first-aid kit," I told Jake.

He headed back toward the Jeep; I looked up to see Lonny still staring blankly downward. "What's the matter?" I asked.

He shook his head. "I just can't believe it," he said slowly. And then, "My father killed himself."

"He did?" I hadn't known this.

"He shot himself. In the head. I found him." Lonny recited these facts quietly enough, but I sensed that the emotions behind them were roiling wildly through his mind.

"It's okay," I said soothingly. "This guy's alive. I can see Ted coming," I added.

Sure enough, headlights were bouncing along the main trail—Ted or somebody.

Jake handed me the first-aid kit; I opened it and began making a pad with gauze and cotton. This I pressed firmly against the wound. Lonny and Jake stood over me, wordless.

After a few minutes two others joined them. I looked up. Ted and Jake's older brother, Luke.

"My God." Ted's voice. Pain and shock were plain.

I had never heard Ted Reiter express so much raw emotion. About my age, Ted was short, stocky and stout, with a round face, guileless blue eyes, a boyish manner. Lonny had taken him on as a hired hand when Ted was seventeen, then, later, as a business partner. Now Ted was sole owner of the pack station. But you'd never know it to look at him. Wearing dirty jeans and denim jacket, usually messing with a horse or flirting with a girl—that was Ted. And despite his unlikely looks, quite the lady-killer.

But now, in this moment, he looked as devastated as Lonny looked stunned.

"Not Bill," he said. "He couldn't."

Luke and Jake were silent. Lonny put a hand on Ted's shoulder.

Some dark emotion seemed to twine through the little group of men. Not grief, not shock, though they were present, too. Something blacker. I could feel it, but I didn't understand it. I wasn't part of it. I hadn't known this man.

After a minute Ted said quietly, "Chopper's coming. Is he still alive?"

"Yeah," I said.

"Better get out in the meadow with the flashlights," Lonny said to Luke and Jake.

"Come on." Ted turned abruptly. "That chopper will be here soon."

The three of them hurried away; setting up guide points for a helicopter to land in the dark was familiar to them. All serious

23

medical emergencies had to be carried out of these mountains by the medevac helicopter. Other methods were prohibitively time-consuming.

"So, what's the deal here?" I asked Lonny. "You all knew this guy, I take it."

"Everybody knew him. He was up here all the time. I'm surprised you never met him."

"I've only been up here on the occasional weekend in the summer." I pressed the pad gently against the man's chest.

"Bill was virtually part of the crew," Lonny said. "He's been the vet for us up here ever since I owned the place. We all knew him real well."

"So, what was going on with him that he would shoot himself?"

"I'm not sure," Lonny said. "Bill would get depressed. He had these bouts of depression every few years. And he tended to drink when he was in one. It made for problems."

"I can see that."

"His wife left him a few years ago, I think because of his drinking. He's been worse ever since. But I had no idea he was thinking of killing himself."

"No," I said.

"Damn, Gail, I wish I'd known." Lonny sounded sad and ashamed; I thought I could guess what it was that had been in the air as the men looked down at their friend. Guilt. They all felt guilty that he had come to this and that they hadn't known, hadn't helped him.

"Ted threw him out of the bar last night because he was trying to pick fights with the customers. Told him to go sleep it off. Damn."

"Where did he stay?"

"In the lodge."

Faintly, in the distance, I heard a steady *thump, thump, thump*. Lonny heard it, too.

"Here they come."

I pressed my fingers to the man's carotid artery. The pulse was there, thin but steady.

"He's still alive," I said.

The thumping grew louder; I could see the lights of the helicopter in the western sky. Ted and the boys were out in the meadow, waving their flashlights. Steadily the chopper approached, seeming to know where it was headed.

In a minute the noise was overwhelming—*whump, whump, whump*. Floodlights came on in the undercarriage as it hovered over the meadow, and the night receded instantly. The mountains seemed to disappear in harsh white light and the gigantic pounding heartbeat of the blades.

No point in talking; we couldn't have heard each other. Lonny and I stood in silence, watching the odd scene. Slowly the chopper lowered itself in a blaze of light and loud, whirling wind. Willows and grass bent away in waves as the machine touched down on the ground.

The intense noise diminished to an idle; the blades rotated gently; two men in white coats jumped out the door and ran toward Ted, who waved them on and turned in our direction. Help had arrived.

Twenty minutes later, Bill Evans was on a stretcher in the belly of the helicopter as the beast lifted off in the same flurry of noise with which it had arrived. Bill was still alive, they said. When asked if he would make it, they shrugged.

Ted and Lonny and I stood together watching the chopper disappear into the night sky. Luke approached and tapped Ted on the shoulder.

"The sheriffs are here," he said. "They want to ask you some questions."

FOUR

Two sheriff's deputies, as it turned out, a man and a woman. We all trooped back to the lodge, and over cups of coffee in the lobby, they questioned the five of us who had gone up to the meadow.

It wasn't terribly formal. They listened carefully to my recitation of how I had found the man, and the female deputy asked me, "He definitely said he was trying to kill himself?"

"Yes, several times. He said he wanted to be let alone to die." I didn't look at Lonny or Ted as I said this.

"Did he say anything else?"

"He talked about dying horses. At the time, it didn't make any sense to me, but now that I know he was a vet, I wonder if he wasn't talking about treating some colicked horses that died."

Both deputies nodded, apparently familiar enough with horses to understand this statement. This wasn't entirely surprising. They were from Sonora, which has the notion that it's a cowboy town; many people from that part of the world have some understanding of horses, and usually pretend to more.

"Did you see him shoot himself?" the woman deputy asked me. She was apparently the leader of the team, or at least the talker.

"No. Nor did I hear it. When I first saw the car, I didn't see the man. He could have shot himself before I ever got up there, or later, when I was off looking at the waterfall. It's noisy enough there that I might have missed the sound of a twenty-two pistol."

Both deputies nodded again. They had confiscated the pistol earlier, ascertaining that Lonny, Jake, and I had all handled it. We were duly fingerprinted; the pistol was sealed in an evidence bag.

"Did you know this man?" Once again the question was addressed to me by the female deputy. She was a big woman, tall and broad, with black hair, hazel eyes, even features, and a forthright manner. I was getting used to looking at her face.

"No." I left it at that.

"I take it the rest of you did." She glanced around the room as she spoke, but her gaze ended up on Ted.

"Yeah, we knew him. He was our vet." Ted sounded terse, his business manner. His playful streak only showed after a few drinks, or when faced with what he considered a pretty woman.

"So, do you have any idea why he would shoot himself?"

There it was—the big question. The female deputy was looking right at Ted; he kept his round blue eyes candidly on hers, another typical Ted ploy. He always looked customers candidly in the eye while he talked to them.

I glanced around the room. Lonny was seated next to me on the couch; he was staring at his boots, stuck out in front of him. Luke and Jake sat in a couple of battered armchairs off to the side—both of them looking down.

"I think Bill was depressed," Ted said. "He was up here

last night and he got drunk, tried to pick a fight in the bar. I told him to go to bed.''

The deputies took this in. ''Does anybody know why he was depressed?'' the woman asked.

''Oh, Bill's like that. He's a damn good vet, though,'' Ted said.

The woman made a note on the pad in her lap. ''Any other possible reasons?''

''Not that I know.'' Ted kept meeting the deputy's eyes. ''He was staying in the lodge here, room number seven,'' he added.

''We'll check it out. And we'll take the car back down to the department, have a look at it.'' She stood up. ''If you'll give me his room key?''

''Sure.''

Ted went to the main desk, found a duplicate key, and handed it to the woman. She headed for the stairs, her quiet partner in tow, and turned back to give us a look.

''This seems pretty straightforward; however, I'd like to ask you all to stay here and be available for questioning tomorrow, in case there's a problem.''

''Okay if I go out for a ride during the day?'' I asked.

''As long as you come back.'' She smiled.

The two of them turned and creaked their way up the stairs. We all stared at each other.

''I wonder if he made it?'' Ted looked directly at me as he spoke.

''I don't know,'' I said. ''It would depend on whether that bullet hit something vital.''

''I'll call the hospital in Sacramento in the morning.'' Ted said it with decision—another Ted trait. I'd noticed before that he tended to deal with difficult situations in a black-and-white fashion.

Now, having settled the matter of Bill Evans, he stood up. ''I'm going to bed.''

He looked at Luke and Jake as he spoke; the two brothers stood up with him. Both tall and lean with light brown hair, brown eyes, fair skin, unremarkable faces, they were hard to tell apart from a distance. Closer up, Luke had a squarer jaw and looked older. Jake's hair was curlier, his expression shyer.

They followed Ted up the stairs now; we all knew that they would be up at 4:00 A.M. Saturday was a big day at Crazy Horse Creek—lots of pack parties going in. Feeding and saddling began early.

Once they were gone, I looked at Lonny. He still stared at his boots, his face withdrawn. Tracing his familiar features with my eyes, I felt a disturbing sense of frustration.

I'd been with this man for five years. Like all long-term relationships, ours had its ups and downs, but we'd survived them well, or so I thought. Until this last six months.

Lonny had finally gotten a divorce from the wife he'd been separated from for seven years. The divorce had entailed a fair amount of financial dickering; by the time all was said and done, Lonny had sold his home in Santa Cruz County and his interest in this pack station. True to his announced intention, he'd purchased sixty acres in the Sierra Nevada foothills and moved. Two months ago, to be exact. He'd packed up his furniture and his cats, put his three horses in the stock trailer, and gone.

Not without asking me to marry him, though. Which had caused me a lot of grief.

Lonny's idea was that I would marry him and move with him to the foothills, giving up my job and my home, in order to make a new life with him. Although the offer was flattering, it didn't fit into any of my plans, and therein began to lie a problem.

For Lonny was determined to pursue his plan, with me or without me, as I came to see; no amount of lobbying on my part for a compromise had much effect on him. Going back to the mountains was his goal, and back he was going.

I'd adjusted, in a sense. I'd acknowledged that it was my choice not to go with him. I'd agreed that we would continue to have a relationship. But as anyone who's ever been in one knows, a long-distance relationship is not the same as having a boyfriend a few miles down the road.

Lonny and I had never lived together, but we'd lived near each other, and we'd always spent most of our nights together. Suddenly I was sleeping alone. And Lonny lived three hours away.

I didn't like it. And I didn't know what to do about it. I loved Lonny, but I did not love the direction our relationship had taken.

"So," I said to him, "how's it going?"

He stared at his boots. "All right, I guess. Until this."

"How are things on the ranch?"

"Okay. The barn's getting built. Feels like I don't have a lot of time for anything else."

I studied him, mingled exasperation and affection welling up inside of me. I'd been with this big, untidy, rough-featured man for long enough to understand him pretty well.

He still stared at his feet; I was quite aware that he felt the estrangement between us and was as uncomfortable with it as I was, but there was no way in hell he was going to bring it up. Ignore it out of existence—that was Lonny's way. Pretend everything was all right.

What do you want out of him, I asked myself, looking at the lines framing his eyes, the strong, thick, callused hands that had touched me so often. An answer jumped into my mind: that he make some space for me in this relationship.

Lonny loved me, of that I was sure. But he loved me in much the same way he loved his horses. He'd do what he could to take care of me; he thought I was great. But I was supposed to be part of his life.

30

What I wanted, what I needed, was to have my feelings, my ideas, my agenda acknowledged. Especially when it was different from his. I needed to have him take my goals as seriously as he took his own.

I sighed. This dialogue was rattling around only in my head; Lonny and I still sat in silence, sipping our cooling coffee. And that was just the trouble. I'd spoken these thoughts aloud before, too many times, always with the same results.

Lonny gave lip service to the notion that my feelings and needs were important, but when it counted he followed his own road, as he always had. And I had to admit, I did the same. As I told him once, neither of us was really a team player.

Trying to distract myself from the direction my thoughts were leading me, I stared around the lobby. The Crazy Horse Creek Lodge had been built in the late 1800s and still looked the part of the stage stop it had once been. No one had ever remodeled, or "cuted up," the rugged post-and-beam construction or the utilitarian pine plank floors and siding. From earlier owners through Lonny and on to Ted, the proprietors had all been satisfied to repair what broke and leave what still functioned alone.

I smiled as I looked at the room. The armchairs and couches were threadbare and battered, the photos and prints tacked on the rough walls were torn and dusty, the floor was scuffed and none too clean. Crazy Horse Creek was no multi-star resort. But the fire chugged away in the woodstove, making the lobby warm on chilly mountain nights, feet were welcome on the furniture (as were dogs), and nobody had to take their boots off to come inside.

"So, is it good to be back up here again?" I asked Lonny.

"I guess. If this hadn't happened with Bill. I have a hard time getting it out of my mind."

"You said your father shot himself." I scooted closer to him on the couch. "I never knew that. It must have been hard on you."

"I was in my early thirties. My mom had died a few years earlier and my dad came to live with me. We lived here in the summers." He gestured in a general way at the lodge; I knew what he meant.

Lonny had owned a small ranch near Sonora where he kept the pack station horses and mules in the winter. But from May till October he and his family and his crew had lived here. The Crazy Horse Creek Pack Station opened every year on Memorial Day weekend and closed when the snow drove them out of the mountains.

"He seemed okay," Lonny went on. "I knew he drank too much; I knew he missed my mom. But he didn't complain. He wasn't really well a lot of the time, but he tended bar when he felt up to it. I thought he liked being here.

"And then one Monday morning he didn't show up at breakfast. It got later and later, and finally I went to check on him. He was living in the log cabin; you know where I mean?"

"I know." The log cabin, one of the many cabins scattered around the pack station grounds, was the oldest structure. The story ran that it had been built by one Justin Roberts, who lived in it while he built the lodge. The log cabin was just that—a genuine log cabin, with all the logs neatly notched and fitted, big squared beams for a floor, and no milled wood anywhere.

"So, anyway," Lonny said, "I went out there and banged on the door, and when he didn't answer I went in. And there he was, in his chair, with a hole in his head. He left me a note. 'Doctor says I have cancer.' That was it."

I leaned my shoulder into his. "That must have been really hard for you."

"It was. I kept wondering what I'd done wrong. How I'd failed him."

"Maybe he just didn't want to go through it all."

Lonny was about to answer when we both heard feet clomping on the creaky stairs. The deputies were returning.

They stopped at the bottom of the stairs and looked at us. The male deputy was about the same height as his partner, a thick, square fireplug of a man. He looked strong as hell, with a heavy neck and a quietly pugnacious face. I revised my opinion that she was the dominant one of the pair.

"Did you find anything?" Lonny asked them.

"Not really." She spoke; he watched us. "Some paperwork that suggests he was doing some work for," she looked down at her notepad, "Dan Jacobi."

"That's right," Lonny said affirmatively. "Bill did a lot of work for Dan Jacobi."

"Do you know him?" she asked.

"Sure. He's a horse trader. A big one. He's got a ranch in Oakdale. I'd guess he buys and sells more horses than anyone in California. Bill was his vet. Dan comes up here a fair amount," Lonny added. "Ted buys quite a few horses from him."

The deputy nodded. I nodded. Her partner watched.

I'd heard of Dan Jacobi. He was well known as a supplier of horses, particularly western-style horses. Lonny's two older team roping horses, Burt and Pistol, had come from him.

We all waited. I watched the male deputy study Lonny and me in turn. He didn't seem inclined to speak.

The woman said, "Well, we're headed back down the hill. We'll be in touch if there's a problem."

She nodded at us both; the two of them tramped across the floor and dragged the heavy wooden door open and shut behind them.

I looked over at Lonny. He was staring down again; it struck me that he was genuinely distressed. This silent contemplation of his feet was his way of saying that he hurt.

Snuggling my body closer to his, I asked him gently, "Does

Bill Evans's shooting himself remind you of your dad?''

"Yeah, it does. I didn't know my dad was thinking of killing himself. I didn't know he had cancer. I thought he was doing all right. But I never asked him. And it turned out he wasn't.

"Same with Bill. I've known him for years. He was a friend, in the way people you've known for a dog's age become friends.

"I would have helped him if I'd known he needed help. But just like my dad, I didn't know. I watched him get drunk last night, watched Ted throw him out of the bar, and I never said a word. I thought he was a silly ass.''

I sighed. Wondered what to say.

"It bothers me," Lonny went on, "how completely ignorant I was of what those people were feeling.''

Here it was, the perfect opening. I could say, once again, that maybe Lonny needed to try and be more aware of other people, more responsive to their needs. That if he weren't so wrapped up in getting done what he wanted to get done, he might notice how someone else felt. Like me, I added to myself.

But I didn't say it. Instead I said, "No one can do everything right." Trite and not very helpful, I guess. I put my hand in his. "What do you say we go to bed?''

Lonny stood up. "Let's go," he said.

FIVE

I awoke the next morning to the familiar sound of Lonny snoring. Lying on my side, head propped on my hand, I watched him sleep. He'd made love to me last night with enthusiasm, and I'd responded with pleasure; we'd fallen asleep relaxed and sated. Still, this morning, studying his face, vulnerable with unknowing, I felt not only tender and protective but also stymied.

Lonny snored on, oblivious. What is it about snoring that causes a person to look so pathetically ridiculous? Suddenly I wanted to get up, get out, be on my own.

I dressed quickly—jeans, a tank top, another denim shirt—and pulled my boots on, all without waking Lonny. Then I was out the door, stepping quietly on the creaky floor as I headed down the hall.

The second floor of the lodge was arranged along the lines of old-fashioned hotels—long, narrow halls with small rooms on either side, and a couple of communal bathrooms near the stairway. Stopping at one of these, I performed brief morning ablutions and then creaked on down the stairs and out the back door of the lobby.

The mountain air met me, cold and fresh, tingling in my nose like the icy water of a high lake. Everything sparkled. I shut my eyes for a moment, dazzled by the brilliance of the sunlight. The whole world—pine trees, meadow, granite ridges—was sharp and clear and pure. So different from the soft atmosphere of the coastal hills I called home.

I walked out into the morning, half-startled, as I always was, by the intensity of these mountains. Yips greeted me as I approached my pickup. Roey leaped out when I opened the tailgate, bounding around me with shrill, excited squeaks.

"Don't bark," I admonished her firmly.

Grabbing her tail in her mouth, she spun in frantic circles, her usual response to this command. I had the notion she felt she needed something in her mouth to stop herself from talking.

Exuberance overcame caution and she leapt around me, barking happily.

"Knock it off," I warned, about as amused as I was deafened.

In this noisy fashion we approached the corrals. Plumber and Gunner neighed at me, their "Hey, where's breakfast?" neigh. I broke a couple of flakes of alfalfa hay off the bale I had brought and threw them into the corral. Both horses turned to eagerly.

I was watching them eat, making sure they both looked healthy and unscathed, when more excited yips from Roey got my attention. I looked in her direction; she was sniffing noses with a dog.

I laughed out loud. This had to be the funniest-looking dog I'd ever seen. About Roey's size, it had short white fur extravagantly speckled and blotched with red-brown spots, a long whiskery muzzle, perky ears, and blue eyes, with a big blotch over one of them. It wagged its tail furiously as it nuzzled

Roey, who was wagging hers equally furiously back.

In a second the two dogs were leaping and running happily together in a game of chase. The stranger dog looked to me to be female and still a pup.

I was watching them play with a grin on my face when a voice said, "Hello, Stormy."

I turned around. A man on a dun horse, leading a pack horse. Tall man, with red hair and a gray fedora-style hat. Blue Winter.

"Stormy?" I said.

He smiled at me. "I spent a few years in Australia. Every woman named Gail gets nicknamed Stormy in those parts. I thought you might have heard it."

I shook my head, smiling.

"That's where they started calling me Blue. All redheads get that. Blue or Bluey." He smiled again. "Nobody thought about how it would sound with my last name."

I smiled back at him, thinking that he seemed much friendlier out here on horseback than he had in the bar last night.

"I had a dog named Blue once," I said.

He laughed. "Don't tell me, he was a blue heeler."

"That's right."

"Is she yours?" He gestured toward Roey, who was racing madly after her new playmate.

"Yeah," I agreed.

"The other's mine."

"You're kidding," I said.

He laughed again. "Why would you say that?"

I smiled at him. "I don't know. You don't seem the type to have such a, let's see, different-looking dog."

"You mean funny-looking. She's half Australian shepherd, half Jack Russell terrier. She's just a pup." He snapped his fingers. "Come here, Freckles."

The spotted dog raised her ears in his direction and veered

37

away from Roey. Still going full blast, she dashed up to the big dun horse and stopped by his left foreleg, waving her tail at her owner.

The dun horse didn't flinch. Blue Winter said, "Good dog."

I studied his horses. The saddle horse was a gelding and had to be sixteen hands tall. Big-boned and heavy-muscled, he looked like a Quarter Horse type. He was a medium dun, a soft dusty gold all over, with a white blaze and a faint dorsal stripe down his back. An easy horse to pick out of a crowd.

The pack horse was less conspicuous. A small sorrel mare with a little white on her face and a couple of socks, she had no obvious distinguishing characteristics.

"Are you on your way in?" I asked him.

"Yeah, we're headed to Snow Lake tonight."

I looked at him curiously; Snow Lake was my chosen destination for my first day's ride in. "Staying there long?"

He shrugged. Once again his face seemed withdrawn. Whatever. I waved a dismissive hand.

"Well, have a good trip."

"I hope to. You, too."

"Thanks."

He clucked to his horses, said, "Come on" to the dog, and the small entourage moved off, the pack horse dragging a little on the lead rope. I smiled. Plumber had a tendency to do that, too.

I watched them head down the main trail, small puffs of dust rising around the horses' feet, the dog running in a big curving circle through the meadow. Ahead of them Relief Peak glowed in the early sunlight. Snow Lake was quite a ways on the other side of that mountain, over Brown Bear Pass. A twenty-plus-mile ride.

Blue Winter and his horses were a small vignette now. A cowboy riding down the trail. I couldn't see the dog.

Turning, I headed toward the pack station barn. The crew

was busily saddling horses and loading packs; it looked as though they had several parties getting ready to go out. Ted stood by the loading dock, talking to a strongly built man with a white straw cowboy hat.

Both men turned to look at me as I approached; the stranger had a square bulldog jaw and high cheekbones and seemed vaguely familiar. He said something affirmative to Ted and turned away, nodding civilly in my direction. Now where do I know him from, I wondered.

His back gave no clue; a long-sleeved blue shirt, pressed Wrangler jeans, and dusty boots were so typical as to be almost a uniform. But I'd seen him before, somewhere.

"Morning, Gail," Ted said.

"Hi, Ted. Did you call the hospital?"

"Not yet." His blue eyes looked candidly into mine. "I'll do it when I go in for breakfast." The eyes traveled over me a little, then moved back to my face. "I saw you down there talking to old Blue Winter."

I smiled. "I'm sure you did."

Crazy Horse Creek Pack Station was familiarly known as Peyton Pines by everyone who visited it often. New romances, one-night stands, illicit affairs . . . the place was known for these, and the whole crew, Ted in particular, loved to gossip.

"So, do you know Blue?" Ted prodded. "He comes from your part of the country."

"That's what he said. No, I never met him until yesterday in the bar. Do you guys know him?"

"Sure. He comes up here every year. Brings his horses, stays a few days, and rides in on a trip. Lonny knows him." Ted laid a little extra emphasis on Lonny's name.

"Is that right?" For some reason this conversation was annoying me. "Who was that guy you were talking to?" I asked. "I'm sure I know him from somewhere."

"Dan Jacobi."

"The horse trader."

"That's him."

"He was here last night?" I asked curiously.

"Nah. He drove up this morning from Oakdale. He comes up here a lot. Takes a pack trip every summer. He was pretty shook up when he heard about old Bill."

"I'll bet."

Ted and I stared at each other a moment. The same thought must have been chasing through both our minds, because he dropped his eyes and said, "I'd better go call. Find out how he is."

"Yeah," I said. "Let me know."

"Okay."

Ted headed for the lodge; I called Roey and wandered around the meadow for a while, letting the dog run. Eventually I felt a cup of coffee calling me.

Going into the lobby, I walked past the small cafe, where paying customers could get meals, and through the kitchen door. Here, amongst an odd, old-fashioned collection of stoves, refrigerators, cupboards, counters, sinks, and shelves, Harvey the cook had his domain.

A big, stout barrel of a man, as befit a cook, Harvey was autocratic in tone and mercurial in temperament, in the time-honored tradition of camp cooks. He grunted at me as I poured myself a cup of coffee. Apparently Harvey was not in a talking mood this morning.

Carrying my coffee, I walked through the open doorway that led to the cowboy room, a large dining room with one big table in the middle where the crew and friends ate. Lonny was seated alone near the end of the table, working his way through a plate of pancakes, sausage, and fried eggs. I sat down next to him and sipped my coffee.

Besides a brief and muffled "Morning," Lonny's attention remained on breakfast. He ate neatly and steadily, in a workmanlike fashion, until all food items had been dispatched. Then, cradling a coffee cup in his hands, he leaned back in his chair, with the air of one who had just completed a pleasant chore, and smiled at me.

I took a sip of weak but very hot coffee and smiled briefly. "Have you heard anything about that guy . . . Bill?" I asked.

Lonny's smile faded, but his green eyes looked clear and untroubled as they rested on mine. Apparently last night's distress had gone.

"I heard Ted went to call the hospital," he said. "I don't know any more."

We looked at each other; after a moment his eyes crinkled slightly at the corners. "So, are we going for a ride?"

"I guess so."

True to form, Lonny was now focused on the day's possibilities. He didn't carry pain around much; a night's sleep usually restored him to his typical optimistic good humor. A nice trait, I had always thought; it was only lately that I'd begun questioning its implications.

"What do you say we ride to the cow camp at Wheat's Meadow and have a look at Ted's cattle. It's only a few miles; it ought to be a good warm-up for your horses."

"All right." I'd made the short ride to Wheat's Meadow before, using Ted's horses. The trail was good and there wasn't too much rock. About what Gunner and Plumber needed.

"And you get to ride over the bridge."

"Yeah."

A mile out of the pack station, the main trail crossed Crazy Horse Creek in the middle of a steep canyon, via a stout wooden bridge. In Lonny's packing days, the trail had taken a lengthy detour to reach a spot where the creek could be forded. Ted had built and placed the bridge (via helicopter) in the early days of his tenure. The cowboys reckoned it saved them half an hour in each direction.

This was great, and of course, all Ted's horses were quite used to crossing the bridge. Mine, however, weren't. I'd taken them on numerous trail rides in the coastal hills around Santa Cruz in preparation for this trip, and a couple of these rides had included small bridges. Gunner and Plumber hadn't been crazy about them, but they'd agreed to walk across them, despite being nervous about the hollow echo their hooves made on the wooden planks. None of these bridges, though, bore much resemblance to the Crazy Horse Creek bridge, which spanned a hundred feet, with a drop of a couple of hundred to the crashing water.

"Better to go across it following me the first time," Lonny said.

"Yeah," I agreed. I had thought of this.

"So, what do you think? We'll saddle up in an hour or so, after you've had breakfast and the horses have finished theirs."

"All right." I was about to ask Lonny which horse he planned to take when Ted walked into the room.

Instantly our eyes swiveled to him.

Ted stood by the end of the table, his round face quiet. "Bill didn't make it," he said.

SIX

Damn." Lonny stood up. "Did he make it to the hospital?"

"They said he died there." Ted's voice was uninflected.

We were all quiet. I thought about the man lying under the night sky wanting to die. I hadn't saved him.

Lonny and Ted were still staring at each other. Aside from Lonny's angry "damn," neither man showed much recognizable emotion. And yet I was quite aware that both were very upset.

Bill Evans had been part of their world; he was one of the family. Such were not supposed to give up, give in, put a bullet into their heart. They were supposed to carry on.

I tried to think of something comforting to say. Nothing seemed possible. We all stood in silence.

Lonny turned abruptly toward me. "There isn't a thing we can do now," he said. "I'll go saddle the horses."

Without waiting for any response I might have made, he banged out the screen door at the back of the room; I watched his long, hasty stride as he headed toward the barn.

Ted looked at me questioningly. "We're going to ride up to Wheat's Meadow," I said. "Give my horses a chance to get used to the rock, and the bridge," I added.

Ted nodded, still not saying anything. For a moment he reminded me of a small boy, mute and sad.

"Do you want to come with us?" I asked.

He hesitated. His eyes were blank, all their playful sparks in abeyance. "I could have a look at those cattle," he said at last.

"Yeah, you could," I agreed. "Let me just go up and use the bathroom and I'll be right with you guys."

When I got to the barn ten minutes later, three horses were saddled and tied to the hitching rail, Gunner among them. Plumber stood next to him with the pack rig on his back, but no pack bags. I walked over and checked the cinches.

It was like Lonny to have saddled my horse as well as his. I couldn't decide whether I was mildly pissed off that he didn't let me deal with my own livestock, or mildly grateful that he had done one of my chores for me.

Tightening the cinch on Gunner, I looked at the other two saddle horses. The bay was Chester, Lonny's young horse. The buckskin I recognized as Hank, the horse Ted usually rode.

Ted and Lonny emerged from the barn, carrying bridles; I noticed Lonny had hung Gunner's bridle on the saddle horn. I got it off and offered my horse the bit. Opening his mouth obligingly, Gunner accepted the metal bar; I pulled the bridle on over the halter and fastened the lead rope around the saddle horn with a couple of half hitches. This would make the horse easy to tie up if need be.

Ted was tying saddlebags on Hank. "I brought us some lunch," he said.

Lonny carefully fastened a long case made of PVC pipe to Plumber's pack rig.

"You plan on doing some fishing?" I asked.

"Might as well," he said. He patted Plumber's neck. "Just about the right kind of a load, huh kid?" Plumber sniffed Lonny's elbow and then tucked his nose into the crook of his arm. Lonny rubbed the horse's forehead and smiled at me. "What a puppy dog he is."

"I know," I said. "I like him that way."

No need to justify my preference for friendly horses to Lonny; he felt the same as I did. Ted, however, was a different matter. Like many cowboys, he treated his horses standoffishly; a slap on the rump was about all they got in the way of affection.

Ted swung up on Hank. I called Roey. I had left her to wait on the pack station porch, something she was reasonably good about. In a minute she appeared from that direction, bounding through the grass. She ran up to the group of us and barked happily. She knew what the horses meant.

"Be quiet," I said, as I swung up on Gunner.

Lonny handed me Plumber's lead rope and climbed on Chester. The little bay started to move off as Lonny got on; Chester was a restless, lively horse who always wanted to do something. Lonny hung in one stirrup for a moment before he was able to get his right leg up and over the horse's back.

"You better teach him to stand still," I said. "You're getting a little stiff for that kind of a running mount."

Lonny grinned at me from Chester's back. "I know it. But it's so hard for him. He just wants to go so bad."

Ted grunted. "This so-and-so knows better than to walk off when I get on him."

Lonny and I said nothing. We were both familiar with Ted's ways.

Ted clucked to Hank and turned him up the trail; Lonny and I followed. I took a half turn around the saddle horn with

Plumber's lead rope, encouraging the little horse to come along. In a moment we were moving down the trail in a caravan, Roey frisking around us.

Deadman Meadow was a vivid, even green in the morning sunlight. The main trail ran along one edge of it, and Crazy Horse Creek ran along the other, with the exception of a narrow channel of water that the original owner of the pack station had created. This branched off the creek shortly after it emerged into the meadow and ran along the pack station side of the little valley. Eventually it fed into the horse corrals, through a couple of big stone troughs and a beautifully constructed granite-lined channel that provided an endless supply of fresh water for the horses.

I looked back at the pack station, seeing a picture right out of an old Western movie. The two-story shingled lodge build-ing, with its long front porch and gray stone chimney, was outlined against a towering granite cliff. Scattered clumps of pines surrounded it, and the meadow spread out like a carpet in front of it. Add in the old barn and wooden corrals with their granite troughs, and picturesque was a mild description.

Turning, I gazed up the valley to where Relief Peak raised a snowy head in the sun, feeling a sense of amazement that I was actually here, riding down this trail on Gunner. I still couldn't quite take it in.

Lonny and Ted rode ahead of me, Roey scampered along-side, and Plumber plodded behind. I watched Gunner's black-tipped red ears, seeing them flick forward curiously, cock back toward me, and flick forward again. The old cowboys used to say that you could tell a good horse by the way he "works his ears."

Ted had fallen back beside me, and I glanced over at Hank. His ears moved forward and back, like Gunner's. I smiled at Ted. "How come you always ride him?" I asked.

"Oh, I like him," Ted said, a little sheepishly.

46

I studied the horse. He had some obvious faults; he carried his head too high on a neck that was too straight, and he had one front leg that was noticeably turned out. On top of which, he was jigging a little as we moved along the trail, and I'd noticed before that this habitual prancing was a trait of his—a trait most cowboys are not fond of. But he did, indeed, seem likable, with his bright gold buckskin color, kind eye, and good attitude.

"He's not too smart," Ted said, "but he's willing." He laughed. "He's a good son of a bitch. I tell the kids I keep him for my own riding horse 'cause he's got a smooth trot. But I just like him."

I smiled back at him, knowing what he meant. Liking a particular horse was a lot the same as liking a particular human. Often the feeling was inexplicable, as much because of as despite what others might regard as faults.

We were almost at the end of the meadow now. I glanced at the spot where Bill Evans's sports car had been, and noticed that Lonny turned his head away, keeping his eyes on Relief Peak. None of us said a word.

We started up the steep piece of trail that led out of the meadow. The horses were on granite now, but the trail had been blasted out by crews with dynamite and carefully built, and the footing was good. Gunner seemed confident, following Hank and Chester. I kept a careful eye on Plumber, but the sheer drop off one side to the boulder-strewn creek below didn't seem to intimidate him any more than it did the others. Like Gunner, he cocked an alert ear at the noisy water occasionally, but both horses picked their way over the rockier sections of the trail like good mountain ponies and seemed happy enough to be there. Gunner stopped dead when he saw the bridge, though.

I couldn't really blame him. It was a narrow one-horse-wide wooden ramp, and the railings only reached about to stirrup height. It looked insubstantial as hell, stretching from one rim

47

of the canyon to the other, with the long drop beneath it to the cascading roar of the creek. At first sight most people tended to stop, as Gunner was doing now, and stare at it apprehensively.

Lonny smiled back over his shoulder at me. "He'll follow the other horses," he said reassuringly.

I nodded. Hank was on the bridge now, and Chester followed him. I clucked to Gunner and urged him forward. He obeyed, but I could feel his trepidation. Plumber was leaning back a little on the lead rope, but he was coming, too. No horse likes to be left behind.

The bridge was spooky enough, even for me. The horse's hooves banged hollowly on the wooden floor, the water far below crashed and echoed on the canyon walls, and the sense of being exposed and vulnerable, high above the railing, was extreme. If a horse did jump, and either he or you went off, you'd be dead for sure.

We made it across with no problems and began the mile of steep switchbacks on the other side to reach the top of Camelback Ridge.

"Are there many bridges like that in this part of the Sierras?" I asked Lonny, as we climbed.

"A few. You're liable to meet a couple of them, the way you're planning to go." Lonny knew my proposed itinerary; he'd helped me plan this trip last winter. I wanted to get to several of the high mountain lakes that I'd heard about for years but never seen. And I wanted the easiest possible route. After all his years of packing, Lonny was a veritable mine of information.

"Sure you don't want some company?" Lonny grinned at me; he knew what my answer would be. It had been somewhat of a sore spot initially, but as time had passed Lonny had accepted and understood my need to go on this trip alone. Goal-oriented himself, he had a lot of sympathy for my desire to achieve a dream I'd held for so many years.

I smiled back at him as the horses worked their way up the ridge. All the time, half my mind was on Gunner; I kept a light feel of him through the reins, guiding him to the easier side of the trail, checking him when he started to hurry. Lonny, in contrast, left Chester's reins completely slack, allowing the horse to pick his own course and speed. Chester had been up in these mountains several times in the last few months; he understood about rock.

But Gunner didn't. Nor did Plumber. All the intricacies that to a mountain horse like Hank were automatic reactions, were uncharted territory for my ponies. Avoiding V-shaped clefts, stepping slowly and cautiously through scree, being wary of loose rock, and above all, staying off the slickrock, were things they were learning as we proceeded up the ridge.

I tried to help, guiding Gunner toward better footfalls, making sure Plumber had plenty of slack in the lead rope and wasn't hurried when we crossed rough ground. And the horses did well, seeming, in my estimation, to gain a sense of how to move on rock as we went along.

We stopped twice to let the horses breathe before we reached the top of the ridge. The pass, such as it was, was inconspicuous, but the views as we started down the other side were wonderful. All around us the granite glowed with light. Pine trees lined the distant ridges, blue-green in the sunshine, stiff and erect like soldiers. The sky was an endless, clear Sierra blue. I smelled the sharp scent of pine resin and dust and felt completely happy.

Gunner picked his way down the ridge like a pro, following Chester. Plumber seemed to be doing fine. Roey was following the pack horse now, tongue hanging out, a grin on her face.

The wind made a rushing noise in the pine trees, like big

trucks on some distant highway. I thought of my friends in Santa Cruz County, perhaps driving to work right now on just such a highway. And here I was, I thought in amazement, here I was.

The trail forked when we reached the creek in the bottom of the canyon. The main trail continued on toward Relief Peak and Brown Bear Pass. Wheat's Meadow trail crossed the creek and headed over a different ridge.

We let the horses drink; Roey splashed about happily. Neither Gunner nor Plumber turned a hair when we waded across the creek. Fording creeks was a routine part of our trail rides back in the coastal hills. This was a good ford, shallow and not too rocky. No problem.

One more ridge, and then through a shadowy pine forest. A sudden dazzle of light and openness ahead, and we emerged from the trees into Wheat's Meadow, as from dark to daylight—the wide, sunny grassland was so vastly and dramatically different from the dim, shady silence under the pines.

Wheat's was a green jewel of a meadow in a setting of silver granite. There was an old cow camp at the north end—a log cabin and a barn—which was deserted. The uneven chiming of bells marked the presence of Ted's cattle in the trees behind the barn.

We reined our horses to a stop, standing in the bright, breezy openness of the meadow. Lonny smiled at me and I smiled back. "It's great, isn't it?" I said.

"It sure is."

Ted said nothing, just gazed out over the grassland. After a minute, he reined Hank toward the barn. "Let's go have a look at those cattle."

The cattle were in a little grove of willows on the other side of Wheat's Meadow Creek. We rode around and through them, while Ted counted heads and checked to make sure all were healthy. They looked good, their red and black backs sleek and shiny, and we could all see that there was plenty of feed left in the meadow. A Brahma cross heifer stepped toward Plumber and sniffed noses with him curiously. Plumber snorted and pinned his ears. I laughed.

"I love the bells," I told Lonny.

He nodded, a brief downward motion of his chin, his eyes on the cattle. The cowbells were hung around the necks of the older cows with leather straps like collars. They clanked and chimed with every step, helping the cowboys to locate strays that were holed up in the brush. Up close as we were, the noise could be cacophonous when the whole herd was moving, but from a distance it made a strange music, half-harmonious, half-discordant, almost eerie. Fairy music.

"Ready for lunch?" Ted asked.

"Sure," Lonny answered for both of us.

We tied the horses to some pine trees by the old barn and sat down by the banks of the creek to eat. Ted had packed us each a sandwich as well as a beer apiece, wrapped in a plastic garbage bag full of ice. The beers were icy cold and perfect. We ate and drank contentedly and watched the creek. When we were done, Lonny broke down his case and put two fishing poles together.

Ted declined fishing in favor of napping, so Lonny and I creek-stomped together for an hour. Wheat's Meadow Creek was full of trout, and they were quick and eager. I got at least one hit at every hole. Ten inches was a big fish, but they fought hard and were fun to catch. We hooked a dozen or so apiece, on lures, turned them all loose, and went back to the horses and Ted.

The ride out was pleasant and uneventful; I slouched a little on Gunner's back as we worked our way down Camelback Ridge, feeling confident in him. Plumber, too, looked sure and poised as he picked his way over the rock. It was all going to be fine, I told myself.

This trip, the trip of my dreams, was coming off just as I'd planned. Everything would be great.

In retrospect, I can't remember when I've ever been so spectacularly wrong.

SEVEN

Once we were back at the lodge and the horses were unsaddled, turned out, and fed, Lonny was keen to go to the bar and have a drink. I acquiesced, not altogether enthusiastically. I enjoy a cocktail in the evening as much as anyone, and mostly, I find bars pleasant. But the Crazy Horse Creek Bar on Saturday night was often a madhouse, and I wasn't sure I was up for it.

Stopping to put the dog in the camper and give her food and water, I arrived at the bar a few minutes after Lonny to find my fears confirmed. The place was a zoo—the tourists three-deep at the bar itself, the few tables full. Several couples were dancing—well, frugging in place—to Johnny Cash on the juke-box. I scanned the crowd for Lonny.

He was in the corner, talking with Ted and Luke. I made my way toward them, pushing gently through the throng. Chatter and laughter roiled around me; I heard the cowbell over the bar ring, a signal that somebody had bought the place a round. A rich somebody, I reflected.

Which wasn't surprising. Most of the folks who were up here

to be packed into the mountains by the pack station crew had plenty of dollars. Horses, mules, and packers did not come cheap; those who weren't long on money carried their gear in a backpack. Shoe buckaroos, as the cowboys called them.

There were probably a few shoe buckaroos in the bar tonight, and some who were just car camping in the Forest Service campsite at the other end of Deadman Meadow. But the majority would be what Ted called "customers," heavily emphasizing the first syllable. Most would be staying in the cabins that clustered around the lodge, eating in the cafe and drinking in the bar, en route to being packed into a mountain lake. These were the people who made Ted a lot of money, and he was always very happy to see them.

On the other hand, he didn't much like to talk to them, and usually avoided the bar. Lonny's presence had created the exception, I surmised.

I started to work my way as unobtrusively as I could between two men in cowboy hats in order to get to where Lonny was standing.

"Excuse me," I said, as one of the men turned around.

He was in his late twenties, blond and handsome, and arrogant with it. He was also, I realized a quick second later, very drunk.

He looked me up and down. I was pinned by the crowd behind me, and he was firmly blocking the route to Lonny.

"Excuse me," I said again.

"Well, you're a pretty thing." He drawled it out.

I sighed. "Thanks. I need to get through here, if you don't mind."

"I don't mind at all. Just you squeeze your pretty backside right in."

He shifted slightly to one side, leaving a six-inch gap between himself and his neighbor.

I shrugged and insinuated myself shoulder first; at the same time I felt him grab my ass—hard. It pissed me off.

I'm used to drunks and I'm used to cowboys; I'm used to drunk cowboys, for that matter. But I didn't like this guy. I kicked him in the kneecap with the pointed toe of my boot.

"Fuck off, asshole," I said clearly.

I wasn't prepared for his reaction. He yelped and grabbed me by the breasts. "You like this better?" His eyes were mean.

"You son of a bitch." I said it loudly enough for the people around us to hear.

The cowboy-hatted man next to us turned, took a look, and said, "Knock it off, Steve."

His voice was deep and hard and familiar. Dan Jacobi, I realized.

Steve let go of me.

Dan Jacobi gave me another glance, in which recognition dawned. "Apologize to her," he said to his companion.

Steve looked sulky. "The hell I will. I work for you; you don't own me."

"Apologize to her." Dan Jacobi enunciated each word clearly.

Steve shrugged and turned back to the bar. "The hell with it."

Dan Jacobi put a hand on his shoulder. Steve looked at him. Effortlessly as an ax splitting firewood Dan drove his fist into Steve's gut.

The blond gasped and grabbed his stomach and sat abruptly on the floor of the bar.

"I'll apologize for him," Dan Jacobi said. "He's busy."

Wheezing and retching, the unfortunate Steve half crawled and half walked to the door, doubled over with both hands holding himself. I had the impression he would be puking for a while.

"Sorry about that," Dan Jacobi said. "He's had too much to drink. Can I buy you something?"

"It's not necessary," I said.

Lonny had witnessed our little scene, along with the rest of the barroom crowd, and stood by my side.

"What did he do?" he asked me.

"Grabbed me." I grinned. "I kicked him; he didn't like it."

"Good for you." Dan Jacobi smiled briefly. "How about I buy you both a drink?"

"Sure." Lonny answered for both of us. "Gail, this is Dan Jacobi. Dan, Gail McCarthy."

"Nice to meet you, ma'am," Dan said. "What'll you have to drink?"

"A Stoly vodka tonic with an extra squeeze of lime," I said.

"Jack Daniel's and soda for me." Lonny grinned at Dan. "Gail's my horse vet."

"Is that right?" Dan Jacobi looked at me with mild curiosity.

I studied him back. He would be about the same age as Lonny—fifty or close to it. His thick, big-chested body looked powerful, an impression that was bolstered in my mind by his quick dispatch of a much younger man. Everything about his face, from the square, bulldog jaw to the hard, dark eyes, confirmed this sense of inner force. Dan Jacobi was clearly a man to be reckoned with.

He handed Lonny and me our drinks; we thanked him. I took the first cold, sharp sip and sighed.

Dan Jacobi addressed both of us. "That was a terrible thing about Bill Evans."

Lonny looked somber. I could feel Ted stepping up on the other side of me, a drink in his hand. Dan continued talking about Bill, saying what a nice guy he was, that he'd been his vet for years, that he, Dan, had never imagined that Bill would do such a thing.

I listened with half an ear, most of my attention focused on Lonny and Ted. Lonny still looked blank and sad; Ted's face was expressionless, but I could feel the tension in his body.

Dan Jacobi was talking to me now. "I heard you found him."

"Yeah, I did."

"And that he was still alive and talking."

"Yeah."

Ted's voice was high and sharp. "So what did he say?"

"Nothing that made any sense, really. That he was trying to kill himself. That he wanted to die. He said something about horses with fire in their bellies. I guess he was talking about colicked horses, since he was a vet."

"Did he say anything about any people?" Ted again.

"No, not that I recall."

Dan and Ted were both watching me; Lonny was looking at the floor. I took another swallow of my drink and felt it tingle all the way down to my stomach.

Around us the barroom crowd talked and laughed, oblivious to our strange, tense conversation. I ignored the men next to me for a second, feeling the eager, excitable ambience of the place—everybody here on vacation, ready to have a good time. The cowbell clanged again; I could see Ernie and Luke, who were both behind the bar tonight, hustling to make another round of drinks.

Next to me, Ted shifted, took the whiskey and water that Ernie handed him, and looked at Dan. "I heard you were looking for Blue Winter."

Dan's eyes moved to Ted. "That boy owes me some money."

Ted grinned; all the tension in his body dissolved. "You're too late. He rode in this morning. Nobody knows when he'll come back out." He took a long swallow of his fresh drink.

"Why does he owe you money?" I asked Dan.

"That big dun gelding he's riding. He bought the horse from me and he never paid for him."

"Oh." I took that in. "He didn't seem like that kind of person."

Dan shrugged one shoulder.

"Maybe you'll see him while you're in," Ted said to Dan.

"Do you know where he was headed?" Dan's voice was quiet.

"Snow Lake, I heard," Ted said. "That's where you're going, too, right, Gail?"

My turn to shrug. I wasn't real keen on the whole world knowing exactly which lakes I was headed for.

"Gail's going on a pack trip," Ted went on, seeming unaware of my discomfort. "All by herself."

"Is that right?" Once again, Dan Jacobi looked at me curiously. "Ted's packing us in next week. To Huckleberry Lake."

I nodded. Sounded like it would be a busy time in the backcountry. Well, mid-July, what did I expect? With any luck at all, though, I would still find myself alone at some of the high country lakes and meadows.

Taking another sip of my vodka tonic, I wished suddenly to be out of this bar, out of this crowd. I looked at Lonny.

"You ready to go?" he asked.

"Yeah."

"I'll buy you dinner," Dan Jacobi offered.

"I'll buy you all dinner," Ted said. He finished his drink and grinned at the group of us, seeming restored to good humor. "Steak on the house."

No use protesting. I was clearly in for a social evening. I followed the men out of the bar and down to the lodge, listening to Lonny and Dan talk about team roping horses. Ted added nothing to this conversation.

Ted didn't rope, or rather, he didn't team rope. He roped enough to catch and doctor his cattle when they needed attention and no chutes were handy. But, like many ranch cowboys, he disdained the competitive rodeo sport of team roping, considering it impractical, for dilettante cowboys with no real chores to do.

Lonny, on the other hand, had never been a rancher. Unlike Ted, when Lonny'd owned the pack station he'd kept only the horses and mules. Lonny roped for fun and was a keen competitor, although he was also perfectly capable of roping cattle out in the open, in order to help Ted or some other ranching friend.

We settled ourselves in the cowboy room and were served dinner and beers by a silent Harvey, to the accompaniment of a nonstop conversation about horses. I contributed the occasional question or story, but mostly I just listened.

Dan Jacobi had a knowledge of horses that was wide and deep and eclectic. Though he was primarily known for cowhorses, particularly team roping horses and ranch horses, he appeared willing to deal in any kind of horse, as long as he could make a profit. He talked of buying Thoroughbred horses off the track and selling them to be jumpers; he mentioned buying horses from the livestock auction, destined for the killers, and sorting through them to find which might be suitable pack string and dude horses for Ted.

"And you've been buying those gaited horses, what do you call them?" Ted asked him.

"Pasos. Peruvian Pasos. People with bad backs like 'em. They've got real smooth gaits."

"Where did you say you got them from?" Ted asked.

"South America."

Ted grinned at me. "Old Dan's a real wheeler and dealer."

Well, sure, I thought. Dan was a horse trader. Where you could make a dollar on a horse, there he would go.

Seeming to catch my thought, Dan Jacobi smiled at me. "I was raised by the gypsies, back in Oklahoma," he said. "I grew up buying and selling horses. Sometimes I like it; sometimes I hate it. But it's what I know how to do." He was quiet a moment. "I sure am gonna miss Bill," he said reflectively. "He was a friend. And he knew a hell of a lot about horses."

I nodded sympathetically.

He smiled at me again. "Sure you wouldn't like to move to Oakdale?"

Before I could reply to this sally, Lonny asked Dan a question. "Do you have any idea what was on Bill's mind to make him do a thing like that? Was he sick?"

"Not that I know of," Dan said.

"Maybe it was seeing Blue," Ted interjected.

"Seeing Blue?" I asked.

There were a couple of seconds of quiet. Lonny looked uncomfortable; Dan Jacobi looked impassive. Ted's eyes were sharp with prurient interest. I had the distinct sense all three men knew something I didn't.

"Seeing Blue?" I asked Lonny. "You mean that guy, Blue Winter? What does he have to do with it?"

Lonny looked at the remains of his dinner, then at me. "When Bill's wife left him, she lived with Blue awhile."

"That's right," Ted said. "She left him for Blue. And then she left Blue and went back to Bill. And then she left Bill again."

"I thought you said Bill's wife left him because of his drinking." I was addressing my remarks to Lonny; Ted's gossipy tone got on my nerves.

"She did," Lonny said. "Blue just happened to be in the right place at the right time. I don't think Katie was ever very serious about him. She left him within a year and went back to Bill."

"Blue was pretty broke up about it," Ted said.

"But then she left her husband again?" I asked Lonny.

"That's right. He was drinking a lot."

"What happened to her?"

"She left the country," Dan Jacobi said. "Nobody knows where she went."

"Oh."

"Maybe Blue shot Bill," Ted said. "Over Katie."

I looked at Ted. "You don't like this guy Blue much, do you? And Bill Evans told me he was trying to kill himself."

"Maybe Bill was covering up." Ted said.

"Why would he do that?" I was feeling fairly annoyed at Ted. "And what is it you have against Blue Winter?"

Ted shrugged. "He thinks his shit don't stink."

Belatedly it occurred to me that Ted had had several drinks in the bar and a couple of beers with dinner. He was now more than a little drunk, his straw cowboy hat tipped back on his head, his eyes slightly unfocused, his voice sloppy. There was no way I was going to get a straight answer out of him.

Besides, I thought I could answer my own question. No doubt Ted disliked Blue Winter partly because Ted didn't make any money on him. Blue packed his own horses into the mountains; he didn't use Ted's stock or his crew. And more than that, I imagined that Blue Winter probably didn't kowtow to Ted the way most of the customers did. Ted was a czar in his little fiefdom; he didn't have much use for those who weren't interested in paying homage.

So what's the big deal, I asked myself. You know Ted's that way. What do you care about Blue Winter? You're getting to be a grouch in your old age, Gail.

It was true, kind of. Once again I was getting tired of the situation I was in. I was bored with Ted's gossip and posturing; I wanted out of here. When I was younger I was more patient, more enthralled with the lengthy business of cowboys talking about horses—and other cowboys.

I stood up. "I think I'll go check my horses. Nice to have met you," I said to Dan Jacobi.

He stood up. "Likewise, ma'am."

Lonny stood up, too. "I'll go with you, Gail."

Ted remained seated and didn't meet my eyes.

Turning, I walked out the back door, Lonny following me. I wished he weren't. I wanted to go into the Sierra night alone, check my horses in peace and solitude.

Well, you will, I told myself silently. You will. You'll be alone soon enough.

EIGHT

Sunday passed uneventfully. I spent it going over my gear, checking my lists, packing the last of my food items. My horses rested, the dog rested, I rested.

Monday morning I was up early. Dressing in the cool, sharp air, I went over my mental lists one more time. Had I forgotten anything? If I had, I would be doing without it. There were no convenience stores, no human habitations of any type, where I was headed.

I selected my clothes with a little more care than usual, thinking not about looks but comfort. Comfort and safety. I picked a soft cotton tank top in dusty brown, a faded sage-green shirt, and some old jeans. I wanted clothes that wouldn't restrict me at all, and in the unlikely event I needed to conceal my presence, would help me blend into the landscape.

The issues to do with being a woman alone had not escaped me when I planned this trip. Of things that were genuinely a threat to me, there were few: rattlesnakes and bears, in the way of animals; lighting and trail accidents, in the line of natural phenomena; and of course, other humans.

The likeliest danger was probably a slip on the slickrock, but I had tried to prepare for other possibilities as well. Were I, for instance, to be camped alone at a lake with a party of drunken men nearby, I wanted to be able to hide if need be. And if that didn't work, to defend myself.

So I had chosen the colors of my clothes with care, and my .357 pistol was at the bottom of my saddlebag, under my rain gear. It wasn't, strictly speaking, legal; however, the law wasn't going to be much help to me where I was going.

I zipped a shelled pile jacket (dark green) over my shirt, and pulled my boots on. Creaking down the stairs, I could feel my heart thumping away, adrenaline rushing into my system. I was getting ready to ride into the mountains alone. For two whole weeks I would be completely on my own, cut off from civilization, dependent on my own resources. I was excited and scared, both at once.

I let Roey out of the camper for a brief run, gave her food and water, and locked her back up, hoping she'd eat as much as possible before we left.

When I got up to the horse corrals, I found that Gunner and Plumber had already been fed. Lonny leaned on the corral fence, talking to Ted.

The pack station was much quieter this morning, most of the parties having gone in on the weekend. Ted's crew was saddling a few horses; I didn't see any pack rigs in evidence.

Ted himself looked wide awake as usual; I heard him tell Lonny that he would be packing Dan Jacobi in himself.

I made a mental note to stay away from Huckleberry Lake, and smiled at the two men. "Morning," I said.

Lonny grinned. "So, are you ready?"

"As ready as I'll ever be."

He slapped my shoulder. "You'll do just fine."

"The horses look good," I said, running my eyes over my two happily munching equines.

"You bet. You go on in and have some coffee and breakfast and I'll saddle and pack 'em for you."

I started to protest and shut my mouth. I would be leaving soon enough. Why argue with Lonny now?

"Come on in and have a cup of coffee with me first," I said instead. "Let these guys finish eating."

"All right."

We trooped down to the cowboy room, Ted in our wake. So much for a few romantic moments together before I left. Instead I had breakfast with virtually the whole crew; the cowboy room bubbled with laughter and jokes.

Ted was telling Lonny about the horses Dan Jacobi had brought with him. I listened with half an ear.

"Best-looking gray gelding you ever saw in your life. Big and strong and pretty-headed. I told him he was crazy to take that ten-thousand-dollar horse up here in the rocks. Take one of my horses, instead, I told him. But he just says, 'That's what I own 'em for.' " Ted snorted. "I'd say he owns 'em to sell 'em, and there's no use crippling 'em up. But him and those two boys of his are riding those three fancy geldings to Huckleberry Lake."

Lonny shrugged. Ted had made the same point to me—I ought to ride his horses and leave my flatland ponies at home. Lonny didn't agree.

"I like riding my own horses. Maybe Dan does, too." Lonny grinned at Ted. "So you make a little less money."

Ted's turn to shrug.

I worked my way through a plate of French toast, more or less forcing myself to eat despite my chattering nerves. My mind flipped constantly from item to item—had I brought enough dog food, would I wish I had a heavier jacket, did I have enough painkiller in the vet kit?

Horse talk drifted past me; I barely heard it. Soon now, I would be on my own.

Lonny got up and poured me another cup of coffee. "I'll go get your horses ready."

"I'll go with you."

I stood up, carrying my coffee, and followed him out the door. Cold, clean early-morning air washed over me; the ridge line glowed in the pale gold sunlight. The Sierra Nevada, the range of light.

Lonny was catching Gunner and Plumber; I began ferrying my gear up from my truck. I'd packed the panniers yesterday, weighed them to be sure they were even, and organized my top load. Packing Plumber up this morning would be a relatively simple process.

I lugged my saddle up to the corrals, wondering yet again if I was making a mistake. The heavy roping saddle was familiar and comfortable, both to me and Gunner, but it weighed much more than necessary. Built to tow six-hundred-pound steers around, the saddle was certainly nothing a long-distance endurance rider would choose. But I reckoned the comfort factor was most important, and I wasn't planning on any really long rides. Twenty miles was the most I intended to cover in a day.

Lonny put the pack rig on Plumber while I saddled Gunner. Working as a team, we lifted the pack bags onto the forks, set the top load in place, and covered the whole deal with a plastic tarp. Lonny watched as I lashed the tarp in place, using the diamond hitch and the trucker's knots he'd taught me.

Plumber pinned his ears crossly when I cinched everything tight; like most horses, he disliked that part.

Almost ready now. I tied my saddlebags to the back of my saddle, let the dog out of the camper, locked the truck, and handed my keys to Lonny.

"I should be back two weeks from today," I told him. "You know my route."

"That's right." Lonny was bridling Gunner, and didn't look at me as he spoke. "If you don't show up, I'll come looking for you."

"Okay." Watching his back, the long muscles strong despite the roll over his belt, I felt a surge of affection. "Give me a hug," I said.

He turned, holding Gunner's reins with one hand, and hugged me roughly. "Have fun," he said. Then he handed the horse to me. "You'd better get going."

I smiled at him, knowing from long experience that he disliked protracted farewells. Well, so did I.

Setting my foot in the stirrup, I swung up on Gunner. Lonny put Plumber's lead rope into my hand and our fingers touched. He met my eyes, and his own eyes crinkled at the corners. "I envy you," he said.

I smiled. "See you soon." Taking a half turn around the saddle horn with Plumber's lead rope, I clucked to Gunner and called Roey, feeling slightly light-headed. Here we go, I thought, here we go.

The sun shone in my eyes as I rode out from under the pine trees; I was headed east. I turned to wave good-bye to Lonny, saw him standing in front of the old corrals, waving to me, and my heart twisted. Why so many choices, I wondered, not for the first time. To fulfill my dream, I had to leave Lonny behind. Just as he'd had to leave me behind in order to fulfill his. Why did life have to be like this?

I didn't know. I only knew I was riding down the trail on a bright summer morning in the High Sierra, headed for Snow Lake. This was the here and now, the present moment. It was time to toe that line.

Relief Peak glowed ahead of me; the ridges rose around me. I was where I'd wanted to be for so many years.

I reached down and smoothed a strand of Gunner's heavy black mane over to the right side of his neck. He walked down the trail, looking alert. Roey swished through the meadow grass beside us, a wide grin on her face. I grinned back at her.

So here we were. I began, slowly, to lapse into the trail rider's mind-set. Part of my attention stayed on the horses; I guided Gunner to the safer, easier parts of the trail, looked over my shoulder every few moments to take note of how Plumber was doing. I admired the scenery meanwhile, watched the dog scampering through the rocks, enjoyed the sun on my face. At the same time my mind drifted, going over the route ahead, touching on Lonny, wondering briefly what was happening back at the veterinary clinic.

In this way we progressed uneventfully up Camelback Ridge. I felt some trepidation as we approached the bridge, but did my best to hide it, knowing my own attitude would influence my horses. I talked out loud to the dog as we neared the spot, speaking in a light, conversational tone as though I were talking to a companion about the weather. Nothing settles a spooky horse better than the sound of his rider's voice sounding happy and unconcerned.

So I told Roey what a nice day it was, and sat easy and relaxed in my saddle, and though Gunner hesitated briefly and snorted, at a gentle thump on his ribs, he stepped forward onto the bridge. Snorting again and cocking a watchful ear at the odd-sounding thunks his hooves made on the wood, he tiptoed forward, as if he were walking on eggs.

But he went. Plumber followed. They'd been over this bridge before. They knew it could be done.

Once we were on the other side I heaved a deep sigh of relief. There was nothing too scary ahead, as far as I knew.

Upwards, ever upwards we went. Then, topping the ridge, we came down to the trail fork that led to Wheat's Meadow. I let the horses and the dog drink at the creek and then continued on, headed over the next ridge.

I was starting to relax now. The horses' necks were slightly damp with sweat; they appeared to be handling rocky areas easily and confidently. We climbed a small area of switchbacks that had been dynamited into a solid granite face, and despite the rock and the exposure, neither horse hesitated or slipped once.

Good. Very good. I let my eyes wander over the rock-and-pine-tree country spread out around me. In some ways, the Sierras, through dramatic and beautiful, were repetitive; how many ways can gray stone, blue sky, green pines be arranged? The tumbling streams and startling lakes and meadows were a motif constantly repeated. Although I never grew used to the flicker and dazzle of the aspen, or the human-sounding voices in the white water, or the stark moonscapes of the granite passes, they became familiar.

We were approaching a small meadow called Saucer Meadow. Relief Creek ran along the far side of it, and the whole thing was a blaze of brilliant wildflowers. Bright red-orange, sharp yellow, deep blue-violet, brilliant magenta pink. As the trail dropped into the little basin and flowers were all around me, I could identify some.

Lupine and paintbrush and asters in impossible profusion, wild columbines and leopard lilies, penstemons, larkspur, and monkey flower—to name only the ones I recognized. Arranging themselves in perfect harmonies and rivulets of color along the stream, colonizing a fallen log, grouped around a solitary gray granite boulder. I stopped Gunner and stared in amazement and delight.

There were no more flowers than butterflies. Small brown ones and blue ones the color of forget-me-nots, slightly larger ones like bright orange mosaics, large black-and-yellow striped swallowtails, and lots of monarchs. In the mid-morning sunshine, the meadow was a blaze of green, slashed with colors and flashes of colors.

Roey was delighted. Despite the five miles or so she'd covered already, she gamboled about, showing me the proper way to appreciate a meadow. Rolling in the long grass, wading in the creek, chasing and bounding after the butterflies—I laughed out loud to see her.

Gunner gave an impatient tug on the reins. Either let me eat some grass or let's get moving, he said. I thought about it. Saucer Meadow was lovely, but we still had roughly fifteen miles to go. I had planned to stop for lunch at the aptly named Lunch Meadow, another five miles ahead. Better keep moving.

I clucked to the horses and rode on. The breeze brushed my face gently, as I tried to take it all in. The sunny expanse of green and flowers, with the wind blowing through the willows and cottonwoods that fringed the stream banks. Such warm, open, friendly greenness, so free and full of light. It was an amazing contrast to the hard stone country all around it; it seemed almost magical.

I looked over my shoulder as we entered the pine forest once again, saying good-bye.

Another rocky ridge ahead. Pine trees and granite. The wind moved, that clean, lonely Sierra wind that blows in the pines. Around me the rocks seemed to tumble in a frozen cascade, a jumbled silver granite landscape ever restless in its heart. The meadows and lakes were tiny flecks of stillness in a great, rough tapestry of hurled rock.

I rode on. Slowly the feeling of being alone in these mountains was coming back to me. Each mile that took me farther from the pack station, from civilization, from my real life, brought me closer to that old feeling, that elusive sense of place.

I'd been here alone before; I knew these mountains. They weren't a place of close, warm, familiar beauty, they won't cuddle up to you as some gentle hills and pretty valleys will. I felt dwarfed, always, by the roughness of this place, by its indifference.

And I felt honored to be here. To be tolerated by these bizarrely lovely mountains—this place not made for man. Only in the meadows, and in those little pockets of meadows on the shores of the lakes, did I ever feel briefly at home, as though perhaps I could really live here.

I clucked to the horses, called to the dog. For now, I was a sojourner; for the present moment, my home was on my back. Or, more literally, on Plumber's back.

I was getting hungry. By my reckoning, it was almost noon. Reckoning was all I had to go on; I hadn't brought a timepiece. By choice, not error. I'd learned from my solitary backpacking expeditions that I could tell time well enough for my own purposes by the sun, and it was an extraordinarily freeing feeling to do without a watch.

We should hit Lunch Meadow between noon and one, I thought. I would eat there and let the horses rest for half an hour, then push on and hope to reach Snow Lake in time to make camp before dark. Today's ride was the longest one I had planned for the entire trip. But I felt that the horses were fresh, and I wanted to get as far into the backcountry as possible right away.

The farther I went, the fewer people there would be. More or less. As a matter of fact, the way to avoid people was to avoid the lakes and the big meadows with good fishing creeks. The trouble was that like most of the other folks in the backcountry, I really liked the lakes. And I needed to camp where there was plenty of feed for my horses. So I was liable to run into a few other travelers.

Amazingly enough, I hadn't seen anyone yet. This was probably because it was Monday. Weekends in the mountains were a lot more crowded than weekdays.

The trail was following the banks of Relief Creek now, and the terrain was leveling off. I passed the old Sheep Camp, knowing Lunch Meadow wasn't far ahead.

It was getting warm. I'd shed my jacket several miles back; now I took off my overshirt and tied it around my waist. The sun felt good on my bare arms. Absently I brushed flies off Gunner's neck.

The landscape was opening up, and I could see the wide spaces of Lunch Meadow ahead. I rode until I was out of the forest and then sent the horses off the trail to a pocket-sized hollow along the creek. Here the water made bathtub-like pools in the rocks, perfect for soaking feet.

Dismounting stiffly, I tied Gunner and Plumber to trees, and hobbled around, taking saddlebags off and loosening cinches. Damn. I wasn't used to riding this many miles. God knew how stiff I would be when I got into camp this evening.

Settling myself by the banks of the creek, I cut hunks of dry salami and mozzarella cheese and rolled them in a flour tortilla. Humble but very satisfying. Long swallows from my water bottle washed it down. I eyed the icy cold water of the creek, but didn't drink it. *Giardia*, an intestinal parasite, was a problem in these mountains. I would only drink from springs that had not had a chance to become contaminated. Either that or pump my drinking water through the filter I'd brought.

Once my hunger was satisfied, I took off my boots and socks and soaked my feet in the creek. The water was so cold it hurt, but my skin tingled and I felt invigorated. I let my feet dry in the sun with my soles pressed against the warm, scratchy surface of the granite.

Time to go. I put my boots on, tied the saddlebags back on the saddle, and tightened Gunner's cinch. Plumber nickered at me. I looked him over carefully. The sweat had dried on his neck and flanks and his eye was bright. He was my chief concern on this trip. I had used Gunner a lot in the last couple of years, and knew him to be a trouper—a horse who traveled well and was tough. Plumber was more of an unknown quantity. Younger, smaller, and perhaps less tough-minded, he was also somewhat inexperienced. Although he'd been shown quite a bit as a youngster (by someone else), he'd spent his last few years turned out because of a lameness. Since he'd been sound, all I'd done with him was some gentle trail riding and the legging-up necessary for this trip. I wasn't sure how he would tolerate it all.

He looked okay, for the moment. I untied both horses, climbed on Gunner, and headed off across Lunch Meadow.

It was really more of a desert than a meadow. A big, open flat covered with low-growing, scrubby sagebrush, Lunch Meadow had been decimated many years ago by sheep. The four-footed locusts, who were both tended and decried by John Muir, had spent many summers here, while their shepherds relaxed and played cards at nearby Sheep Camp. Too many. Overgrazed and beaten down, the meadow had never recovered.

I rode across it, thinking about the ecological issues the sheep brought to mind. For the subject wasn't ancient history—far from it. Sheep were no longer pastured in Sierra meadows, but cattle, Ted's cattle, for instance, were. And there was a vociferous group of folks who thought that this should not be so.

An even more extreme contingent wanted to ban livestock altogether, including saddle horses and pack horses. Their thinking ran along the lines of preserving the meadows, and looking at the waste of Lunch Meadow, I couldn't help but feel some sympathy for their position. Trouble was, they didn't seem too long on facts.

I'll admit I'm prejudiced. I like horses; I like riding into the mountains. I've backpacked a fair amount, and I prefer taking my horses. These issues aside, I didn't see that the occasional use of livestock to travel through the mountains was likely to do any great and irreversible harm. Pasturing them in the meadows for the summer was another thing altogether.

Though Ted would hate to hear me say it, I'd several times wondered if his contented heifers were slowly turning Wheat's

Meadow into the desert that Lunch Meadow had become. I didn't know. I was pretty sure Ted didn't either.

I could see the steep slopes of Brown Bear Pass in front of me; my horses were on rock again. Red-brown lava rock now, rather than silvery granite. Brown Bear Pass was hot, dusty, exposed, and bare, the long slog up it a matter of plowing steadily through the scree. The trail was good, though.

Stopping to let the horses rest a number of times, I progressed steadily toward the ridge line. No trees up here. Several small, chattering creeks made green rivulets. Wildflowers clung to the dusty slopes—blue flax, white yarrow, bright red California fuchsia—all lovers of dry, well-drained places.

Everything was empty and quiet. A hawk circled in the blue. Gunner snorted. Roey trudged behind the horses, starting to look tired.

The jagged red-brown crags around us were peaceful with the peace of supreme unconcern. These constant, ever-changing, ever-similar vistas—stone in sunlight—seemed prehistoric in their inviolate purity.

Steel-shod hooves clicked sharply against rock; Plumber grunted as he struggled to haul the pack up the steepening trail. I could see the pass ahead of us—a curious collection of rosy pink, more-rounded boulders marking the spot.

Slowly, and then suddenly, we were there. Over the top, the wind in our faces, and all of Emigrant Meadow and Emigrant Lake spread out in front of us. I grinned in sheer delight.

Brown Bear Pass might have a steady slog of an ascent, but it also had a breathtaking view from the top. Looking over my shoulder, I could see the long vistas of granite and pine trees—the country I'd just ridden through. Relief Peak raised its head in the middle ground; in the distance were the shoulders of the mountains around Sonora Pass, where the pack station was.

And ahead of me was a vast, treeless meadow with a sheet of blue water in the middle. Beyond that the sharp outlines of the little ridge between Emigrant Meadow and Summit Meadow. And right next to Summit Meadow was Snow Lake. We were getting there.

I clucked to the horses and called the dog, who had plopped herself down in the shade of a boulder. She got up slowly, looking tired and a little footsore. Damn. I'd been afraid this long day might be hard on her paws.

Still, everybody seemed to be moving okay as we worked our way down the gradual slope to Emigrant Meadow. As I got closer, the meadow began to appear as blue as the lake—wide swathes of wild lupine carpeted it, the sweet, elusive fragrance as heady as the deep blue-violet color.

Riding through heaven, riding through the sky, I thought, as the lupine surrounded us. Flowery images, for sure. But what else could one say? How many people had ridden through fields of lupine, solitary on horseback, alone with the wind?

I sang. The dog pricked up her ears and lapped water from a stream. The horses drank; I took a long swallow from my water bottle.

"Not too far now," I told them all.

And it wasn't. Not too far, and not too steep. Just a gentle dirt trail, running through a series of small meadows and pothole lakes, climbing only briefly here and there. Until, an hour later, we reached the wide, grassy openness of Summit Meadow, with the peaks of Bonn Pass hovering above it.

I stopped to let the horses water one more time by the old stone cabin in Summit Meadow. Still plenty of daylight left. And Snow Lake was just ahead. No problem.

No problem at all. In fact, all my problems seemed to have dropped away as I'd ridden. I forgot about my job, I forgot about Lonny and our strained and tired relationship. As for the dead man in Deadman Meadow, he'd never crossed my mind, even once.

NINE

Snow Lake was a quarter of a mile from Summit Meadow. I rode over the little ridge that separated them, and was unprepared for the feeling of apprehension that hit me at my first sight of the lake.

I'd camped at Snow Lake before, with Lonny; I'd chosen it for my first camp on this trip because it was the right distance away, and there was a particular campsite I liked. I called it the lagoon camp. But I'd forgotten how dark and forbidding Snow Lake can seem.

Every mountain lake and meadow has its own particular character. I never wanted to camp by Emigrant Lake, for instance; it always felt too exposed to me. Snow Lake was sheltered enough, in a rocky hollow near the ridge line, but it seemed darkly opaque, mysterious, and even ominous. It never struck me as a pretty, sunny mountain lake.

This evening, already in the shadow of the ridge, riffled with little waves, Snow Lake looked more forbidding than welcoming. Oh well. We were here and we were staying, I told myself.

Just ride on to the lagoon camp; you've always liked that spot.

The lagoon camp was half a mile away; we skirted the lake, riding west. And sure enough, as we rounded the tip, where Forest Service workers had built a little stone dam in the forties, I saw the small lagoon below the main lake lit with evening sunshine. It was empty; I hadn't seen another soul so far.

Once again my heart lifted, my mood as mercurial as the light. There was a meadow next to the lagoon, and a campsite in some boulders near the meadow. This was all going to be just great.

I tied my livestock to trees near the campsite and unsaddled the saddle horse and unpacked the pack horse. Judging that both were tired and hungry enough not to wander, I left them turned loose while I strung a picket line out in the meadow between two pines.

Both horses lay down and rolled right away, choosing a sandy spot near the lake. I smiled, watching them. Once they'd gotten up, shaken off, and taken one more drink, I caught Gunner and tethered him to the picket line. He was tied long enough to reach the grass, and short enough that (I hoped) he wouldn't tangle himself up.

Methods of dealing with livestock while camping were as various as the people who went. Some hobbled their horses, some staked them out, some built rope corrals, some tied everything up, some left everything loose. The last method was a bit fatalistic in my opinion: the traveler trusting to his horse's loyalty and love of grain to stay in camp.

I didn't care for hobbles; many horses could move along at a fair pace in them. Nor did I like staking out; I'd seen too many horses get tangled up. Rope corrals were notoriously unreliable. My preferred method was to keep one horse on the picket line and one off, during the daylight hours, and tie both up at night. Generally speaking, a horse is very reluctant to go off on his own; I had no doubt that Plumber would stay within sight of Gunner.

Keeping half an eye on the horses as I worked, I unpacked and set up my small dome tent, unrolled and laid out my pad and sleeping bag, gathered firewood and built a fire. Then I tied Plumber up and turned Gunner loose.

Next I fetched a pot of water from the lake and pumped it through a filter, unfolded my collapsible chair, got out some salted peanuts and a bottle of Jack Daniel's, and made myself a drink.

The light slanted low and golden over the meadow and the lagoon, raising bright sparks on the surface of the water and gilding the feathery stems of ryegrass. In fifteen minutes or so, the sun would drop behind the rim of the canyon behind me. I leaned back in my chair, watching the fire flicker, and took a long swallow of bourbon and branch water. Ah, the cocktail hour.

The horses cropped grass peacefully; the dog lay sacked out flat on her side, taking a well-earned rest. I put my feet up on a boulder, ate a handful of peanuts, and sighed with contentment. I was here.

Content lasted until dark. I had two drinks, not because I'm so fond of Jack Daniel's, but because it was all I had. Wine and beer are prohibitively heavy to pack in, and nothing seems to mix as well with lake water as bourbon. So I drank my whiskey and water, ate peanuts, and watched the light die out of the sky.

When the air began to grow dim, I caught Gunner and tied him up, made myself another tortilla with salami and cheese, and gave the dog a bowl of dried dog food, which she disdained. All she seemed to want was to sleep.

I put another log on the fire and thought I'd do the same. This long day was trailing its way toward night, and I was tired. I'd brought some steak and cans of chili, and other more labor-intensive dinners, but I really didn't feel like cooking.

What I felt like, suddenly, was having somebody to talk to. Dusk gathered around me; smoke rose from my small fire and curled out over the lagoon. Flickers skimmed over the water, hunting flying insects. A fish jumped with a splash, making a ring on the still surface of the lake.

I could go fishing, I thought. If Lonny were here, he'd go fishing. If Lonny were here, he'd be sitting next to me now, happy to be in camp. And whether I felt frustrated with him or not, I'd also feel safe. And I'd have someone to talk to.

I made myself another drink and put my jacket back on. Why the hell had I wanted to come on this trip alone, anyway? Had I forgotten just what it felt like to be alone in the mountains as dark closed in?

I got up and got my gun out of my saddlebag. There was still enough light to see by. I checked to make sure there was no shell in the chamber, though I knew this was how I'd left the gun. Five bullets were what I had; I'd brought no spare ammunition. The pistol was for self-defense in an emergency, for scaring off bears in the unlikely event it was necessary, for shooting a horse in what I hoped was the extremely unlikely event of a broken leg. I sincerely believed I would get through the whole trip without using it.

Putting the gun back in its leather holster and snapping the safety strap over the hammer, I hung it on my belt and sat back down. The pistol was bulky and awkward there around my waist, but comforting, too.

I took a long swallow of my drink. Bright against the darkness, flames crackled in dry pine boughs. I could hear something moving in the trees and scrub, probably a deer.

What is it about sitting by a fire and hearing animal noises outside in the night? Despite the fact that I knew perfectly well that deer were the likeliest cause, I felt nervous. Fixing my eyes on the fire, I listened to the sounds of brush breaking and wondered what exactly was out there. Bears? Bigfoot?

I took another swallow of my drink. You knew this would happen, I reminded myself. You've been alone here before. Some kind of caveman instinct kicks in as it gets dark. The animal noises seemed to scare me almost automatically, a reaction as simple and primitive as hunger.

Time to go to bed. I put another log on the fire, wanting the companionship of its flickering light as I went to sleep. Roey looked up at me as I dug my flashlight out of my duffel bag, her first sign of life since we'd made camp.

"You can sleep with me," I told her.

Clicking the flashlight on, I followed its beam out to where the horses were tethered. They stood quietly, unperturbed by the deer or whatever it was. I ran the light over them. Plumber looked pretty ganted up, his flanks sucked in high and tight. Damn. This was not a good sign.

I checked him over closely, but he seemed okay otherwise, one foot cocked in a horse's typical resting pose. I'd just have to see how he was in the morning.

Back to the fire. I took off my jeans and boots, left my underwear and tank top on, made a pillow of my jacket, put the pistol under it, and crawled into the sleeping bag.

"Come on," I said to Roey.

She got up stiffly and picked her way over the ground toward me, looking pretty damn sore. I lifted her paws and checked them in the firelight; the pads were intact, no cuts or scrapes. She wagged her tail when I was done, stepped carefully into the tent, and curled up in a fold of my sleeping bag.

I left the tent door open, so I could look out at the night sky, and the fire made comforting orangy shadows on the nylon. The dog's warm weight pressed against my side and I snuggled deeper into the bag. In a rush as sudden as it had come, the fear went. I felt cozy and happy lying there alone, miles from any other human. The distant white sparkle of the stars seemed friendly. I dozed. Then I slept.

Sometime later I woke up. I didn't know how long I'd been asleep; it was still dark. I lay in my sleeping bag with the feeling that something was wrong.

The fire had died; I must have slept for a few hours, anyway. What had woken me?

Then I heard it. *Thump, thump, thump.* A familiar sound. The sound of a horse pawing the ground.

I scrambled out of the sack, fear twisting inside of me. Shoving my bare feet into my boots and grabbing the flashlight, I went to check the horses.

As I'd more than half suspected, it was Plumber. Pawing the ground and looking unhappy. Colicked.

Damn, damn, and damn. I had known this might be a problem. What Plumber probably had was a stress colic; I had seen it before with other young horses on their first pack trip. The long day and unaccustomed circumstances produced a mild bellyache.

Trouble was, in horses a mild bellyache could be life-threatening. The equine digestive system is constructed such that a horse can't vomit. Thus, upset stomachs could result in ruptured guts and death. Colic, a general term for any sort of intestinal disturbance, is a common and often serious problem that I frequently had to deal with in my role as a veterinarian.

But it was different when it was my own horse and we were twenty miles into the backcountry. The sort of help I would need with a severe colic—the ability to hook the horse up to an IV, a surgery center if need be—was simply not available. And Plumber was my friend. The distress in his eyes upset me in ways that overrode the detachment I'd cultivated in my veterinary career.

Still, I'd come prepared. Taking a deep breath to calm myself, I patted Plumber's neck and walked back to camp to get my vet kit.

In the kit was a bottle of banamine and a syringe and needles. Setting the flashlight down on a rock, I filled the syringe with eleven cc's, my hands shaking a little with chill and anxiety.

Back to Plumber, who was pawing the ground again. I took his pulse briefly and watched his respiration in the flashlight beam. Both were only slightly elevated, and he wasn't sweating. There was every chance in the world this shot of banamine would put him right.

I slipped the needle into his jugular vein, watched the blood well into the syringe, and injected the shot. Then I waited.

Plumber had accepted the pinprick of the needle quietly; now he watched me watch him. In a minute I could see a change in his expression. The worried look in his eyes vanished, and the normal curious brightness returned. He bumped me with his nose.

Good. The painkiller had kicked in. I studied the horse while I shivered in the night air. My bare legs were covered in goose bumps.

Should I turn him loose? The type of colic he had was probably due a great deal to stress and tension. Plumber was unaccustomed to being tied up all night, and this confinement could be contributing to his discomfort. If I turned him loose he could relax. Lie down, crop a little grass, move around when it suited him.

On the other hand, he could also run off. Or eat too much and make his digestive problems worse. Or, worst-case scenario, the pain could return and he might lie down and thrash. In which case it was possible his intestines would twist, like a hose with a kink, and he would die. I would never be able to get him to a surgery center in time to save him.

I stared at him and he tugged impatiently on his tether. He wanted to be turned loose. I made a decision and slipped his halter off. Without hesitation, he walked over to a nearby patch of grass and started eating. He felt fine, for the moment, anyway. Thank God for drugs.

Running the flashlight over Gunner, I ascertained that he looked okay. I gave him a pat on the neck and marched my by now thoroughly chilled body back to camp. I pulled off my boots, soaking wet from the dew-covered grass, and crawled back in the sleeping bag.

Roey grunted. She'd never even moved. I doubted that she'd even woken.

I, however, was now wide awake. I listened to the sound of Plumber munching grass and worried. Given that his colic was as mild as I supposed, the banamine should relieve his pain for at least six or eight hours. And, if I was right, when the drug wore off, the horse would be perfectly fine.

But if I was wrong and he was, or became, worse, the pain would come back and I would be forced to decide what to do. I would go out, I decided, lying in my sleeping bag and shivering. I would go right back out and try and save my horse.

I watched the dog snoring gently next to me and made another choice. I had planned to ride to Dorothy Lake, a mere five miles away, the next morning, but I would not. My dog was sore and tired, my horse was sick. I was pretty worn out myself. I would give us all a rest day. Make sure Plumber was completely okay before we moved on.

Choices made, I rolled over, hoping to doze before I got up to check the horse. It looked like I would be spending a little more time at Snow Lake.

TEN

Everything seemed better in the morning. I'd checked Plumber twice during the night and he appeared to be fine. The second time I'd tied him back up and turned Gunner loose. I woke several hours later to the soft gray light of dawn and a feeling of calm.

Little white mists rose off the silvery surface of the lake. The sky over Bonn Pass was a paler gray, announcing the approach of the sun. I could see Gunner, out in the meadow eating. Plumber stood quietly on the picket line. All was well.

I snuggled back down in my bag and waited for warmth. I am not one of those people who springs up early on camping trips, building a fire while fingers and toes grow numb. I like to luxuriate in the sleeping bag until the sun gets me up.

The lagoon camp was ideal for this, which was one of the reasons I liked it. When the sun rose over the ridge, rays streamed across the lake and hit my tent—pale yellow light as cheering as a fire at night.

Light and heat, how wonderful. I watched with satisfaction

as the sun rose, stronger and more golden every moment. And warmer. The lake gleamed; the sky went from gray to blue. Not a cloud in sight. A perfect Sierra morning.

I lay quietly and peacefully in the sleeping bag while the sunlight dappled the tent, content. When it grew warm enough to be encouraging, I got up and slipped my wet boots on, caught Gunner and tied him up, and turned Plumber loose.

The little brown horse looked absolutely normal; nickering at me as I walked toward him, eager to eat. This was good, but I wouldn't be sure he was all right until noon or so, when the last effects of the banamine would be out of his system.

Building a fire, I heated a pot of water and made cowboy coffee. Strong and rough, the coffee suited the place and my mood. I sat in my chair in the morning sunshine, wearing my tank top and underwear, and took hot, harsh sips from the insulated cup I'd brought.

Motion in the woods. Turning my head, I saw a buck step from the trees into the meadow. I froze. Moving only my eyes, I checked the dog. Still asleep in the tent. Oblivious.

I watched as the buck, a four-pointer, began to crop grass. Another stepped out of the trees. Six points. And another. Seven bucks in all emerged from the pines—one with an enormous twisted rack, like nothing I'd ever seen. I wondered how he managed to walk through the trees.

They grazed in the sunshine, apparently unworried by the horses or the fire. Park bucks, no doubt. The boundary of Yosemite National Park was right on top of the closest ridge, and hunting was not allowed in the park at any time. These bucks probably spent hunting season safely holed up—thus their indifference to my camp.

Seven big sandy-colored bucks, grazing by the shore of a bright lake in the early-morning light. I smiled and took a carefully unobtrusive sip of my coffee. Now this was living.

Ten minutes or so later, when they'd drifted off toward the

forest, I relaxed my muscles and stood up. I was hungry.

Putting a cast iron skillet on the fire, I got out a package of bacon and some scones. I laid the strips of bacon on the skillet one by one; they sputtered and hissed and steamed. The sweet, salty smell rose into the air, and the dog woke up.

She blinked at me from her position on the sleeping bag, ascertained that I really was frying bacon, and got to her feet. A long, stiff stretch, a big yawn, and a shake—then she walked toward me a little gingerly, wagging her tail.

I patted her wide, wedge-shaped head. "Yes, you can have some."

Taking the cooked strips out, I let the grease cool a minute, then poured it on the dry dog food Roey had ignored last night. She wagged her tail enthusiastically when I set the bowl in front of her. Now this, she seemed to say, is more like it.

The dog dug in; I munched strips of bacon and bites of cinnamon raisin scones, washing them down with hot coffee. There was some real strength in the sun now.

When I was done eating, I stripped off my clothes and boots, pulled on a bathing suit and some rubber and nylon water sandals, and prepared for a morning bath. Had the lake been a little more isolated, I wouldn't have bothered with the bathing suit, but just my luck, a whole party of good old boys would probably ride up as I dove in.

Not that I dove in immediately. First I walked down to a small pebbly beach and tried the water. Cool, not cold, as this lagoon had been the last time I camped here. So far, so good.

Spotting a good diving rock that I remembered, I walked over and stretched myself out on top of it, waiting for the sun to warm my skin. It took half an hour of concentrated sun bathing; I let my mind wander.

This was the thing about life in camp; this was the reason I'd come to these mountains alone. This sense of timelessness, this freedom from schedules and pressure, from other people's expectations. If I wanted, I could spend my whole two weeks at Snow Lake, dozing in the sun and swimming. No reason not to. No reason to do anything, except by my own inclination.

In the mornings I was always happy to be alone. The fear that came with darkness seemed inexplicable and slightly ridiculous in the morning light.

I rolled over, sunning my front side. The sky above me was a deep, pure cobalt blue. Turning my head, I could see the lake coming at me in gentle green swells rimmed with gold; the breeze had come up. I snuggled into my rock.

Being here, just being here, was what I wanted. Aware of myself as a still, solitary speck on the great rolling sweep of the globe. All my thoughts, all my worries reduced to insignificance.

The sun grew hotter on my skin. I turned over again, propped my chin on my hands, let my eyes drift over the granite slopes on the far side of the lake. Sometimes I felt like a small vulnerable animal up here, a house cat mistakenly lost in the wilderness.

When I was younger, I had come to these mountains with expectations, seeking a comfort that they would not give. In love with their beauty, I returned again and again, to see if in some way they would condescend to seem familiar.

I put my cheek against the rock. This is the intimacy you can find, I told myself. Just this. Alone with yourself in the present moment. Quiet in this austerely lovely place.

Now I was hot. I stood up, stretched, walked to the edge of the rock. The lake was blue-green, clear, deep. I could see the stones on the bottom. I put my hands over my head, chose my spot, and forced myself to spring off the bottoms of my feet and part the water with my hands.

My God, it was cold. Cold, green, silky, wet. I came up, gasped, and swam. Water clear and soft around me, clean as air. In a moment, it was cool, not cold.

I swam under the surface, stroking quietly through the underwater world. Green and shadowy, mysterious and dim, so different from the bright, sharp-edged land up above.

A few strokes later, I turned back. Never swim alone, they say. And particularly not miles away from any help, they would probably add. Whoever they were.

I swam back to shore, washed my face, armpits, crotch, and hair with the biodegradable soap I'd brought, dumped a pot of water over myself to rinse off, and swam again. Then I lay back down on my rock.

So, what about Lonny? Could I find some clarity in my aloneness here that would help me in my relationship? I loved Lonny in much the same way I loved Plumber and Gunner and Roey. He was part of my life. But were we really well suited as a couple?

Just what was it I wanted that he didn't give, I asked myself, staring at the big gray boulder in front of me.

Someone who was sensitive to who I was, who could make room for my way of being—that was the answer. I wanted a man for whom I would be more than a pleasant addition to a satisfactory life.

My skin and hair were drying rapidly. I sat up. Maybe there was no right man for me. I certainly didn't have another one in mind. I also doubted that Lonny would ever change much. He liked himself; he liked his life. He could, as he was proving, get along without me.

And me, I was lonely. In some ways, I was lonelier at home than I was here. I missed having a partner. I was thirty-five; there were lines around my eyes, some gray strands in my dark hair. I was past the point of being a cute young thing, if I'd ever been one. I had zero interest in checking out the dating game.

Maybe I needed to reacquaint myself with solitude. Maybe that was why I was here.

I was dry now. Getting up, I walked back to camp. Roey was asleep in the sunshine, full and content. I hoped she would rest all day and be able to travel tomorrow.

Plumber grazed in the meadow, looking fine. I caught him and tied him on the picket line and turned Gunner loose. Then I pulled off my wet swimsuit, hung it on a bush to dry, and put on some clean, dry underwear, shorts, and a tank top. Grabbing some dried fruit and nuts to nibble on, I sat down in the shade of a pine tree with a book.

Not just a book. With *Walden*. Henry David Thoreau's masterpiece was a tradition for me. When I'd first gone backpacking in the Sierras I'd brought *Walden* to read; in fact, it was *Walden* that inspired me to attempt some solitary camping in the woods. And on every trip thereafter, I brought it as some might bring the Bible. Brought it and read it.

"I went to the woods because I wished to live deliberately, to front only the essential facts of life, and see if I could not learn what it had to teach, and not, when I came to die, discover that I had not lived."

I put the book down. Here I was, alone in the woods, following in Henry David's footsteps. Looking up, I watched the white streak of a jet trail progress across the sky. Some things had changed, others were the same. People were crowded into the cabin of that jet, reading, writing, thinking, twenty thousand feet up in a little metal box. On their way to Chicago, maybe, or New York. And all the while I sat here by the side of my lake and built a fire to cook my breakfast.

I read some more. Ate a chunk of dried pineapple. Swatted at the pesky and persistent flies. A hummingbird zoomed into camp and swooped up to each red object she saw, exploring them for signs of nectar. Disappointed, she whirled away, in search of better feeding ground.

Thoreau was beginning to pall. I looked up, saw that Gunner had quit eating and was resting in the shade, idly swishing flies with his tail. He could just as well do that on the picket line.

I caught him and turned Plumber loose. By now all effects of the banamine would be gone—and Plumber looked fine. His flanks were no longer ganted up, his eye was bright, and his attitude seemed good. As soon as I unclipped his lead rope, he put his head down and started eating.

Sitting back down in my chair, I watched him meander around the meadow. He wasn't really hungry; he ate a bite, walked a few steps, took another bite. Then he walked down to the shore and had a long, leisurely drink.

Done with that, he looked around, took a step forward into the lake, splashed the water once with his foot, and lay down. I leaned forward in amazement as he rolled in two feet of lake water, putting his whole head and most of his body underwater and getting himself thoroughly wet. I laughed out loud.

"Haven't you ever seen a horse take a bath?"

The voice came from behind me; I jumped up with a lurch, heart thumping. Even as I whirled, I registered a familiar voice.

Ted. Ted sitting on Hank, in the woods behind my camp, watching me.

"How did you get here?" I demanded.

"Rode from Bigelow."

"Oh." The trail from Bigelow Lake, a mere mile away, came down the opposite slope from the trail I'd ridden in on.

"So what are you doing here?" I asked.

"I packed Dan Jacobi and his crew in there yesterday."

"I thought he was going to Huckleberry."

"He was. He changed his mind. He wanted to be somewhere less crowded. I told him Bigelow."

This made sense. Huckleberry Lake was big, with a few large islands, pretty campsites, and great fishing. Though a long ride in, it was very popular. Bigelow, smaller and much higher in elevation, was rocky and almost treeless, seldom visited. The fishing was equally good, though.

Ted smiled at me. "I thought if I took him to Bigelow I could come visit you."

I stared at him, wondering if he could possibly be as obtuse as that sounded. I hadn't ridden into the mountains alone in search of company.

"But I wasn't sure you'd still be here," Ted went on.

"I didn't mean to be. Plumber colicked last night. I thought I'd give him a layover day."

"He looks all right," Ted said.

We both watched the horse, who was eating grass, his back wet and shiny.

"I've never seen a horse roll in water like that," I commented.

Ted smiled. "They do that."

We were both quiet. Ted made no move to dismount, just sat on Hank and watched me. For my part, I did not invite him to sit down. I was feeling intruded upon and mildly resentful. Why in hell had Ted considered it his civic duty to come check on me?

Ted's eyes moved around my campsite and then back to me. "You look like you're doing okay."

"I'm fine." A thought struck me. "Lonny didn't send you to check on me, did he?"

Ted raised one hand. "Lonny has no idea I'm here." He met my eyes. "I didn't say a word to him."

I shrugged my shoulders, puzzled. "Well, when you get back to the pack station you can tell him everything's going well. Are you riding back out tomorrow?"

"Yep. I'm leaving Dan and his boys at Bigelow for a week. They're keeping their saddle horses and two pack mules, in case they want to make an overnight ride. The one kid knows enough to pack a horse."

"Uh-huh." I nodded, not much interested in any of this. I would avoid Bigelow Lake, and with any luck at all, would never run into Dan Jacobi and his crew, which included the obnoxious blond Steve.

"Well, I'd better get on back." Ted was still watching me. He seemed to be waiting, I didn't know what for. I was damned if I was going to invite him to sit down with me. I hadn't ridden all these miles to gossip with Ted.

"See you later, then," I told him.

"You bet." Ted turned Hank and looked back at me. "See you later."

Once he was gone, I got up and made myself a tortilla with peanut butter on it for lunch. It was too early for a drink. Or was it? The sun's over the yardarm somewhere, as my friend Lisa Bennet used to say. What the hell. I was on vacation.

I made a Jack Daniel's and water, weak, and sipped it with my impromptu peanut butter sandwich. I read some more of *Walden* and took another swim. Then I took a nap. Life in camp.

By the time late afternoon arrived, I could tell that all my animals were feeling rested and more chipper. Roey quit snoozing and found a pinecone to play with. Plumber trotted off across the meadow, looking like he wanted to go somewhere. I caught him and let Gunner loose.

Tonight, I thought, I'll make myself a proper dinner. Salad and steak and garlic bread.

I had these luxuries because I had packed a small cooler with a block of ice in it. It wouldn't last the whole trip, but for the first few days, anyway, I was traveling in style.

First I made myself a drink. Who can cook without a drink in hand? Then I built a fire, made a salad, buttered bread and wrapped it in foil, and marinated my strip of skirt steak in soy sauce and garlic.

All things prepared, I sat in the sun and sipped my drink and read *Walden* for an hour. Camp seemed peaceful; I was no longer worried about Plumber; dark was several hours away. Life was good. I felt all set to enjoy my solitary evening.

But it wasn't to be. Just as I got up to put another log on the fire and freshen my drink, Gunner nickered. Plumber echoed him. Roey barked. I looked up to see two horsemen picking their way down the trail from Bigelow Lake. Even at this distance I recognized Ted's big buckskin. The other horse was a gray. Looked like I was having company.

ELEVEN

Ted and Dan Jacobi rode up to my camp and dismounted while I was catching Gunner. By the time I had both my horses securely tethered to the picket line Hank and Dan's gray gelding were tied to nearby pine trees and Ted and Dan were sitting on convenient boulders near my fire. Roey sniffed them in turn and wagged her tail.

"We came to have a drink with you," Ted said.

"That's nice," I replied, doing my best to keep the chagrin out of my voice. "I'd ask you to stay to dinner, but I'm afraid there's only enough for one."

"We won't stay," Dan Jacobi said politely, rubbing Roey behind the ears.

"No, but we brought you a drink." Ted was carrying his saddlebags. He opened them up and produced a bottle of Stoly's, a bottle of tonic, three limes, and a plastic bag of ice. "Your favorite."

I had to smile. I might not welcome their company, but a vodka tonic on ice sounded just fine.

"Thanks," I said, as Ted made and handed me the drink.

He produced a small bottle of Jim Beam and proceeded to make whiskey and waters for himself and Dan. It took a minute, but finally it dawned on me that the elaborate vodka tonic preparations had been brought solely on my account. And they had to have been thought of and organized back at the pack station. Had Ted intended to come visit me all along? And if so, why?

This question occupied my mind while we all sat around quietly and sipped our drinks. I waited. Damned if I was going to make conversation. This whole visit was their idea; let them talk.

Ted tried a smile. "I told Dan he should stay in camp," he said. "When a man rides out to have a drink with a pretty lady, he wants to go alone. But Dan, here, he had to come with me."

Dan Jacobi smiled briefly. I had a moment's sense of his inner force, then his expression became even and unremarkable. An odd man, I thought. He wouldn't stand out in a crowd, really, but he seemed a good deal more intense than the average person when you paid attention to him.

"So how's it going?" Ted asked.

"Fine." I was still feeling uncooperative.

"How's your horse?"

"He's fine." I took a cold sip of my drink and sighed. What the hell did Ted want?

There was some more quiet.

"I been thinking," Ted said at last. "Thinking about Bill."

"Oh." Sad to say, I'd more or less forgotten about Bill Evans. His death had been striking and tragic, but I'd had more than enough on my mind for the last two days.

"I keep wondering why he did it." Ted took a swallow of his drink and stared at the fire. "He didn't say anything about me, did he, Gail?"

"No. He talked about colicked horses. Horses with fire in their bellies. Said he wanted to die. That was it."

"Nothing else?" Ted still watched the fire.

"Well, there was some more along those lines. Green fire, I think he said, and he couldn't save them. Something like that. It really didn't make any sense."

"But he didn't talk about me throwing him out of the bar or anything?" Ted was still off on his own track. "I been telling Dan, I'm worried about that. If I'd known he was thinking of killing himself, I never would have done that."

Dan gave Ted a level look. "What did I tell you? You heard what she said."

"Yeah." Ted drank some more whiskey. "Dan, here, he told me to ask you. I'm still worried it was on Bill's mind."

"Well, I can tell you he never said anything about it while I was there." I looked away.

I wasn't liking this conversation. Talking about Bill Evans was bringing the whole thing back to me, and I wanted to forget. The sight of that man, lying on his back, shot through the chest, waiting to die . . . I shivered. Wanting to die all alone, staring up at the distant stars. And I hadn't saved him.

It brought mortality, my own mortality, all too close. Those same indifferent stars would watch me die, if something went dramatically wrong up here. All alone.

We all took sips of our drinks. Dan Jacobi spoke. "It's a bad deal, but it's not your fault." He looked at Ted. "Let it go."

Ted said nothing.

I handed him my empty glass. "Since you're here, why don't you make me another. That ice will just melt."

Ted seemed to rouse himself with an effort. He smiled, a faint echo of his usual cocky grin, and took my glass. Slowly, carefully, he began to make the drink.

I turned my attention to Dan Jacobi. The man was beginning to interest me. I liked his quiet assumption of power, his apparent lack of the need to assert it. I watched his eyes as he watched the fire. It struck me that they were eyes that were accustomed to looking straight at problems, whether dissatisfied horse buyers or unruly colts. He had spoken firmly but not unkindly to Ted, whom he seemed to regard as just such a problem, at least for the moment.

Dan was aware of my eyes on him, I could tell, but he said nothing.

Ted handed me my drink, and poured a splash more whiskey in his own and Dan's. The sun had dropped behind the canyon rim, and dusk was beginning to gather. The flames of the fire were brighter. I was ready for these guys to go any time. I had no wish to cook and eat my dinner in the dark.

Ted didn't seem to be in a hurry. He squatted back down on his boulder and regarded the fire. After some seconds of this, he said, "Bill didn't say anything about Blue Winter, did he?"

"No," I said shortly. "I told you what he said, as well as I could remember. What have you got going about this guy, Blue?"

"Blue's a thief," Dan Jacobi said evenly.

"So you said. How did he happen to steal your horse?"

Dan shrugged. "Took him home and never paid for him."

I waited. The man said nothing more. I had the definite impression that the subject was off-limits.

Oh well. So what? I had only a passing interest in the whole thing anyway. If Dan Jacobi didn't want to talk about it, fine.

"You haven't seen Blue out here, have you?" Ted's voice held the familiar gossipy tone.

"No." I was really getting tired of this. I stood up. "I haven't seen anybody except you two. If you'll excuse me, I need to cook my dinner before it gets dark."

"Of course." Dan Jacobi stood up, too. "We'll be going."

"Thanks for the drink," I said, as he turned toward his horse.

"Any time." He tipped his white straw cowboy hat briefly. Ted followed him more slowly, stopping to look back at me.

97

"Sure you don't want some company tonight?" He grinned at me, his barroom grin, the little-boy smile that had won several dozen hearts. Or if not hearts, at least bed companions.

"I'm sure." I laid the skirt steak on the grill.

Dan was already mounted. I looked his gray gelding over curiously. He was, indeed, big and pretty. Too big and pretty for me. I don't like horses with that sort of heavy, massive muscling; I think they're prone to problems. And I've often thought that overly pretty horses are like overly pretty men— not as likely to be good ones as their plainer counterparts. To top it all off, I'm not crazy about dapple grays, everybody else's favorite color. They're more likely to get melanomas, for one thing. And they're just so obvious.

Still, I did the polite thing. "Nice-looking horse," I said to Dan Jacobi.

"Thank you."

Ted laughed. "I told him he shouldn't take that ten-thousand-dollar son of a bitch up here in these rocks. He should rent one from me."

Dan said nothing.

Ted was on Hank now. I heard him cluck, and the two horsemen moved off. I waved. "See you later," I said.

"You take care." Ted looked over his shoulder at me.

"Night." I could just hear Dan Jacobi's low voice.

Turning back to my fire, I got to work on dinner. But even as I warmed the bread and cooked the steak, I thought. What in the world was in Ted's head? Was he feeling that guilty over Bill Evans's death? Belatedly I wondered why, exactly, Ted had thrown Bill out of the bar. Could that have something to do with Ted's excessive and morbid-seeming curiosity?

Too late to ask him questions now. I wasn't sure I would have bothered, anyway. I wanted to forget the whole thing, not think about it more.

Try as I would, though, I found I couldn't. I thought about

Bill Evans's death as I made and ate my dinner, as I fed the dog and checked my horses, as I got ready for sleep. I thought about it to the exclusion of anything else, despite my intention to do otherwise.

Why had the man shot himself, really? Why was his death upsetting Ted so much? And what, if anything, did it have to do with me?

Naturally I had no answers to any of these questions, but that didn't stop them spinning uselessly around my mind. Along with unwanted images of Bill Evans's face, and bloody chest, and confusing words.

Damn. I didn't want this. I didn't want anything to do with it. Why in hell had I happened to find him?

The fire gave me back no reasons. It flickered and smoked. I stared at it from my sleeping bag, wishing I could drop the subject of the unfortunate man's suicide.

Roey snuggled up against me, and I reached down to stroke her head. "I can't even go to sleep," I told her pointlessly. "This is bad." Little did I know.

TWELVE

The next day, I saw Blue Winter. I'd saddled and packed up in the morning and was on my way to Wilma Lake. I met him in Grace Meadow.

I was in new territory now. Once I left Summit Meadow and crossed Bonn Pass, I was on trails I'd never seen, only traced on my map. Of course, I'd heard plenty of stories. All my years with Lonny had been filled with recounted pack-trip sagas and I knew many secondhand details about the trail to Wilma, and Jack Tone Canyon, and Benson Lake.

Still, everything I saw was new to me. Bonn Pass, the highest pass I'd cross on my trip, was less spectacular than I'd supposed. Dorothy Lake, which I passed en route, more severe and dramatic than I'd ever imagined. And, unlike my ride to Snow Lake, I had to stop and consult my map often.

Unfamiliar trails were challenging. I didn't know where the tricky spots were ahead of time; I found myself getting tense when I saw steep, rocky climbs or descents ahead of me. I never knew whether they would be easy or downright dangerous until I was right in the middle of them.

Experienced packers can tell slickrock at a glance, at least sometimes. Sometimes they can't, until a horse slips. Slickrock doesn't always look much different from less slippery granite.

And though I knew the basics—enough not to let my horses step in V-shaped wedges, and to keep them off obviously loose stepping stones—I wasn't experienced enough to eyeball a section of rocky trail and know immediately where the worst sections were.

Thus, although I enjoyed the new scenery, I was pretty tense by the time we'd worked our way down Bonn Pass. So far, so good; no cuts or scrapes on either horse, and we were in level forest land, a ride in the park.

Grace Meadow appeared up ahead of us, a long, rambling grassland that followed Hetch Hetchy Creek down to Jack Tone Canyon. I rode until I found a pretty spot along the creek with a sandy bank and a convenient pine grove nearby. Lunch time.

Roey plopped herself down next to me when I sat. She'd traveled well today, neither wearing herself out with unnecessary excursions nor falling behind. She trotted patiently in Plumber's wake, conserving her strength. She was learning.

I took my boots off and soaked my feet in the truly bone-chilling water. It was snowmelt, and I could only bear it for a minute.

Burying my toes in the warm sand to thaw and dry them, I busied myself making a tortilla sandwich. Roey snoozed next to me; my horses dozed in the shade of the pines. None of them saw the approaching horseman. Only me.

Riding along the trail through Grace Meadow, going the same way I was going. At first he was just a distant rider; I watched him curiously. First person I'd seen today. The details began to sink in. A dun saddle horse, a smaller sorrel pack horse. A gray hat with a fedora slant. I could see a small white dog running alongside.

My immediate reaction was mixed. I'd liked this man when I met him, but Dan Jacobi's insistence that he was a thief, and Ted's obvious mistrust, had made me wonder. I could see his red hair under the gray hat now. I wonder if he knows about Bill Evans, I thought.

He had left the pack station the morning after we'd found Bill. I hadn't known, then, whether the man was dead or alive. I didn't know that Blue Winter even knew that Bill Evans had shot himself, though surely he couldn't have missed the chopper.

And Ted had said that Blue had lived with Bill's wife for a while. The solitary rider was close enough that I could see his face, as well as the red-brown freckles on the white dog. What should I say, or not say?

Blue Winter rode up the trail until he was fifty feet away from where I sat on the banks of the creek. Reining his horse to a halt, he watched impassively as his young dog raced up to me, wagged her tail in my direction, and sniffed noses with Roey. The two dogs began an elaborate greeting ritual, composed of much tail wagging, sniffing, and leaping about.

"Hello, Stormy," Blue Winter said.

I smiled. This man had that effect on me. Reminding myself that Dan Jacobi had said he was a thief, and I didn't know what, if anything, he might have had to do with Bill Evans's suicide, I let my smile die.

"Hi," I said.

We were both quiet for a moment. Normal backcountry etiquette called for a least a few words of pleasant conversation here. And normally, I would enjoy exchanging some polite talk with another traveler; it made a nice break from the solitude of my own thoughts. But I was wondering what in the hell I ought to say to Blue Winter.

For his part, the man seemed quite content to be quiet, a trait I'd noticed in the bar. He regarded me without a sign of impatience, seeming happy to sit on his horse in the sunshine and watch me.

His stolen horse, if Dan Jacobi was to be believed. The big blaze-faced dun gelding looked worth stealing. Unlike Dan Jacobi's gray, this horse had the sort of long, flat muscling that I liked, and he wasn't overly pretty. He looked to be in good flesh, too; traveling in the mountains didn't seem to have stressed him any. If Blue Winter had stolen him, at least he was taking care of him.

"So, how's it going?" I said at last.

"Good enough. How about you?"

As I'd remembered from our previous conversations, his face remained remote, giving no clues to his thoughts. If I had any curiosity at all about him, I was going to have to work at satisfying it.

"I'm doing okay," I told him. "I've been camped at Snow Lake the last two nights. How about you?"

"I'm going to Tilden," he said briefly.

Well, it was one piece of information. Tilden Lake was several miles from Wilma Lake, and a popular backcountry destination because of its large size and good fishing.

"Planning to catch some golden trout up at Mary?" I asked. Nearby Mary Lake had one of the few remaining populations of native California golden trout. Most of the other lakes had been overrun by imported rainbows and brookies.

Blue Winter smiled. "I'm not much of a fisherman."

We watched each other with what I thought was mutual curiosity. I had the idea we both wanted to ask, "So, what do you come here for?" but courtesy forbade it. There was no answer to the question, anyway, but the discussion would be interesting.

103

Instead, I said, "I ran into Dan Jacobi and Ted Reiter at Snow Lake."

If I'd been hoping for a reaction to this, I'd have been disappointed. As I expected, Blue Winter's face showed nothing. Since it wasn't a question, he made no answer. Just sat there on his horse, watching me.

Suddenly I felt self-conscious, sitting on my sandbank, barefoot and defenseless. I stood up, scanning the meadow for my dog. She was wrestling happily with Blue's dog, twenty yards away. My two horses were still safely tied to pine trees. I turned back to my visitor.

"They mentioned you," I said.

He continued to say nothing. He was a master at it.

Then to my surprise, he dismounted. Holding his reins in one hand, he said, "Mind if I have lunch with you?"

"No, of course not." I stumbled over the words, too startled to consider what to say. I wasn't sure if I minded or not. But Blue Winter was already tying his horses up. He returned and sat down on a log, a polite ten feet from the sandbank where I'd settled back down. He was carrying his saddlebags, and produced an apple and some beef jerky.

Eyeing my tortilla, cheese, and salami, he smiled. "I'll trade you some apple for some cheese."

"Deal," I said, smiling back. Damn, he had a nice smile.

We swapped food and munched. The apple was a fine complement to my sandwich. I was still wondering what, if anything, to say to him, when he spoke.

"Did Dan Jacobi tell you I stole the dun horse?"

"Uh, yeah, he did." I swallowed a mouthful of tortilla and regarded the man cautiously.

I should have guessed. His face remained quiet; he said nothing. Just ate a piece of cheese.

As a conversationalist, he was difficult. But I was genuinely curious now.

"So why did Dan say that?" I prompted.

"He thinks I did, I guess," was the reply.

"And did you?"

"We disagree about that." Blue Winter ate a piece of apple and watched me quietly. "I'll tell you the story, if you're interested."

"Yes, I'm interested."

"All right, then." He paused. "I've known Dan awhile, and he knows me. About a year ago a friend of mine wanted a rope horse. He had plenty of money, but not much knowledge. He came to me to help him." Once again Blue Winter smiled. "I'm the opposite. I've got some knowledge and no money to speak of.

"Anyway, I went with this guy to Dan's and helped him try horses, and eventually we settled on this one." He looked over at the dun.

"My friend took him home, pending a vet check." He looked at me and I nodded. I knew about buying horses with the caveat that they would pass a veterinarian's inspection. I was often the vet in question.

"Of course, you know all about that. Anyway, that night the horse colicked, bad." He looked at me, and I nodded again.

"My friend didn't even realize something was wrong until the horse was in pretty bad straits. He called me; I came out and had a look and called Bob." Once again, the look.

I nodded and said, "Uh-huh." Bob was Bob Barton—our main competition for the equine veterinary market in Santa Cruz County.

"Bob said the horse needed to be operated on right away. You know what that costs."

I nodded and said, "Uh-huh" again. I did.

"My friend didn't want to pay that kind of money to fix a horse he didn't own yet. I called Dan and explained things to him. Dan wasn't willing to pay for it either. 'Just keep treating him,' he said. 'He'll either die or live. I'm not paying five thousand dollars for surgery.'

"But Bob was sure the horse had a twist. He'd die." Blue Winter shook his head.

"I don't have a whole lot of money. But the horse was just five years old. And he was a real nice horse and a hell of a rope horse. I called Dan back and asked him if I could have the horse if I paid to have him operated on. He said, 'Take him. I don't care.' " Blue shrugged.

"I didn't have five thousand dollars to spare. So I convinced Bob to do the operation at his place in Watsonville. He didn't want to, but it was either that or let the horse die. He has enough of a facility to do minor surgeries on horses, and I convinced him that I wouldn't blame him if the horse didn't make it."

I nodded again. I knew that Bob, just like Jim and I, did not normally do colic surgeries. We all sent those off to the major surgery centers, where they did, indeed, cost five thousand dollars, minimum.

"Bob operated on the horse and fixed him. Cost me a thousand dollars." Blue Winter's face stayed quiet. "That was all the money I could spare, period.

"Dan called and asked me what became of the horse a few weeks later. I told him, and said I was taking care of the horse and that in six months or so, I'd know if he'd really be all right."

I nodded and said, "Uh-huh," yet again. Colic surgeries have a long recovery period.

"So eventually I knew the horse was all right, and I took him to a couple of ropings. Dan rides up to me at one of them and says, 'You owe me six thousand.'

"And I said, 'Why is that?'

"And he tells me, 'That's a seven-thousand-dollar horse, and you paid one thousand for his vet bill, and you owe me the other six thousand.'

" 'Well,' I said, 'wait a minute, my understanding was that I could have him for the price of his vet bills.'

"And Dan, he said, 'That's not right. You owe me for what he's worth. For all I know, that horse would have been fine without the operation. You only paid a thousand dollars for him. You owe me six.' "

Blue looked at me. "You can see the position I was in. I couldn't afford to give Dan six thousand dollars, even if I thought he was right, which I didn't. I could give him the horse back, but I'd spent every spare cent I had to fix him, and I'd taken care of him and fed him for a year. As far as I was concerned, he was my horse.

"So I didn't say anything. I just rode off. I figured if he thought I'd stolen him he could take me to court."

"So, did anything come of it?" I asked.

"He rode up to me one other time and said he owned Dunny; he still had the papers and I had no bill of sale. The horse was his, he said.

"I told him it was true enough about the papers and that I had no bill of sale. But I told him he knew and I knew what had really happened. And Bob Barton knew. And my friend who had originally taken the horse knew."

"So, what did he say?"

"Not much. He just said it was his horse, and he wanted me to pay for him or give him back. I said I had done what I thought was right and left it at that. So far as I know, the only thing he's done about it is go around telling everyone I stole the horse."

"How does that make you feel?"

Blue Winter shrugged his shoulders. "People can think what they like."

The cowboy ethic in action. Still, there was one thing that puzzled me. "Why would Dan want to do something like that? He's got plenty of money, from all I hear."

Blue Winter shrugged again. "You'd better ask him. He didn't get to be rich by giving money away."

We were both quiet. I stared at the big dun gelding. He was standing quietly, one back foot cocked in a resting pose. Blue Winter's story made sense. There is a gray area when a horse is being "tried." The former owner has relinquished control of him, and the new owner isn't committed to buying him. Problems like this can result. But I wouldn't have thought it was in Dan Jacobi's best long-term interest to take this particular tack.

"Did you hear about Bill Evans?" I asked. As soon as the words were out of my mouth, I regretted them. Talking to Blue about the horse had caused me to drop my guard; I hadn't stopped to think what would follow from the question.

"No, what happened?" Blue's face was as unreadable as ever.

"He shot himself the night before you rode in. Didn't you hear the chopper come to take him out?"

"I heard the chopper. Didn't figure it was any of my business."

More quiet. I waited for him to ask a question.

"Is he dead?" he said at last.

"Yeah."

"That's too bad."

And that was it. Blue Winter nibbled his apple core and volunteered nothing more. I wondered if I wanted to ask him a question or two and decided I didn't. What was it going to achieve? If he knew something about Bill Evans and his suicide, he clearly wasn't going to tell me.

I could tell him the story of my finding the man, but again, why? And I could hardly haul off and ask him if he used to live with Bill Evans's wife.

I began putting my socks and boots on. Blue stood up, all six-and-a-half feet of him. He looked down at me.

"Thanks for listening to my story," he said. "I didn't want you to think I stole a horse from Dan."

"I understand. Have a good trip," I added.

"You, too. Maybe we'll run into each other again." Blue was tying his saddlebags back on the dun gelding.

I wondered if he knew more about Bill Evans's suicide than he was letting on. He'd dismissed the whole matter pretty abruptly. Surely that wasn't natural.

He was on his horse now, pack horse in tow. He whistled for his dog, who bounded up obediently. I stood by the side of the creek looking up at him.

He stared down at me for a moment, then touched the brim of his hat briefly. "It was good to see you. Bye, Stormy."

Before I could make any reply, he'd turned and ridden off.

Well, well, well. I watched him disappear down the trail, then set about organizing myself to go. As I tied my own saddlebags back on and tightened cinches, I wondered. I found I'd become very curious about Blue Winter.

THIRTEEN

I made camp at Wilma Lake in good time. It turned out to be a pretty lake, but there were two parties of people in, one group complete with teenagers, rubber rafts, and boom boxes. This, I supposed, was because Wilma, though two days' ride from Crazy Horse Creek, was a short day away from Hetch Hetchy Pack Station. Though I saw no horses in evidence, it was apparent from the amount of stuff both groups had with them that they had been packed in. No doubt the packers had ''dropped'' these parties and would be back to collect them later.

The worst part of all this was that Wilma was not a huge lake, and fully one half of the shore line consisted of vertical rock wall dropping into blue-green water. Pretty for sure, but providing no campsites. The other half of the lake was open enough, but the two biggest (and best) campsites had been taken by the large parties.

Had I been backpacking, I might have found an obscure ledge somewhere on which to pitch my tent, but my two horses required a patch of level ground and some grass. The only likely-looking spot I saw was right along the trail. A stone ring showed that it was used as a campsite, and there was a good-sized pocket of meadow and a nice rock wall against which to set the tent. But the trail ran right through it.

It isn't good manners to camp alongside a trail, nor did I like to do it; traffic through one's camp is disturbing. But I didn't see that I had much choice. It was either that or park myself cheek by jowl with one of the other groups, which was equally rude.

Reluctantly, I unsaddled and unpacked the horses at my chosen site, then put them both on a picket line out in the meadow. I wouldn't turn them loose, not with this many people around.

Chores done, I wandered about, finding that the river that departed the lake just beyond my camp featured a wonderful granite drop-off festooned with many small waterfalls and bathtub-sized cascading pools. Golden-orange leopard lilies overhung one of these in combination with nodding red and yellow columbines—a vignette more telling than any carefully arranged garden feature I'd yet encountered.

After a brief foray I returned to camp, unwilling to leave the horses for long. Once again I made a drink, collected the jar of peanuts and *Walden*, and parked my camp chair where the last rays of sunlight would hit me. For an hour I read, sipped, and munched, relatively undisturbed.

Every so often the teenagers in the next camp, who were engaged in water fights out on their rubber rafts, would emit particularly loud squeals and shouts, enough to cause me to look up. It was during one of these brief lifts of the head that I saw the two women.

They were coming toward me on the trail, from the direction of Hetch Hetchy. One tall, one short, both with backpacks on their backs, walking with end-of-the-day weariness. Hetch Hetchy might be an easy day's ride, but it was a good long slog of a hike, and all uphill.

111

These two hikers looked understandably beat. They also looked miffed as they surveyed the lake with its all-too-obvious complement of campers. I knew how they must feel. Despite the fact that we all know it's unreasonable, those of us who frequent the backcountry always hope to find our destinations of choice pristine and undisturbed. After a long day's journey through the wilderness, it's somewhat of an anticlimax to search for an empty campsite as though you were looking for a vacant space at an RV park.

After a minute the two women halted, not twenty feet from me, and surveyed the situation at Wilma Lake. I watched them idly, wondering where they would choose to camp. If it were me, I thought, I'd cross the creek and camp on the other side. The shorter woman said something to her companion.

I stared. The short women's face was turned directly toward me, with the setting sun full on it. It was Sara. Lonny's ex.

I recognized her with a jolt of emotional resonance all out of proportion to my actual acquaintance with her, which was virtually nil. I'd met her twice, and only briefly then. But she'd been a part of my life for many years, a shadowy, threatening presence, a woman I'd found myself almost fearing.

Sara had left Lonny two years before he and I had started dating, so I had never felt even peripherally responsible for the end of their marriage. Several years later, Sara had decided she wanted to move back in with the man who was still, technically, her husband, and she had been extremely angry when Lonny had chosen to continue his relationship with me. The ensuing fireworks had, more or less, precipitated their divorce. Thus Sara blamed me for, as she had once put it, "coming between" her and Lonny.

I thought this unreasonable, and I'd said so, which hadn't made her like me any better. In short, our one conversation had not been a friendly chat. I regarded her now with considerable apprehension.

How in the world had she happened to appear here and now, on the shore of Wilma Lake, in the Sonora wilderness, just when I happened to be camped here?

It was Sara; I was sure of it. The year since I'd seen her hadn't treated her kindly; she'd gained some weight, cut her hair short, and dyed it blond, none of which was flattering. But she was, quite recognizably, the woman who had worried me and haunted me for so long. Lonny's wife.

His ex-wife, I reminded myself. And the last time I saw her she was dating another man. Sara had no real reason to resent me.

I was still uncomfortable. For a second I contemplated getting up, turning my back, hiding by my horses . . . anything to avoid a confrontation.

But self-respect, and for that matter, curiosity won out. I stayed where I was, facing the trail, and waited.

In the quiet evening air, I could hear bits of their conversation. The unknown woman looked somewhat younger than Sara; a Viking of a human being, she was taller than I, perhaps about six-foot-even, with long brown-blond hair in a braid down her back and a strong Scandinavian face.

Sara was addressing her in querulous tones, and I caught the phrases "nowhere to camp," "too noisy," and "too many people."

Eventually the two moved forward again and stopped when they were ten feet from me, just where the trail ran past my camp.

"Hello," the tall woman said.

I looked up from my book. My eyes searched Sara's face. "Hi," I said.

I saw Sara start. She knew me, just as I knew her. Perhaps she, too, had thought about me for years—the woman who had stolen Lonny's devotion away from her, as she would see it.

We stared at each other. On her face I saw a range of expressions—surprise, hostility, and yes, curiosity.

"It's Sara, isn't it?" I said.

She said nothing to me, just looked at her companion. "Lee," she said urgently, "that's Lonny's girlfriend."

The woman so addressed stared at me with equal curiosity, but a complete lack of hostility. She had pronounced smile lines around her eyes and a strong chin. Like Sara, she wore regulation walking shorts and hiking boots, topped with a fleece jacket for the cool evening air.

"Hi," I said again.

For a second it seemed we were at an impasse. Sara, stony-faced, wouldn't look at me. I had no idea what else to say. We all stared awkwardly.

The tall woman finally chipped in with, "I was just going to ask you if you knew of any other good campsites nearby, since this lake seems so crowded."

"It looked like there was a nice spot across the creek," I said.

I watched Sara as I spoke, finding myself fascinated. Perhaps all women who have shared a man have this odd connection. It isn't often friendly, but it's there. He who has loved me has also loved you. In a strange way, I almost felt as if Sara and I were related.

These thoughts raced through my mind in short order as Lee asked me how I'd gotten across the creek.

"I didn't," I said. "I just saw a nice spot over there. I guess you'd have to wade."

I didn't quite make it to the end of this statement before Sara interrupted me. "Come on, Lee," she said. "We don't want to talk to her."

Lee looked taken aback at this piece of overt rudeness; I wasn't terribly surprised. Sara had shown herself quite capable of being rude the last time we'd spoken.

To my amazement, I found myself speaking to her. "I didn't

114

take Lonny away from you, Sara. I had nothing to do with the failure of your marriage. You know that.''

Why in the world I said it, I had no idea. Perhaps because it had been on my mind for years. Whatever the reason, it just came out of my mouth as though it simply needed to be said.

As I might have expected if I'd thought about it, this direct form of address triggered all the anger that Sara had been somewhat unsuccessfully bottling up.

''How dare you say that to me? If it wasn't for you, Lonny and I might have gotten back together. He might have been willing to work on our marriage. You were the reason he wouldn't.'' The words came tumbling out of Sara with a force and velocity equal to my own.

Something raw leaped inside of me. I looked her right in the eyes. ''You know as well as I do that you left Lonny. You found a boyfriend. That was the reason your marriage ended. And I know just how unhappy it was for years before that. You blame me because you don't want to look at your own failure.''

Sara's eyes flashed hot sparks at that. ''Did you ever once think what a rotten, selfish thing you were doing?'' she demanded. ''Lonny and I had a long history together. Our marriage wasn't perfect, but we could have saved it if it weren't for you.''

Sara's chin tilted up as she said it. Taking a step toward me as if she would have liked to hit me, she stopped abruptly. ''Someday you're going to find out what it feels like.'' She enunciated the words clearly. ''You're going to be the one who suffers.''

Her fine-boned face looked almost contorted, the somewhat thin-lipped mouth twisted over her teeth. I held perfectly still and wished distinctly that I'd never provoked her.

Her companion seemed as aghast as I was. ''Come on, Sara,'' she muttered. ''Let's go.''

Without a word, Sara turned and marched down the trail in

the direction from which I'd originally come. The tall woman followed her, looking back once over her shoulder.

Whew. I took a swallow of my drink as I watched them disappear up Jack Tone Canyon. I couldn't imagine a stranger encounter. Although this was a popular hiking area and Sara could be expected to know it well, having spent many summers with Lonny at Crazy Horse Creek . . . still. What odd chance had brought us to this meeting?

For a second paranoia kicked in and I wondered if Sara might have found out somehow about my solitary pack trip. A moment's reflection ruled that delusion out. Sara had been as surprised to see me as I was to see her. It had been plain on her face.

The sun had now set. I got up and made another drink, grubbed some dried fruit and more peanuts out of the pack bags, and turned my camp chair so that it looked out over the darkening lake. This was not going to be a cooking night.

One of the advantages of traveling alone—it incommoded no one if I preferred simply to eat peanuts and drink.

Roey still snoozed by the pack bags; I didn't think she'd even been aware of the two hikers. I hadn't built a fire yet, and now I wondered if I would. My neighbors' fires glowed, bright orange torches in the evening air. I could hear occasional friendly shouts and bits of music; I certainly didn't need a campfire of my own to dispel the loneliness of solitude.

I sat and watched the dark water of the lake, thinking of Sara. I wondered if she knew Lonny had moved away. Wondered how she'd feel if she knew how much I was struggling in my relationship with him. Vindicated, probably. I was getting what I deserved in her opinion, no doubt.

Taking another swallow of Jack Daniel's and water, I wondered where Sara and her friend had camped. I couldn't see their fire.

It was getting well and truly dark now. I could hear the peaceful sound of my horses cropping grass in the meadow when the neighboring campers were quiet. I'd move them along their picket lines before I went to bed so that they'd each have a fresh patch of grass to graze on.

At the thought, I heard a voice. Low and soft, almost a whisper. "Fucking horses."

At least that's what I thought I heard. I leaped up and spun around to face the trail.

A figure stood there. In the dim light I could see that it carried a backpack, with what looked like various oddments tied on here and there. Short, square, apparently male. The figure turned toward me and I could see that he had a dark beard. He stood on the trail and stared at my camp.

"What are you doing?" I demanded.

"Nothing." The same soft, low tone. "Nothing to do with you."

For a second we stared at each other. I could see the gleam of his eyes in the dim light, but I couldn't make out his expression. But surely I had heard him cursing my horses?

"You shouldn't be camped so close to the trail." His teeth showed white in the dark beard when he spoke.

"I know," I said. "There are a lot of other people here. I couldn't find a better spot."

"None of you would be here if it weren't for the damn horses. None of you could make it in here with all that stuff. Fucking horses," he said again. "Ruining the mountains."

Oh no. A genuine tree hugger, as the cowboys were apt to put it. I knew that many hikers were resentful of horsemen, but I had never run into any who cursed me openly.

The man still stood on the trail, regarding me and my camp. Slowly I made out little details of his kit. Shorts with ragged edges, what looked like a canvas rucksack—sleeping bag and pots and pans tied all over it—a floppy hat on his head. He would have presented a rather engaging gnomelike appearance, if it weren't for the animosity in his voice.

"I'm sorry," I said at last. "I know my camp's in the way here. Have a good night."

Turning, I stepped back toward my saddlebags, where the pistol was. If, God forbid, this guy was really a nut, I wanted to be able to get it out fast.

His strange voice stopped me in mid-stride. "You'd be better off leaving your horses at home," he said. "Bad things can happen to them up here. The last bunch of horses I saw were at Deer Lake. They aren't there anymore."

"What do you mean?"

"I turned them loose. People left them tied to trees and went fishing. Fucking horses were pawing the ground, tearing up the trees' roots. I turned them all loose."

"That's wicked." I edged toward my saddlebags, not turning my back on the gnome. "It's wrong for people to leave their horses tied like that; it is bad for the trees. But those horses could be hurt or killed, running around loose."

I could see him shrug. "Leave them at home then. They don't belong here. This is the most beautiful spot on earth, and the fucking livestock is ruining it."

I took one more step toward my gun. Roey woke up at the motion, lifted her head, saw the man on the trail, and gave a startled woof.

"Stay," I told her.

She subsided; the man continued to watch me. I had no idea what to say, or do, next.

He spoke again. "You got anything to drink, or smoke?"

"No," I said shortly. This was a palpable lie; I held a mug of bourbon and water in my hand. But I was damned if I was going to share my precious store of liquor with this horse hater.

"I've been in for two months now." There was a faint whine in his voice.

"Is that right?"

"I just walk around, look at things. The more I see, the more I understand."

I was standing right next to my saddlebags now, fighting the urge to get the pistol out and wave it at this guy, yelling, "Go away!"

Instead, I said, "I'm sure that's true."

"We need to ban all livestock from these mountains and most of the people. That's what it will take to save this place."

"Uh-huh." How in the hell was I going to get rid of him?

"All I carry with me is beans and rice. That's all I need." He sounded plaintive again. "Sure you don't have anything to drink?"

"I'm sure," I said. "Good night."

After a minute more staring in my direction, he turned and moved off.

Jerking my pistol out of the saddlebag, I hung it on my belt and hustled over to check the horses. They were fine. I moved them to new spots on the picket line, and then put my tent as close to them as was practical. I turned the tent so that its open doorway faced the horses and climbed inside.

Stripping my boots, jeans, and jacket off, I wiggled into the sleeping bag, and put the pistol under my folded jacket.

Damn. What an evening for company. I definitely preferred being scared of dark solitude to being over-impacted by people.

Looking out of the tent, I watched the distant glitter of stars over Wilma Lake. An image of other nomads, in other times and places, looking out of other tent doorways at the selfsame stars came into my mind. That's what I was, for now, merely another nomad. And tomorrow, I thought, I'll move on.

FOURTEEN

I left Wilma Lake early the next morning, in search of more solitude. The plan called for me to go to Benson Lake next. It would be a long day, but I could just possibly do it. Or I could stop and camp somewhere in the middle. I thought I'd decide when the time came.

Riding toward Seavey Pass, I worried about how tough the trail was going to be. En route, I had passed the cutoff trail to Tilden Lake, and wondered briefly if Blue Winter was still there, or if he, like me, was moving on. No way of knowing.

I kept riding, casting occasional glances at the sky. Unlike the previous three days, big thunderheads were building up. I could be in for some weather.

This was not a surprise. Afternoon thunderstorms during the summer in the Sierras were more the rule than the exception. I had merely been lucky so far.

Well, I had rain gear in my saddlebags. I had a tent, and a couple of tarps to cover my stuff. I'd do fine.

Gunner plodded down the trail, half-asleep. A few days in the mountains had inured him to pine forests and granite boulders. It took something more dramatic to spark his interest. Maybe thunder and lightning would do it.

Damn. I cast another glance at the rapidly graying sky. Despite my preparations, I was not looking forward to a storm. I didn't much like lightning myself. Not to mention the granite got slipperier when it was wet.

Gunner plodded on through the pines, undeterred. Plumber followed, leaning back a little on the lead rope from time to time. Roey trotted behind Plumber, accustomed to the caravan life.

I began to think about alternative destinations as the sky grew darker. Red Can Lake was maybe two miles ahead and half a mile off the trail. I would reach it in an hour or so, all going well. The only trouble was, there was no trail to it.

Lonny had told me that Red Can was a wonderful little lake, one of his favorites. But the half mile between it and the main trail was unmarked except for a few ducks.

"Ducks?" I said.

"Yeah, ducks. You know."

"No, I don't know." I'd had an odd mental image of mallard ducks squatting at strategic spots, pointing the way.

"Ducks are little stacks of rocks. People mark routes with them."

"I thought they used blazes on the trees."

"Not anymore. Forest Service doesn't like it."

"So I look for little stacks of rocks?"

"That's right." Lonny had gone on to describe the route into Red Can Lake; I thought I could remember it well enough.

"All right, I'll go there," I said out loud.

Gunner cocked an ear back at me. I looked up at the darkening sky. The wind was starting to blow—an ominous sign. I could see the granite of a steep ridge up ahead. As I understood it, Seavey Pass was at the top of that ridge, and Red Can Lake was a little way down the other side.

Without warning, Gunner spooked—a sudden, violent sideways leap. I clutched at the saddle horn and clung with my legs and stayed on, barely. I could hear the scramble of Plumber's hooves behind me, even as another noise registered. A buzzing noise. Rattlesnake.

Gunner stood still and snorted, looking at the rock from which the buzzing emanated. I straightened myself in the saddle and looked at it, too.

No sign of the snake. The rock was (now) twenty feet away, a safe enough distance. And fortunately the forest I was riding through was open; detouring around the rock would be easy. Still, if Gunner hadn't jumped when he did . . .

I stared at the rock. It was right by the side of the trail. The snake had stopped his rattling. No doubt, though, that he was coiled under that rock. If Gunner had walked past, there was a distinct chance he would have been snakebit at this point.

It wouldn't kill him, I told myself. My knowledge of rattlesnake bites in horses was sketchy and secondhand. Where I practiced, on the coast of California, rattlesnakes were rare. I had never had occasion to treat a horse who had been bitten.

Rattlesnakes were fairly common in the Sierras, though. I knew something about them, mostly through Lonny. I knew, for instance, that they had two types of bite—a fear bite and a food bite. When they struck at a large object, such as a horse or a human marching down the trail, they attacked out of fear and did not inject much venom. Thus, rattlesnake bites were seldom fatal, especially not in animals as large as a horse. A dog now, would be another thing.

I looked back. Roey was lying down just behind Plumber, showing no inclination to investigate the snake. She'd learned to rest when she could.

The worst thing about a snakebite in a horse, Lonny'd told me, is the swelling. "The horse will swell up something terrible," he said. "It's a nuisance if it's in one leg, but if the snake bites the horse on the muzzle, it can kill him because he swells so much he can't breathe."

The other thing he'd warned me about was the food bite. "That's the most dangerous. If you're climbing through the rocks and you reach your hand up on a ledge and the snake sees something small he thinks he can eat, and strikes at you, that's bad. They inject a lot more venom in a food bite."

"So, what do I do?" I asked.

"Ride out, if you can. It still won't kill you, probably. But it'll make you damn sick."

"Great."

Thinking dismally about how it would feel to embark on a two-day ride while I was deathly sick from a rattlesnake bite, I guided my caravan on a wide detour around the snake's rock.

When we were once again moving down the trail, I found I was a hell of a lot more jumpy. The sky grew darker; the wind blew.

I could see jumbled rock and a steep climb up ahead; it looked like the storm would be upon me in an hour or so. Still, I could make it to Red Can Lake, if I hurried.

Or I thought I could make it to Red Can Lake. If Seavey Pass wasn't too tough. If there were no more rattlesnakes. If I didn't get hit by a bolt of lightning. If, if, if.

Get a grip, Gail, I admonished myself. A storm is not the end of the world. And Lonny said the trail over Seavey Pass was okay.

But my mind jittered. I didn't like lightning at the best of times, and alone on a high pass on top of a steel-shod horse was not the best of times. Not to mention Lonny's idea of an okay trail and my idea of an okay trail were apt to differ greatly. Lonny rode across country in the same style in which he team roped—balls to the wall. Many times he'd told me, "Come on, this is fine," and I'd found myself on some frigging cliff.

I could see Seavey Pass ahead of me now, and it did not look good. A steep tumbled slope of boulders, it had the appearance of a giant avalanche. And the trail ran right up through the middle of it.

Reining Gunner to a stop, I stared upward. Shit. The sky was a deep, blue-violet gray. There were distant rumbles in the general direction of Nevada. The storm would be here soon.

I clucked to Gunner and started up through the rocks, feeling distinctly nervous. The trail looked reasonably well made, but the country was ungodly rough.

Gunner picked his way slowly and cautiously, allowing me to guide him. He had a characteristic I found useful: he would let me change his intended footfall in mid-stride, just by the lightest indication of the reins. Thus I could select which rocks he put his weight on.

Plumber I couldn't help much. All I could do was be sure he had plenty of slack in the lead rope when he was crossing a tricky section.

We progressed. Slowly. The wind blew my shirt away from my body, and I wondered if I should have stopped to put my rain gear on before we began the ascent. There were no places to dismount here.

Just for a second I let my concentration wander, looking away from the granite slabs of the trail and scanning the steep jumbled slope around us, the wild gray windy sky above. My God, I thought, it's beautiful. And I am really out here.

The next second I heard a horrifically loud rumble crashing above me, and my mind spun. Thunder? No. Rockfall.

"Jesus." I had time only for the one word before I saw the rocks crashing down on the trail behind us, coming from somewhere up above.

The noise was terrifying; both my horses leaped forward. Too rapid for thought or fear . . . I corrected Gunner's tendency to plunge, did my best to hold him and Plumber steady and to the trail. Rock was still falling, landing, so far, behind us; I let the horse scramble forward, keeping everything controlled as well as I could.

No time to look for the dog. No time for anything but go, go as fast as I could. Rocks pinged and clanged behind me, not so loud now. The worst of it was over.

But rock was still falling. My heart thudded in great leaping bounds. I could feel Gunner's heart thumping between my legs. My God, my God.

We clambered up the trail at the long trot. I could see Roey's small foxlike shape right on Plumber's heels. I said a brief prayer of thanks.

The last of the rocks was rattling down the canyon. Taking a deep breath, I checked Gunner down to a slower pace. Keep moving, not so fast, no need to break a leg getting away.

Up and up we went, climbing an increasingly steep trail. I could see what I thought was the top of the pass. My heart thudded steadily. I wanted off this rock slope so bad I could taste it. I didn't think I'd ever been so frightened in my life.

Eventually we topped out. I stopped for a moment and dismounted, looked both horses over carefully. Plumber had a small scrape on his right front pastern, down near the hoof. Besides that everybody seemed fine, including Roey.

Hastily I put my slicker on, mounted, clucked to Gunner, and moved out. I was well and truly spooked. Thunder boomed above me; as soon as I could find a decent spot, I was making camp.

But a decent spot demanded that it have horse feed and water, and I couldn't find one. No convenient meadows appeared by the side of the trail. The map told me that Red Can Lake, a mere quarter of a mile away as the crow flew, was my closest campsite. Next was Wood Lake, a full five miles distant, but right on the main trail.

Drops of rain spattered around us; a cold wind blew out of the heavy gray sky. I was shivering with fear and chill. Casting my eyes over the countryside around me, I recognized the landmark Lonny had told me of. "A great big fallen pine by the side of the trail, just after you top Seavey Pass. Turn off there."

Here was the fallen pine. That was it. No trail, no sign, no ducks even. Should I?

I stared off through the trees and rocks. I could get myself in a pretty bad situation out there. But I really wanted to make camp before it started pouring, and Red Can Lake was close. I went for it.

Clucking to Gunner, I guided him around the log and down the gully Lonny had described. Sure enough, in fifty feet or so, I saw a duck.

"Follow the ducks until you come to the fern meadow," Lonny had said. "From there you can see the lake."

I followed the ducks. It was easier said than done. The wind blew in fitful gusts, whipping scattered drops of rain along. The horses were antsy and uncooperative, still upset, just as I was myself. Whenever I had to stop and reconnoiter, Gunner pranced and Plumber tugged on the lead rope.

At one point I found myself on what appeared to be a pathless field of granite, my way marked only by these obscure little rock stacks. I followed where they led, hoping some practical joker hadn't moved them all last week.

I heard a crack of lightning and the accompanying roll of thunder and shivered. The rain came down more heavily, dripping steadily off the hood of my slicker. Gunner's neck was wet. My jeans were starting to soak through where they stuck out beneath my slicker.

Damn. This whole day had gone so far wrong it would be laughable, if I weren't having to cope with it. Here I was, alone

126

in a literally trackless wilderness with a storm about to break overhead. Having just escaped a rattlesnake and some major rockfall.

Lightning flashed again; thunder rumbled almost immediately. Rain cascaded out of the sky, as if someone had suddenly turned up the shower. Visibility was getting difficult. I parked Gunner under a pine tree and stared out at the uncompromising place I'd chosen for my vacation.

Another clash of light—a huge *ka-boom*. The storm was right above. Peering through the half dark, I tried to judge whether my pine tree was the tallest one around. It was providing us with a certain amount of shelter; big drops fell on us at intervals rather than a steady barrage of wind and rain, but this would not be a worthwhile trade for being struck by lightning.

Never stand under a tree in a lightning storm, they say. I wondered again who they were. This advice was ignored by virtually everyone I knew. Who wouldn't take shelter in a downpour?

The horses stood quietly now, heads down. Water ran off them. They lifted their heads sharply at each flash and drum roll, but seemed willing enough to wait out the deluge under the tree.

In the next second my hair stood up. Lightning again, a strange green light and an eerie crackling hiss. Instantaneously, a deafening crash.

Shit. "That was too close," I told the horses. "That hit right near us." They huddled together, their eyes big. Roey was curled in a small, shivering ball at the base of the pine.

I tried to decide whether I should leave the shelter of the tree. Rain poured down in sheets; I stayed put, shivering.

The next bolt of lightning was farther away. I kept thinking about one of Ted's favorite stories—the two cowboys who had been struck by lightning as they were crossing Emigrant

Meadow. "Both their horses killed dead under them." Ted would repeat it with apparent relish.

I trembled with cold and fear and wondered what in the hell I was doing here. What had made me think I could cope with all this alone, what stupid hubris had drawn me out into this godforsaken country to what looked to be my imminent demise.

The rain was abating a little, but I still huddled under my tree, feeling helpless. Jesus, it was all just too much. I didn't feel up to dealing with it. I wanted to crawl into my nice warm bed in my cozy little house. I wanted back to civilization, pronto. I'd had enough of the wilderness.

I stared down at my small red dog, who was shivering even more than I was. Tough luck, Gail, I told myself. You chose to be here, and you have to take care of these animals. They're counting on you; you can't let them down.

"Okay, okay," I said aloud. One thing about being alone in the mountains, you get to talking out loud. "I'll persevere."

The downpour had decreased to a sprinkle; it was time to ride on. I could hear intermittent thunder a ridge or two away, but the sky was steadily getting lighter where I was. I lifted the reins gently, clucked to the horses, and called Roey.

Wet and bedraggled, we moved out, aiming for the duck I could see up ahead. Three ducks later we were in the fern meadow. Through an opening in the trees, I could see the gray, restless water of Red Can Lake. Now all I had to do was get down to it.

Once again, easier said than done. Lonny had explained to me that this was the tricky part. "Follow the ledge to a crack that runs down the rock face. It's a pretty wide crack. Just stay in it. You'll be fine. The crack will take you right down to the lake."

Lonny's directions proved accurate, but, as usual, he'd way underestimated the scary factor. I felt completely exposed, riding a horse along a granite face that looked as if it should have been reserved for rock climbers.

Gunner picked his way obediently down the crack under my direction; I could only hope Plumber would do the same. My heart thumped steadily and I cursed my own foolhardiness. Why, why, why had I ever chosen to put myself and my horses in this much danger?

The lake was just ahead of us now. I could see what Lonny meant. Despite its storm-ruffled appearance, it was truly lovely. Smaller than Snow Lake or Wilma, Red Can nestled in a granite hollow on the rim of a huge canyon. The entire shoreline was granite, except for the small green jewel of a meadow we were descending into.

The meadow was ringed by rocky gray walls on three sides and by the lake on the fourth—a proper box canyon. I could turn both horses loose here.

There was one small grove of pine trees with a little-used fire ring in the middle. I rode the horses up to it and dismounted.

The rain was over; the sky had turned a pale, misty gray. I stared around at the most perfect campsite I'd ever seen and patted Gunner on the neck.

"We made it," I said.

FIFTEEN

The next morning dawned gray, but with no actual precipitation—yet. It hadn't rained all night, either, for which I was grateful. I spent a leisurely few hours in camp, taking my time over coffee while Gunner and Plumber grazed contentedly in the meadow. I figured I'd ride to Wood Lake in the afternoon and camp there. It hadn't been part of my original plan, but what the hell. Plans were for changing.

Eventually I got everything packed back up again—no small chore. The pale, evenly gray sky had resolved itself into a pile of heavy thunderheads over the peaks, and I thought it might rain again in the afternoon. I wanted to be snug in camp at Wood Lake when the storm broke.

Getting out of Red Can turned out to be trickier than getting in. I stared at the steep crack I'd descended the day before and wondered how in hell I'd get back up. Leaving my horses tied to trees, I investigated on foot.

A closer inspection was not encouraging. As Lonny had told me, a horse had to stay in the crack. The steep granite slope on either side was slickrock, and absolutely prohibitive. Any horse who tried to clamber along there was going to fall.

I tried to decide what to do. I could lead the horses up, one at a time, hoping they would stay in the crack behind me. But there were problems with this. I had less control when I was leading them rather than riding; I couldn't really stop them from moving off the dirt onto the rock. Also, they would be anxious, separated from one another, and this might cause them to hurry.

On the other hand, if I rode Gunner and led Plumber, I wouldn't really be able to control the pack horse at all. Odds were he'd follow the saddle horse, but I couldn't be sure. And if Gunner slipped and went down, I'd go with him. Scary thought.

I stared at the crack, my heart starting to pound. There was no other way out of here. I had to go up that thing unless I planned to spend the rest of my life at Red Can Lake.

"We went down it; we can go up it," I said out loud, though I knew this wasn't necessarily true. Horses tend to go very slowly and carefully down steep descents, and they have an equal impulse to hurry on climbs. Trying to get some momentum up, I supposed. Whatever their reasoning, it made going up tricky spots more dangerous than going down. Down felt scarier but was actually safer. All the major wrecks I'd seen on mountain trails involved a horse or mule scrambling while climbing up a tricky piece of rock.

I couldn't stand here all day staring at it. Walking back over to the horses, I untied them and mounted. For lack of a good reason to do otherwise, I was going to do this the cowboy way.

Clucking to Gunner, I pointed him in the right direction; he started up the crack. I tried to keep a steady, gentle guidance on the reins, checking him when he hurried, aiming him toward the dirt footfalls, not disturbing his concentration. I leaned slightly forward so my weight was over his withers where he could balance it best. I kept my eyes on the crack, my concentration straight ahead. I could hear Plumber behind us; there was slack in the lead rope. I didn't look back.

We almost made it. We were near the top of the crack, right where it merged into the ledge, when it happened. The first warning I had was the tension on the end of the lead rope. I looked over my shoulder to see that Plumber had balked, unwilling to make a steep step up that Gunner had taken in stride. I clucked and tugged firmly, trying to stay calm.

Plumber hesitated and then, to my dismay, he stepped to the right, out of the crack, trying to go around the step up. I tugged on the lead rope, said "Whoa," to no avail. The little brown horse took one step on the slickrock and slipped, going down to his knees.

I let go of the lead rope; no use pulling Gunner down, too. Plumber scrambled; his shoes clanged and crashed against the rock, throwing sparks. He was up; he went down again; I thought he would surely roll to the bottom of the slope.

"Please, God, please, God." The words were loud inside my head. Somehow the little horse came up again and stood, all four feet in the crack, shivering.

"Whoa," I said out loud, trying to sound calm. What in the hell am I supposed to do now, my mind shrieked. I didn't have hold of the lead rope; I couldn't dismount. After a moment the only possible answer presented itself. I had to ride Gunner out of here and take my chances on what Plumber would do.

I clucked to my saddle horse and put some slack in the reins. He stepped up the crack. Looking back over my shoulder, I could see that Plumber was following, dragging the lead rope. I prayed he wouldn't step on it and throw himself off balance.

He didn't. We made it onto the ledge, in one piece, more or less. I dismounted and looked Plumber over carefully. He had a few scrapes and he'd lost a shoe. The scrapes were mostly minor, though one on his left front cannon bone was bleeding pretty steadily. The lost shoe, however, was a problem.

I got on and rode off the ledge into the fern meadow. Here I tied both horses up and dug some antibiotic salve and an EZ Boot out of my saddlebags. I rubbed the salve on Plumber's scrapes, and pulled the EZ Boot, an adjustable plastic boot made for this purpose, over his bare left front hoof. Then I walked back down to the crack to look for the shoe.

I found it very near the spot where Plumber had fallen. It was bent; he'd clearly stepped on it with either a back foot or his other front foot when he was scrambling. I wasn't sure what good it was going to do me. I had some minimal shoeing gear stowed in my pack, but my skills weren't really up to straightening this shoe out and nailing it back on.

In the course of my work as a veterinarian, I'd learned to pull horseshoes off. This was a necessity; in order to take X rays of the feet, I needed to remove the metal shoes, and I could hardly demand that the client do it, or expect that a horseshoer would always be handy. But pulling a shoe off was a two-minute job, requiring only minimal skill and some familiarity with the operation. Nailing a shoe back on was a good deal more difficult, and I had never done it, though I had seen it done, often.

I walked back to the horses, carrying the shoe. Plumber could wear the EZ Boot for now. Maybe he could even wear it for the rest of the trip. It was a cinch he couldn't be barefoot in this rocky country. He'd get sore right away.

Stuffing the shoe in my saddlebag, I untied the horses and climbed back on Gunner. Onward.

We retraced our route to the main trail and began descending the other side of Seavey Pass. Big vistas of granite and sky opened up in front of us. Thunderheads were piled high above the ridges, their tumbled gray masses complementing the rough gray rock below.

Beautiful, and slightly ominous, the Sierras beckoned. A siren saying come hither. I smiled to myself. Here I was, hastening to follow the call. To what end?

We went on. Once we were off Seavey Pass and in woodland again, I started to relax. No more tricky trail, and the clouds looked as though they might be breaking up. Perhaps it wouldn't rain after all.

I began to fantasize about a warm, sunny afternoon in camp at the as-yet-unknown Wood Lake. I would take a swim. Two days of no bathing had left me feeling a little grungy. Time for a wash.

The trail continued gradually descending. Wood Lake was a few miles ahead—an hour's ride.

Looking back over my shoulder, I watched Plumber for a while. He was sound, at the walk anyway. Apparently, neither his scrapes nor the lack of a shoe was causing him much grief. The EZ Boot was doing its part and staying in place. If his leg swells, I thought, I'll stand him in the cold water of the lake for a while.

Pine trees and granite, pine trees and granite. Down the trail we went, in a steady procession, Roey trotting quietly behind Plumber. I was half asleep when Gunner jumped up in the air, nearly jarring me loose. I clutched the saddle horn with one hand and jerked on the reins with the other.

"Dammit," I swore. Gunner froze.

It took me a second, but I got it. Rope under his tail. I hadn't been paying attention, and the lead rope had slipped under Gunner's tail. Plumber must have leaned back on it a little and it had become wedged up high.

Gunner was still frozen in place. Thank God. I had seen an otherwise gentle rope horse buck furiously and violently until both its rider and the rope under its tail came loose. But many horses, and Gunner appeared to be one, tended to freeze up.

I got off slowly and carefully, talking soothingly. "Take it easy, buddy, just whoa, I'll get it out, no big deal."

Patting Gunner's rump, I reached for his tail and gently pried it up. Gunner trembled, but he allowed it. I eased the rope out.

Gunner snorted. His eyes were big. I patted his shoulder and told him what a good horse he was as I climbed back on, reminding myself to be more careful. Lonny had broken his shoulder when a horse bucked him off in the rocks—all because of a rope under the tail.

Fortunately my horse was not inclined to bucking. Still, a rope under the tail was just cause, and I needed to prevent it from happening.

We rode on. I stared ahead through the seemingly endless forest, looking for the openness and light that would indicate a meadow or a lake. The ground grew wetter; a stream ran along the far side of the canyon, but the low ground we were traveling on was just plain muddy.

Both Gunner and Plumber snorted and hesitated each time we had to cross a mucky spot. Like most horses, they hated mud. I kept a careful eye on Plumber, hoping he wouldn't pull the EZ Boot off.

The canyon was narrowing and I could see light ahead. The trail was also growing wetter. We scrambled through some spots that were knee-deep, both horses floundering.

I was getting nervous; I didn't like mud either. Visions of quicksand rolled around my mind. At each wet spot I balked right along with the horses, trying to determine where the footing was firmest.

Damn. The trail passed between a rocky bank and a bit of thick forest, and the crossing looked like a tar pit. Thick, gooey, black mud—churned up from all the feet that had crossed it previously. Yesterday's rain hadn't helped any.

The horses and I stared. I felt like snorting, too. It didn't look like there was any way around. Dubiously I selected the right-hand side as being the likeliest, and urged Gunner forward. He hesitated, then lunged.

135

BURLINGAME PUBLIC LIBRARY
480 PRIMROSE ROAD
BURLINGAME, CA 94010

Big mistake. He sank into the mud to his shoulder; the abrupt forward motion and sudden dive to ground level pitched me off. Fortunately it wasn't far to fall. I landed easily in wet black goo and floundered to a purchase on a log. Gunner and Plumber struggled and scrambled, bogging down and heaving themselves out, until they stood on the other side of the muddy crossing. Roey trotted over to me and licked my hand.

Damn, damn, damn. Ignoring the dog, I picked my way toward the horses. At least they stood. They stood on all four feet, black with mud, but apparently okay. I remembered Lonny telling me that he thought a bog was almost as great a danger as slickrock.

Thanking God that neither horse was inclined to run off, I caught them and inspected them closely.

Shit. Damn. Son of a bitch. I wished I knew some better cuss words. Plumber had lost the EZ Boot. It was no doubt at the bottom of that bog, and I knew right away that I'd never find it. I had one more in my saddlebag, and that was it.

Cursing steadily, I climbed back on. Plumber didn't need the boot on this soft ground, and I wasn't taking a chance on losing my last one. I'd put it on him when we got to some more rock.

Mud dripped off me as I rode on. I could see light up ahead but it wasn't cheering me much. Nothing seemed to be going right. I was virtually snarling as I rode out of the trees into a meadow that fringed the shore of a lake. Wood Lake, by my reckoning. And there, camped at the edge of the forest, was Dan Jacobi and his crew.

SIXTEEN

I pulled up. My thoughts were unprintable. These were the last people I wanted to see. And there was no getting out of it. There were three men in camp, and all were staring right at me. Dan, blond Steve, and a third, shorter man with brown hair, whom I didn't recognize.

I was covered in mud, I was in a foul mood, and now I had to deal with these guys. "Hi, Dan," I said, pretty damn ungraciously.

"Howdy, ma'am." He touched his hat. "Looks like you had a little trouble with that crossing."

"I did." I knew I sounded pissed as hell.

He ran a practiced eye over my horses. "They look okay."

"I think they're all right." At this point my brain kicked in, pushing my emotions out of the way. I might not be glad to see these guys, but they could be the solution to one of my problems. "The pack horse lost a shoe," I added diffidently.

Dan nodded. "Did you find the shoe?"

"Yeah, I did."

"Bring any shoeing equipment?"

"A little. Some nails. A hammer."

Dan smiled. "If you'd like, Jim here can nail it back on. He's a shoer."

Since this was just what I was hoping for, I accepted with alacrity. "Thanks. I'd appreciate that."

Patting myself on the back for having some vestiges of intelligence, anyway, I dismounted and tied my horses up. Fishing the shoe out of the saddlebag, I handed it over.

Roey walked up to Dan, sniffed his pants leg, and wagged her tail. He reached down and scratched her absently behind the ears. "I'll need to unpack the pack horse to get at the shoeing gear," I said.

The short, brown-haired man, who was apparently Jim, ducked his chin and smiled briefly. "Don't bother. I've got some nails and stuff handy here. I'll just pound this out flat and nail it back on. Won't take a minute."

"Thank you." I looked around their camp. Two small tents, a fire with a coffeepot chugging on top of it, fishing poles leaning against the trees. Five horses were picketed alongside. Three saddle horses and two pack horses.

"So, how do you guys happen to be here?" I asked Dan.

"Oh, we decided to wander through the mountains a bit, see some more lakes."

"Did Ted go back out?"

"No." Dan looked down. "He said he was going to ride to Buck Lakes, looking for some mule that got left there."

"Oh yeah." I knew about this. "That mule got hurt pretty bad on a pack trip earlier this summer. They said they left her in the meadow at Upper Buck Lake to heal up. Ted must think he can bring her back out now."

"That's right," Dan said. "He thought she might be healed up enough to travel."

I kept my eyes on Dan as we talked, but I was aware that

Steve was watching me with an expression somewhere between hostility and avarice. Not surprisingly, in view of my mud-covered clothes, he also looked amused. No doubt, I thought glumly, there was also mud in my hair and on my face.

Nothing I could do about it now. Pride forbade my scrubbing at myself with the tail of my shirt. I held my head up and looked Steve in the eye. I didn't give a fuck what he thought of me, anyway.

"You look like you could use some help," he said.

I heard the sneer in his voice and worked at remaining detached. "I'm doing all right," I told him.

"A woman doesn't belong out here all by herself."

I shrugged. Judging by his tone, no answer I could have made to this would sink in. I'd met men like Steve before. For some reason, the combination of my competence and lack of sexual interest in them was threatening. They always reacted with hostility, and they were always a pain in the butt.

Though I don't consider myself a feminist, I have a short fuse with the Steves of this world. I'm an individual; I don't feel any more invested in the fact that I'm female than in the fact that I'm a veterinarian, and own horses, and am tall. Whatever. I've never felt that being a woman held me back in any way, and I've dealt with a lot of good old boys.

In my opinion, good old boys mostly respected competence, and if I was competent with a horse and knew my medicine, they noticed it and figured I was all right. I'd heard some women say that "a woman shouldn't have to prove herself just because she's a woman," but I thought that was bullshit. When it comes to fields where there is some risk, where skill is necessary for survival, everybody has to prove themselves. The new guy and the new gal are regarded with almost equal suspicion.

And if the new gal was regarded with a little more suspicion, at least in my line of work, it mostly came down to a simple bottom line. Men are, generally speaking, physically stronger than women. And physical strength is a big asset when you're working with horses.

Fortunately, I'm pretty strong. And I didn't resent people's preference for a vet who could deal competently with all the physical stuff that came along. But once in a while I ran into a Steve. And they were different.

I looked at him now, while various thoughts floated through my mind. Blond, handsome, in his twenties, a white straw cowboy hat on his head, a small butt encased in blue denim, mean brown eyes. Had I flirted with him, he would have acted friendly toward me. But the meanness would still have been there. The Steves of this world just don't like women.

That didn't mean they didn't want to bed them. Guys like this seemed to regard women as prey, scoring them off as notches on the belt.

I stared at Steve's belt, adorned with a holster. This guy was carrying a pistol. I glanced around the camp. No other guns in evidence. Neither Dan nor Jim, who was bent over nailing the shoe on my horse, was wearing a holster.

I looked back at Dan curiously. If I were him, I wouldn't want any help as surly and insolent as Steve carrying a gun.

Dan met my eyes easily. He'd watched my brief interchange with Steve, and he'd seen me notice the gun. None of it seemed to bother him in the slightest.

The man intrigued me. "I ran into Blue Winter," I said.

"Is that right?" Dan appeared mildly interested.

I waited.

Dan smiled. "Don't tell me. He told you all about the dun horse and how he didn't really steal him."

"That's right." Dan said nothing.

After a minute, I asked him, "Do you think he owes you money?"

Dan Jacobi had a poker player's face. Or, for that matter, a horse trader's face. Nothing flickered, nothing changed. "You only know what Blue told you," he said.

I took that in. It was true enough.

"I wouldn't listen to Blue Winter, if I were you," he went on. "I'd be real careful about that guy. He tells you what he wants you to hear."

I stared at him. Two days of struggling through the mountains had pretty much driven everything else out of my mind. In a rush, I remembered all my speculations about Bill Evans.

"Are you telling me you think Blue Winter is dangerous?" I asked Dan.

He shrugged one shoulder. "I'm telling you I don't trust him."

The words had a note of finality. Dan Jacobi turned away from me and went over to inspect the job that Jim was doing on Plumber. This left me face to face with Steve.

Before I could move or flinch, Steve stepped forward until his face was two feet from mine. Reaching a hand out, he dragged a finger across my chin.

I leaped backward and Steve grinned. Holding his hand up so I could see it, he drawled, "Just wiping off a little mud."

Shit. This guy was really a loose cannon. I turned away without a word. I did not want to provoke Steve, not out here in the middle of nowhere.

Plumber's shoe was nailed back on, nice and neat. I thanked Jim and then thanked Dan as I untied my horses and mounted Gunner.

"So where are you off to?" Dan asked me.

"Oh, Buck Lakes, I guess." This was an outright lie. I'd never intended to go to Buck Lakes, and was even less inclined to do so now that I'd heard Ted was there. Some miles past

Wood Lake, the trail forked. Here I planned to take the trail to Benson Lake. But I saw no reason to tell Dan that.

He smiled at me. "Good luck, then."

"Thanks. And you, too."

I clucked to my horses and rode off, thinking with relief that the whole thing had not gone too badly. Steve was downright scary, but Plumber was shod again and I hadn't told anyone where I was headed.

Trouble was, I'd meant to camp at Wood Lake, but I did not want another visit from Dan Jacobi, or more particularly, from Steve. As soon as I was out of sight of their camp, I dug my map out of the saddlebag and looked at it.

As I'd remembered, Wood Lake was a very long, narrow lake—almost a mile long. It had two small, round bulbs at either end with a channel connecting them. Dan and crew were camped at one of the bulbs. If I rode all the way down to the other, I ought to be far enough away that they'd neither see nor hear me.

I rode. The trail followed the side of the lake. I could look down into the clear water and see big brookies swimming along.

Wood Lake was well named. It was in the woods, all right. Aside from the small meadow where Dan Jacobi had been camped the trees came right down to the lakeshore everywhere. I crossed my fingers that there would be a decent campsite down at the other end.

And there was. The far end of the lake, when I finally reached it, formed another circular bowl. The forest sloped down to it for about half its circumference; the other half was rocks and a brief spit of meadow. There was a fire ring in a flat area amongst the rocks and enough feed for one evening anyway. I tied my horses up and started making camp.

Owing to my leisurely morning, assorted wrecks, and bout of horseshoeing, it was now late afternoon. The clouds had disappeared and the sun poured into the far end of Wood Lake with a low golden slant; pine trees and cedars on the ridge stood erect, blue-green shoulders stiff and military, each needle outlined with light. Light sparks glittered on the water of the lake, and all in the world I wanted to do was peel my clothes off and go for a swim.

But camp needed to be built. Dutifully, I unsaddled the horses, put Gunner on a picket line and turned Plumber loose to graze, and began setting up my tent. One by one, I did the familiar chores. By the time I'd finished gathering firewood, building a fire, and pumping water, the sun was behind the ridge and the lake didn't look so inviting. What I needed, I decided, was a drink.

I made myself one and sat down in my chair to enjoy it. Putting my feet up on a rock, I sighed. The last two days had been difficult, to say the least. But we were in one piece, and it felt good to be in camp this evening. All in all, I wouldn't complain.

I made and drank another drink, then heated a can of chili for dinner. Two more logs on the fire, and I leaned back in my chair, alternately watching the flames and reading Thoreau. Slowly the light died out of the sky. I could barely see the print on the page.

Setting a manzanita root on the campfire, I stretched and sighed. Mosquitoes hummed fiercely around me as dark drew in. So far on this trip they hadn't been much of a problem, but the low, boggy country around Wood Lake appeared to be an ideal breeding ground.

I'd smeared mosquito repellent on my face, neck, and hands earlier; now I pulled the hood on my sweatshirt up over my head and tied it under my chin. I wasn't getting bitten much—the repellent kept the little buggers at bay—but the noise was starting to drive me crazy.

143

A high-pitched whine like an engine gone berserk, or a swarm of angry bees, the mosquito hum seemed to fill the evening. It was a nervous sort of sound and always made me antsy. The sweatshirt hood blocked a lot of it.

I stared out at the glossy, darkening lake, then back at the bright flames of my fire. Sweet manzanita smoke, like incense, filled the air. It was a warm night. Suddenly the water looked inviting again.

Why not? It was too dark for anybody—Steve, Dan, or whoever—to be stumbling around the mountains. I could count on being private here. I walked down to the lakeshore. Roey followed me.

Peeling off my boots, jeans, sweatshirt, tank top, and underwear, I waded in. The dog whined anxiously on the shore behind me.

Wood Lake was a warm lake, and the water seemed to be the same temperature as the night air. When I was waist-deep, I made a short, shallow dive and started swimming.

The water felt wonderful against my skin. Cool black silk, soft and shiny and unbelievably sensuous. I floated on my back for a moment, seeing the dark pine tree tops sketched against the deep midnight-blue of the sky—and one star. The evening star. Venus herself.

Mosquitoes buzzed around my ears and I rolled and dove, blocking out the world with cool water. After a few more leisurely strokes, I swam back to shore to pacify the dog, who was most unhappy. Roey swam when she thought it appropriate; apparently swimming in this lake at night didn't seem right to her.

Patting her head, I dripped my way back to camp and stood by the fire. As I dried myself gradually in its heat, swatting at mosquitoes meanwhile, a nearly full moon rose above the ridge, with a few pine boughs traced against it. Smoke curled up from my campfire and drifted across the moon. A witch's night.

I toweled the rest of the dampness off my body, checked the horses, and crawled into my sleeping bag. Looking at my fire and the moon over the lake, I felt content. It was the last peaceful night I would spend in the mountains.

SEVENTEEN

I left Wood Lake early the next morning, determined to put some distance between myself and Dan Jacobi's crew. If I never ran into Steve again, it would be just fine with me.

Cinching the pack rig down with numb hands, I swore under my breath. Leisurely mornings in camp were more my speed; I was no big fan of this move-out-early stuff. Still, I swung stiffly aboard Gunner and pointed my entourage down the trail just as the first pale gleams of sunlight filtered over the ridge.

Today, I thought, I'll make it to Benson. I'd heard about Benson Lake for years—the Riviera of the Sierras, one guide-book called it. It featured a long white sand beach, unusual for a High Sierra lake. I had every intention of taking a sunbath on that beach.

Dan Jacobi thought I was headed for Buck Lakes. Ted was at Buck Lakes. If I wanted to avoid company, I would just avoid Buck Lakes.

The trail to Benson was also the route to Upper and Lower Buck Lakes, for the first seven miles, anyway. However, whichever direction they were headed, I strongly suspected Dan Jacobi and his boys would not get an early start.

They were probably warm right now, though. I pulled some light polypropylene gloves out of the pocket of my jacket and worked my numb hands into them. The sun's coming up, I encouraged myself. In an hour or so, you'll take your jacket off.

I rode down the trail, letting my mind drift. According to the elevation lines on my map, this trail wound through relatively level forest land for several miles. Should be easy riding. Good for a pilot who was still half-asleep.

The banality of my thoughts always surprised me. Alone in the mountains, with the new sunlight poking encouragingly through the branches of the pines and cedars, my mind kept turning incessantly to my hair. Should I cut it? Would I look more attractive with some short, sleek style? I'd worn my hair long, mostly in a ponytail or braid, for years. Maybe I needed a change.

Don't be ridiculous, I chastised myself; think about Thoreau, for God's sake. Think about solitude. Don't think about your hair. Was I about to become one of those sad, desperate middle-aged women who persistently wear too much makeup and too-tight clothes and routinely change their hairstyle in order to appear sexually attractive to men? God, I hoped not.

So why, then, did my mind constantly want to dwell on whether I should try to lose ten pounds? What was going on somewhere deep in my psyche that these odd insecurities popped into my head whenever I wasn't actively engaged in thinking about something else?

Maybe the prospect of breaking up with Lonny. Once again I was surprised. Was I really thinking of breaking up with Lonny? I'd never allowed myself to voice those words before.

Was all this mental nattering about whether I was attractive to do with the fact that I wanted a new sexual partner?

The woods slipped by me unseen, as I tried to decide if this was true. Lonny was part of my life and I loved him, but I was aware that my frustration with him was growing.

I rode. Little puffs of dust rose under Gunner's feet; the air grew drier and warmer. I unzipped my coat and peeled the gloves back off and stuffed them in my pocket. We still had quite a ways to go before we hit the cutoff trail to Benson.

The forest was peaceful in the sunshine, the sturdy pillars of trees thick around us, the warming air filled with the sharp, resinous smell of pines softened by trail dust. Lulled by the stillness and my thoughts, I paid no attention to the warning.

Bees buzzing. I heard it, but it didn't register. In some far-away corner of my mind I filed the sound under honeybees-in-the-garden, a pleasant, innocuous noise. Forgetting that I was in the middle of a pine forest, not the ideal habitat for honeybees.

Suddenly Gunner jumped. I grabbed the saddle horn and looked quickly to see if the rope was under his tail. No. But there were a couple of bees buzzing around him.

Plumber snorted and lunged forward and the buzzing sound intensified. Bees everywhere. Shit. Yellow jackets, not honey-bees, and I must have disturbed a nest.

"Damn!" A red-hot stab in the neck as a wasp stung me. Clinging to the horn as Gunner plunged forward, I clucked to him and kicked his ribs, my one thought to get out of there.

We hit the high lope, Plumber in tow, buzzing yellow jackets swirling around us. I yelped as another sting nailed my wrist, and Gunner crow-hopped in the middle of a stride, pissed as hell.

Clinging to the horn, I thumped on his ribs with my heels. "Don't buck, run," I urged him.

He lunged forward again, just as a wasp stung my forearm. I let go of Plumber's lead rope. The forest was thick around us, no possible escape route but the trail. A big tree leaned across it just ahead. There was room to pass underneath, barely.

Another wasp stung me and I kicked Gunner fiercely, ducking my head as we scrambled under the tree, pushing through branches.

Whump—everything moved, earth shook—a branch cracked across my face like a whip. Dust rose in a cloud.

Disoriented by noise and violent motion, I pulled Gunner up sharply. The tree had dropped like a sledgehammer just behind us, missing Gunner and me by a foot, no more. My God, my God. Where was Plumber? Where was Roey?

My heart drummed frantically. A random wasp stung my arm; I barely felt it. I stared at the heavy trunk and tangle of branches blocking the trail, paralyzed with fear.

A shrill nicker. Plumber was alive, anyway. Was he down? Hurt? I couldn't see him.

I took a step toward the fallen tree and saw a small, neat brown head, ears up, eyes wide, peering at me over the foliage. Plumber. On all four legs and just fine.

"Roey," I called weakly.

The red dog scampered through the branches toward me, wagging her tail. I nearly fell off Gunner in a collapse, the relief was so great.

"Jesus," I said out loud.

What an incredible piece of luck. We had crossed under half-down trees many times on this trip; some of them had obviously bridged the trail for long years before we passed along the way. This tree looked like it had just tipped over. Had it not been for the yellow jackets, I might have inspected it more carefully before I pushed my way through. I might have noticed how unstable it was. On the other hand, had Gunner and I not been moving at the lope, the tree probably would have fallen squarely on us.

The thought caused a visceral shudder. We would be dead. Or very badly hurt, at the very least.

Don't go there, I urged myself. The problem is what to do now. Deal with it.

Thankfully the wasps had dispersed. Either the falling tree had upset them, too, or we were just far enough away from the nest we'd inadvertently disturbed.

"What I need to do now," I said out loud, "is catch Plumber and get him around this tree."

The sound of my own voice sounding calm and logical was reassuring. I climbed down off Gunner and tethered him to a pine branch, noticing that he had several welts on his shoulders and rump. God, I hoped he didn't start into an allergic reaction.

I walked back toward the tree and my other horse, Roey at my heels.

The pine lay squarely across the trail. It was about two feet in diameter—not an enormous tree, but plenty big enough to do some serious damage. Belatedly it occurred to me that had I not let go of the lead rope during our flight from the yellow jackets, Plumber would probably have been much closer on Gunner's heels. The tree would have landed on him.

And Roey had been saved because she'd developed the habit of tracking along right behind Plumber. Even in the confusion, she'd dutifully followed the pack horse. Thank God.

I stared at the tree, which now presented a fairly major obstacle. The trunk bridged the trail at about chest height on a horse—too high to jump or step over. And the thick tangle of stiff branches looked impenetrable. I walked toward the stump end, and stopped dead.

Someone had chopped this tree down. I could clearly see the marks of the ax. The butt end, rather than being ripped and splintered, as it would be if it had fallen naturally, showed the short, sharp indentations of an ax blade. I could smell fresh pine sap.

"What the hell?" Now why in God's name would someone choose to chop a pine down here and leave it. For firewood? I stared around at the forest. Ridiculous. There were downed branches everywhere, and no fire ring to mark a campsite. No obvious spot to camp, either.

I found a route around the fallen tree, and walked toward Plumber, who was nosing at the branches. Had the tree been partially down, and some traveler decided to cut it all the way down with the notion of making it safer? And if so, why leave it hanging precariously over the trail?

Cursing backpackers in general, perhaps unjustly, I caught my horse, who seemed perfectly fine. Leading him on a convoluted route between tree trunks, I guided us back to the trail and Gunner, staring at the downed pine malevolently the whole time.

It was pissing me off. What a stupid, stupid thing to do. Fear receded, anger pumped through my veins. I wanted to throttle the bastard who had almost killed me and my horses.

With a last glance at the tree, I mounted Gunner and started back down the trail. There was nothing I could do about it now.

I rode, looking around with considerably more attention than I had earlier. The hell with how attractive I was, or wasn't. I just wanted to survive.

Another mile of forest, with the trail ascending gradually, and I rode into a small, scrubby, much-eroded meadow that the map called Groundhog Meadow. I stared at the obscure little elevation lines on the paper. Just ahead was Cherry Creek Canyon, which looked big and steep. And after that, the cutoff trail to Benson.

I clucked to the horses and rode on, hoping the trail would be okay through Cherry Creek Canyon.

It wasn't bad. I emerged from a small stand of cedars out into rock with the full panorama of the canyon spread out in front of me.

Wow. Like a softer, more silvery version of the Grand Canyon, Cherry Creek Canyon cut a mile-wide swath through rocky country—a great, deep gorge. I could see glimpses of Cherry Creek itself down in the bottom.

The view was incredible—also the exposure. But the trail seemed well made, blasted right into the rock in the tricky spots. Gunner and Plumber picked their way along, old hands at clambering down granite slopes. I tried to enjoy the scenery.

Wind blew along the slopes of the canyon, fingering the pine boughs with long sighs. The sky was a bright and cloudless blue. A vast emptiness seemed to radiate outward from a gray granite center.

On we went, one switchback at a time. The slope grew steeper. Looking straight down, I could see Cherry Creek, many distant feet away, immediately under my right stirrup. I could also see what looked like a bridge down there.

God, the exposure was severe. If my horse slipped here, he'd be dead for sure. And me, too, if I stayed with him. I took my feet out of the stirrups. If I had to jump off, I would.

We approached another hairpin turn, with a cliff beyond. The wind whistled in the rocks. Gunner moved carefully, one step at a time, seeming aware of the danger. I tried to keep my focus on the trail, not the drop.

Wind moved in a grove of pine saplings as we started into the turn. Gunner stepped down over a rock. With a *whoosh*, something yellow blew into his face. A slicker, for God sake.

For one heart-stopping moment I felt his body tense to spring and thought he would jump. I yelled, "Whoa!"

He trembled; a sapling waved wildly; the slicker landed on the ground at his feet. Gunner stared at it—ears pointed forward, eyes big. He snorted; I could feel his heart thumping. Mine, too.

A bright yellow slicker. Where the hell had it come from? I looked at the drop under my right foot, and said another silent prayer of thanks. Gunner had had enough faith in me to listen to my "whoa" in the face of this new danger. And/or enough sense not to jump when a jump would have killed us all.

The slicker lay next to his left foreleg. Gently I urged him past it, watching to see that Plumber followed. Two switchbacks down, the trail leveled out into a grove of pines. Finding a spot, I tied both horses and walked back up the hill to the slicker.

This isn't right. The words echoed in my mind as I approached the yellow object. A very ordinary rubber rain jacket. I picked it up. Yes, that was what I thought I'd seen. White string. The slicker had a piece of string attached to it. And the string ran up to the tip of one of the pine saplings and was tied there.

Bending down, I investigated further and found two small pieces of wood that looked like they'd been carved with a pocketknife. The trigger. This was, in fact, a snare.

A little more searching revealed the string that had been drawn across the trail. I stared down at it. Someone had rigged the slicker to be a horse-spooker. He had tied it to the sapling, bent the sapling back, and attached it to the carved hook of the trigger. The other string had also been attached to the trigger and then pulled tight across the trail. When Gunner broke it, the trigger flew loose, releasing the pine, which had flung the slicker in our direction.

I looked down at the drop. Someone had rigged this horse-spooking trap on perhaps the most dangerous corner on the entire descent. Someone had meant business.

But against whom? Anyone who passed along this trail was a possible victim. I wasn't necessarily the target.

Could it be some sort of bizarre joke? Or maybe . . . I froze. The fallen tree. I hadn't looked, hadn't considered. The same sort of trigger might have existed. When I brushed through the branches, I had set off a deadfall trap.

In that second I was sure of it. There was no other reason for that freshly chopped pine to be suspended so precariously across the trail. And now this.

These traps were both geared to horses. Oh my God. A crazed backpacker out here with an ecological bee in his bonnet. Rid the mountains of horses . . . now. And I had met the guy back at Wilma Lake. Was it possible?

Slowly I retraced my steps back to the horses, Roey trotting at my heels. If these traps were not the work of an irrational horse hater, then why?

I untied Gunner and climbed back on him, feeling confused, frightened, and undirected. The one thing I did not want to do was run into the author of these traps. But I had no idea if he, she, or they were ahead of me or behind me. Or if more booby traps were waiting.

Keeping my eyes on the trail, I rode on, scanning for string or twine, anything that looked unnatural. Periodically, I ran my eyes over the rocks, looking for color, listening for voices. Was someone out here, hunting me? And if so, why?

The whole thing was beyond belief. Like a bad dream, full of odd and frightening events with no reasonable explanation.

Gunner was walking down the trail, nearing the bottom of Cherry Creek Canyon, and I was looking for snipers. The chatter of the creek grew louder; I could see the white water flashing in the sun. And there was the bridge.

Not as high or long as the one near the pack station, it was still a scary proposition. Particularly in the mind-set I was in. I felt totally exposed and vulnerable as Gunner approached the landing.

He snorted, stopped, bowed his neck. I kicked him in the ribs. "Come on, get on with it."

Gunner lowered his head until his muzzle touched the wooden planks. He snorted again. I kicked harder. "Come on."

I could feel his body tense up. The harder I kicked, the firmer

154

he felt. I thumped him a good one, and he took a step. Back-ward.

There he stood, planted rigidly. Nothing I could do, including whacking him with the end of the lead rope, budged him at all. Gunner, obedient throughout the trip, flatly refused to cross this bridge. Something was wrong.

EIGHTEEN

I wouldn't normally take a horse's refusal to cross an obstacle as anything other than disobedience arising out of natural fear. But I was spooked. I'd run into two booby traps this morning. What if this bridge were another?

Rather than slapping Gunner again with the rope, I sat frozen in the saddle, staring at the bridge with eyes as big as his. What if? What if something were wrong? Gunner had crossed bridges before, including the much scarier bridge over Deadman Creek. Of course, he'd never seen this particular bridge; he might be balking because of the novelty factor. But still.

I didn't hit him again. Instead, I rode him over to some trees by the side of the trail, and tied him and Plumber up. Taking a length of twine out of my saddlebag, I tied Roey nearby. I didn't want her following where I was going. Then I set out to explore the bridge.

Walking onto it was not an option. If something were really wrong, I couldn't take the chance. Gingerly, I worked my way down the bank, trying to see underneath the structure. The bank was no sheer cliff, but it was pretty damn steep. As soon as I lowered myself five or six feet down it, I regretted my choice.

I'm no rock climber. I have no innate ability to cling limpetlike to granite faces, teasing out delicate holds with my fingertips. The whole idea gave me vertigo. Scrambling down this bank, with a fifty-foot drop to the noisy creek below, was scaring me big-time.

Trying to keep my mind on the task at hand, I got a stable foothold on a large flat shelf, and clung with both hands to a couple of bombproof holds. Then I leaned out, peering up at the underside of the bridge structure.

Nothing. Beams and boards, arranged in an orderly fashion, just as one would expect. No loose ends dangling, no fresh saw marks. I stared at the bridge. It looked fine.

Maybe Gunner was full of shit. Maybe he just didn't like the look of this particular bridge. I gave the planks one more cursory evaluation, and started to haul myself up the rocks. I would get back on my horse and we would go across this damn bridge.

I was about to climb up onto the trail when something caught my eye. A different color. Right under my hand. A little patch of golden-pink dust.

I stared; I picked up a pinch of the stuff and smelled the unmistakable tang of fresh sawdust.

My eyes shot back to the bridge. Slowly, I lowered myself back down the bank where I could see beneath the structure. Still nothing obvious. But there was some mud on the two main supporting beams, near where they connected to the landing. Mud that looked fairly fresh.

How in the hell did that mud get there? Had someone sawed through those beams, filled the notches with mud so they wouldn't show, and climbed back up the bank, carrying some sawdust on their clothes or shoes? It was impossible for me to work my way over to the bridge without a rope; the bank was too steep. If someone had undermined the beams, they must have had a support rope to hang from.

Slowly I climbed back up to the trail. Now what? It was the flimsiest of speculations, and yet, I couldn't ignore it. A tree had fallen almost on top of me this morning. The horse-spooking slicker had definitely been a snare. I could not afford to assume this bridge was all right.

I walked back over to the horses. Plumber nickered at me. I patted him, and then Gunner. Gunner turned his head to look at me, and I rubbed his forehead. "You trusted me," I said out loud. "Now I'm gonna trust you."

Dragging my map out of the saddlebag, I studied it. I could still get to Benson Lake, but it was a long damn way around.

I looked back at the bridge. Maybe this was all a bunch of foolishness, but how could I know? The bridge looked solid and respectable in the midday sunshine. My eyes roved the landscape. No one in sight. Just trees and rocks.

Rocks. I laughed out loud. "That's it," I told the horses. "Rocks."

I picked up a handy boulder, lugged it over to the bridge, and pitched it on board. Fifty pounds, more or less. A couple of dozen of these and I'd have twelve hundred pounds on the structure—about what Gunner weighed. If the bridge would hold the rocks, it would hold us.

Carrying rocks was time-consuming and sweaty. I stripped down to my tank top and thought longingly of a swim in Benson Lake. The lake was only a couple of miles away, if I could get across this bridge.

Another rock. The granite was gritty and dusty and abraded my hands and wrists. I lugged another boulder over, and rolled it onto the bridge. I had quite a pile of them out there now. If I was right, the bridge was undermined right next to the bank that I stood on; the rocks were on top of the weak place.

Five more and I would reach my target number of twenty-four. I selected a particularly large boulder. Well over fifty pounds. My biceps ached as I toted it to the bridge. I half rolled it, half pitched it forward and started to turn away.

A long, moaning creak, and the rending shriek of wood tearing. I jerked around. As if in slow motion, the bridge ripped free from its moorings. With a crashing, echoing boom, it twisted and fell, slamming against the opposite bank, wood shards flying.

I stepped to the horses, grabbing their lead ropes. Both were snorting, eyes big. The bridge broke apart, shattering against rocks and bank. Dust rose, wood splintered, noise reverberated off the canyon walls. The whole structure collapsed into the gap it had once spanned.

I gazed disbelievingly at the wreckage. It couldn't be. But it was. The bridge had been booby-trapped.

Implications sank in, one by one. My heart raced at a steady pace as I dug my pistol out of my saddlebag and fastened the holster to my belt. I unsnapped the leather strap that held the hammer down and rested my hand on the butt for a second.

Some crazy lunatic was out here in these mountains. He had to have undermined the bridge from the bank I was on. Therefore if I retraced my route, I was riding right toward him.

There was no other choice. I untied the horses and the dog and mounted Gunner, keeping an eye on the cliff I was about to go back up. The saboteur was out there somewhere. But I had to get back to the ridge.

I clucked to my entourage and started up the trail, planning my new route as I went. I would head back toward the pack station by the shortest possible route. The dangers of the backcountry were one thing, booby-trapped trails were entirely different. I wanted out.

Trouble was, any way I figured it, the pack station was three days' hard ride from here. There weren't any shortcuts.

I scanned the steep walls of Cherry Creek Canyon, wondering who in hell could possibly be booby-trapping the trail, and why. For the first time in my life, I wished earnestly that a forest ranger would appear.

No such luck. The mountains remained ominously silent; the cry of a hawk circling in the blue was the only sound.

This can't be happening. My mind repeated the words uselessly and frantically. I tried to focus my attention in wide-ranging sweeps over the trail and surrounding rocks.

Twenty minutes later, I was most of the way to the ridge when I saw motion up above me on the trail. Gunner saw it, too. He lifted his head, ears straight forward, and neighed.

We both heard the answering neigh. I craned to get a glimpse of the horse and rider, torn between fear and hope.

A brief flash of tawny color behind a rock and then a gray hat and a blue denim shirt were visible. I stared. Blue Winter blocked the trail above me.

"Well, hi, Stormy," he said.

NINETEEN

My hand flew automatically to the butt of my gun. I looked at the man in front of me, saw his eyes follow the motion of my hand, saw them widen slightly. I said nothing. He said nothing.

I kept watching him, waiting for some sign that would indicate whether I was facing a friend or a foe. I could not imagine why Blue Winter would set booby traps for me, but let's face it, I barely knew the man. Dan Jacobi had told me not to trust him. And here he was, blocking my route away from the bridge.

"You look upset," he said at last.

I pondered my reply. "The bridge is out," I said finally.

"You're kidding."

"No, I'm not." I waited, not volunteering any information.

"Damn. Now why would it wash out at this time of year?"

I said nothing. If Blue Winter had set the trap, I was better off appearing ignorant. He would then have no reason to consider me a threat.

His eyes rested quietly on me. "It's a long way around."

"I was just figuring that out."

He glanced at the sky. "I'd say it was about three o'clock." Sure enough, he wasn't wearing a wristwatch either.

He looked back at me, appearing to consider his next words. After a minute, he said, "Were you going to Benson?"

I said nothing. Once again, my mind was racing around in frantic circles, like a rabbit with a cat on its tail. What should I tell him? Why had he asked that?

Blue Winter shrugged. "You can get by me here, if you like."

"All right." I clucked to Gunner and started up the hill. As he'd said, there was room for the horses to pass each other where he stood.

I rode on until we were face to face. He looked at me; I stared right back at him. I was aware, as I had been before, of a sense of inner stillness. His eyes, steady and gray, stayed on my face without a flicker. I wished I could read his mind.

Carefully, I worked my little pack string by his, watching him meanwhile. He didn't move, merely sat like a statue. His dun horse sniffed noses briefly with Gunner; the freckled dog wagged her tail but remained lying down beside a rock, where he'd told her to stay.

I called Roey to heel as we passed, then looked back over my shoulder. Shit. He was turning his saddle horse around, obviously intending to follow me.

He met my eyes. "Looks like we're going the same way," he said.

Oh, great. Once again my hand went automatically to the gun on my belt, but I jerked it quickly away. It wouldn't do me any good, with this guy dead behind me. I would have to gut this out.

If Blue Winter was the lunatic who had set the traps, I would be safest if I seemed not to suspect him. In the interests of which, I ought to act friendlier. But I was finding it hard to do. Riding up Cherry Canyon with a potential killer on my heels was raising my anxiety level to new highs. Chatting seemed impossible.

He might have nothing to do with it, I reminded myself. He might simply have been riding from Tilden Lake to Benson Lake, a very typical route. Tilden and Benson were two of the biggest lakes in this part of the backcountry.

On the other hand, someone had definitely booby-trapped the bridge. And Blue Winter was the someone who was here. A worst-case scenario that kept intruding into my mind involved the notion that he knew perfectly well how I'd escaped going down with the bridge. He'd been sitting up on the ridge watching me through binoculars while I piled rocks. He'd come along prepared to silence me, and was just taking his time.

Damn, damn, and damn. Visions of violent death and nightmares of rape fled through my head; I tried to push them aside, tried to concentrate on the present moment. This man had never struck me as threatening, and usually, my intuition was good. I tried to believe he might be an innocent bystander.

But with each clink of shod hooves on stone, my fear grew. I wanted to get away from this guy. I felt trapped and scared and desperate with him riding behind me.

Risking a glance back over my shoulder, I saw that he was a polite twenty feet or so behind my pack horse. I could see no sign of a gun on him, but that didn't mean he didn't have one in his saddlebags.

I looked back up the trail. We were nearing the ridge. Not far ahead was Groundhog Meadow, where there was a branch trail. There was also a creek. I would stop in Groundhog Meadow, get off, water my horses, and wait until Blue Winter rode on, then I would take another direction. Any direction but the trail he took.

Blocking my mind to the fear that he wouldn't let me go, I

rode toward the grove of cedars on the rim of the canyon. Groundhog Meadow was just beyond.

Gunner's head bobbed gently in front of me with every stride; I could feel gentle tugs through the lead rope as Plumber trooped along behind. Business as usual. It was hard to believe there was some sort of crazed lunatic on my tail.

I was in the cedars now; I could see the light and openness ahead that was Groundhog Meadow. The creek was on the far side—a little trickle with numerous potholes. I would ride to it and stop. If need be, I'd just camp there. I'd run Blue Winter off with the gun, if I had to.

My heart thudded in a steady, frightened tattoo as I envisioned the scene that might be coming. But I was not, I was damned well not, going to keep riding with this man behind me.

We were in the meadow now, the trail dusty beneath Gunner's hooves. Without a word, I veered off the beaten track, headed for the creek. As we neared it, Gunner's ears went forward and he lengthened his stride; he was thirsty.

Roey scampered past me, the little freckled dog running along with her. Both dogs waded into the nearest pothole and paddled around, lapping water as they swam. I wished I could do the same.

I looked over my shoulder. Blue Winter was following me. Well, what did I expect? Maybe he only wanted to water his horses.

I rode Gunner into the creek and stopped. Plumber crowded alongside and I let both horses drink. Blue Winter went a few feet downstream and watered his livestock. Neither of us said a word.

When my horses were finished drinking, I rode them across the creek and over to a small grove of pines near the rocky edge of the meadow. It would be adequate as a campsite if I had to stay. I dismounted and tied the horses up.

Damn, damn, and damn. Blue Winter was following suit, dismounting and tying his stock. What in the hell was going on?

Once again, my hand went automatically to the butt of my gun, but I jerked it away. No use making trouble I didn't need to have. I started walking toward the creek.

Out of the corner of my eye, I could see him walking toward me and I stopped, facing him. Nothing in his body language or demeanor gave me a clue to his thoughts. He looked removed, aloof, and big, very big.

I tipped my chin up in order to meet his eyes as he neared me. Jesus, this guy was tall. Despite my resolution, something of the fear I felt must have shown on my face, because Blue Winter stopped dead. Eyes locked, we stood like statues.

"What's the matter with you?" He said it quietly.

I had no idea what to say. "I just want to be alone." Nothing like the truth.

"Fine, no problem. You'll be alone as soon as I have a drink."

We stood still, staring at each other. He took a step forward and I flinched.

"Jesus." He shook his head. "I'm just going to get a drink out of the creek, okay?"

He took another step and reached a hand toward my shoulder. I jerked sharply sideways, avoiding his grip. Instantaneously, I heard a loud crack.

For a split second nothing made sense. Blue and I stood frozen in place, while echoes bounced off the rocks. That was a shot, my brain chanted.

Crack!

"Shit!" Blue took three running steps and dove into the creek bed, yelling, "Get down, dammit! Somebody's shooting at us."

I scrambled after him, totally confused. Another loud crack

as I crouched behind a rock; I could hear the bullet ripping through pine boughs behind me.

"Knock it off, asshole!" Blue roared.

I huddled behind my boulder. Somebody was shooting at the two of us. Did this mean Blue was innocent, and the crazed hiker was out in the woods with a gun? Or was it some kind of elaborate ruse?

I looked over at Blue; he lay prone on the ground. One hand clutched the opposite bicep; I could see the wet red stain growing under his fingers. His eyes met mine briefly.

"They shot you," I said blankly.

"Looks like it. What in the hell is going on?"

"I don't know."

I started to move toward him, and he stopped me with a quick, "Stay put."

Another shot rang out. It clipped a rock nearby with a sharp ping; a shard of granite flew in the air.

"Knock it off, you bastard!" Blue shouted it at the top of his lungs.

He looked over at me. "You better goddamn well tell me what's going on here."

"I don't know," I repeated. "I think some crazy guy is out there."

Crack!

This time Blue didn't yell. "Get your gun out," he said quietly.

I pulled the pistol out of its holster, and told him evenly, "I only have five bullets and there's no more ammunition."

"All right. He's in the bunch of trees there." One finger pointed. "Can you shoot that thing?"

"Well enough. I doubt I can hit him from here, even if I could see him, which I can't."

"That's okay. Can you put a shot through that grove?"

"More or less."

166

"All right."

I sighted down the barrel of the .357, using one small pine as a target. Without stopping to consider the wisdom of this course, I took a deep breath, held it, and squeezed the trigger gently.

Ka-boom. My ears rang and my arm slammed back with the recoil.

I had no idea if I'd gotten anywhere near the target pine.

As the echoes died, Blue yelled again. "Get the hell out of here, you son of a bitch, or the next one's going right through you."

Quiet. No shooting. No reply.

Blue lay on the ground behind his rock, his eyes fixed on the pine grove. I watched it, too. I could see nothing.

"How did you know the shots came from there? Can you see him?"

"No. But I did a lot of shooting when I was young. That's where he is."

I crouched behind my rock and stared at the pines. No motion; no color that didn't belong. So where was the madman?

A sudden thought struck me and I looked wildly around for Roey. I couldn't see her. I raised my head to look over at the horses.

"Get down." Blue's voice was clipped.

I ducked. Still no shots.

"Your red dog's by the horses," Blue said. "She's hiding in some scrub."

"She's afraid of loud noises," I said. "She hates fireworks. I thought she might have run away."

"Both the dogs are with the horses. I can see the horses and everything's fine. He's shooting at us, not the animals."

Somewhat reassured, I glanced over at my companion. The stain on his arm was growing, and his words seemed to be coming through clenched teeth. He still held his bicep.

"I'd better have a look at your arm," I said.

"Not now."

My eyes went back to the pine grove. "So, if you can't see him and I can't see him, how do we know if and when he's gone?"

"We don't."

"Do we have a plan?"

"Wait."

I thought about it. Waiting made sense. The impatient itch in my muscles didn't. I wanted to be up and out of here. I considered the idea of another shot and rejected it. I had four bullets left. Who knew when I might need them? And I couldn't see the sniper.

Another thought occurred to me. "So, is there someone who has a reason to be after you?" I asked.

Blue turned his head toward me and I got a level look from the gray eyes. "Dan Jacobi," he said.

"He's not going to shoot you over a horse."

"I wouldn't think so."

"No one else?"

"Not that I know of."

We regarded each other, huddled behind our respective rocks. "I found three booby traps on the trail today," I said at last. "Any one of them could have killed me. The bridge over Cherry Creek collapsed because somebody sabotaged it. You were riding down that trail, too. Maybe the traps were meant for you."

Blue Winter took that in. His face stayed still. "I don't know who it would be," he said at last. "Bill Evans had a reason to hate me, but you say he shot himself. And you're right, Dan Jacobi wouldn't kill me over a horse. Bad for business." He gave a brief smile.

"Well, I don't know of anyone who has a reason to kill me either. The only thing I can think of is it's some crazy back-

168

packer who hates horses. I met one like that at Wilma Lake.''

Blue said nothing for a moment. Then, ''That's why you were acting so strange, earlier. You thought I was your crazy man.''

''Maybe.''

''I'd have to be crazy, wouldn't I? To hurt you.'' He kept his eyes on the pine grove.

I stared into the trees and could see nothing. Only blue-green boughs, gray trunks, the soft red-brown duff of the dead needles that carpeted the ground. ''So how long do we wait?'' I asked.

''I don't know. I'll wave my hat, if you want.''

''Forget it. It's what, four o'clock now?''

''More or less,'' Blue said.

''Let's just lay low till the light dies. That'll make shooting difficult. If your arm will wait.'' I looked at the spreading stain.

''It'll wait. Whoever he is, he's shooting with a pistol. And he can't shoot all that well.''

''Okay. So we lie here and wait for dark.''

''That's right.'' Blue turned his head and gave me that sudden smile. ''You can tell me a story.''

TWENTY

Dark took its sweet time in coming. I shifted my weight, tensed and relaxed my muscles in turn. Occasionally I considered creeping toward the horses, but gave it up as too risky. Once I eased my way down to the creek and took a long swallow of water.

Mostly I stayed behind my rock, waiting. I couldn't see the dogs, but Blue reiterated that they were fine, and with the horses. His face seemed to me to grow paler the longer we lay there, and the sleeve of his shirt was dark with blood. Yet each time I tried to move toward him to examine his arm, he told me to wait.

Eventually the sun dropped behind the ridge, outlining the pines and cedars on the western horizon. Then, as the sun sank further below the rim of the world, came the gentle blurring of edges. Dusk crept in.

One moment we lay there, waiting. The next, without a word, Blue took his hat off his head and waved it with his good arm. Nothing. Slowly he began getting to his feet.

I looked at him.

"Stay down," he said.

For a second I had the impulse to get to my own feet right along with him, but rejected it. What the hell. If this guy was so chivalrous as to want to get shot in my stead, I'd let him.

No shots came. Blue climbed awkwardly up the bank, cradling his right arm with his left. After a minute, I followed him.

No response of any kind came from the pine grove.

"They're gone, I guess," I said out loud.

"Looks like it."

We walked to our horses, and the two dogs came to greet us, stretching and wagging their tails. They seemed glad of the rest, anyway.

But Blue looked terrible. He sat down on a fallen tree with an abruptness that made me think the short walk was too much for him. His face was white; he gripped his arm and looked at the ground.

"You'd better let me have a look at that," I said.

"Okay." His response was barely audible.

I dug out my human first-aid kit (small), and my equine emergency kit (bigger). This was all the stuff I had. Bringing my water bottle with me, I approached Blue Winter.

"Let's get that shirt off," I said.

Obediently, he unbuttoned his shirt, and wincing, unstuck the wet red sleeve from his arm. Even as I focused on the wound, I noticed the long, hard muscles. He was built like a Thoroughbred, tall and lean.

The bullet had gone right into the bicep of his right arm; at a glance, I thought it must also have broken the humerus bone.

"Can you move your arm?" I asked him.

I could see him gather himself for the effort. His fingers curled, but the arm barely twitched.

"No," he said. "It must be broken."

"I think so," I said. "The wound looks fairly clean, but I ought to wash it and wrap it, and then splint that bone as well as I can and make a sling. All this is going to hurt. You'd better take some painkillers first."

I looked at him.

"I've got some codeine in my first-aid kit. I've also got some torbugesic. If I put it in IV, it would be a lot quicker," I told him.

"Torbugesic?"

"Yeah. It's a horse drug. I use it for severe colics. It's a great painkiller. It'll work on people, too."

"Are you sure?"

"Yeah, I'm sure." I smiled at him. "I had a friend in vet school who used to try all the drugs he gave the horses on himself. He gave me a full report."

"Better give me the torbu—whatever it is." Blue closed his eyes. "This hurts pretty bad."

I got out a syringe and filled it with one cc of torbugesic. By my reckoning, this was a light dose for such a big man. Still, though I'd tried to sound confident when talking to Blue, I was a long way from sure this was the right thing to do. What if he reacted negatively to the stuff?

I stared at the syringe in my hand. Light was evaporating like rainwater in the sun. In a little while it would be dark. I needed to work on this man's arm in the light.

"Okay," I said. "Here we go."

What I wanted, I thought, was the vein in his wrist. That was where nurses always gave the IV injections.

"Make a fist with your left hand," I told him.

Squinting in the faint light, I rolled the skin of his wrist under my fingers until I could feel and see the vein. "This will sting a little," I said.

Gently but definitely, I inserted the needle. I glanced at Blue. His face was impassive.

172

Attaching the syringe to the needle, I injected the shot. We both waited. In a minute I could see his face relax.

"That's better," he said.

I smiled. "Now for the hard part. I need to clean this, put some antibiotic salve on it, and wrap it. Then we've got to splint it and make you a sling."

"All right." Blue definitely sounded better.

"The bullet is probably still in there, from the looks of it, but I think we're better off just to leave it there for now. I want to get you fixed up to travel."

I paused in the act of swabbing the wound with water and Betadine scrub. "I guess we'd better head straight for the pack station."

"It's a three-day ride."

"I know. Have you got a better idea?"

Blue was quiet a minute. "How about we ride to Bridgeport?"

"Why Bridgeport?"

"It's closer, for one thing. We could make it in two days, if we pushed. And . . ." He stopped.

"And what?"

"Do people," he said carefully, "expect you to ride back out to Crazy Horse Creek?"

"I suppose so." I smeared antibiotic salve on his wound, put a telfa pad on it, and began to wrap it with Vet Wrap (horse Band-Aids). "Are you suggesting whoever is doing this crap is after me, and that it's someone who knows me?"

"I'm not suggesting anything." Blue's mouth was compressed. "I'm thinking out loud here. I don't know who this bastard is after; it's a cinch he shot me. But maybe I was just in the wrong place at the wrong time. Still, if this person is hunting either you or me particularly, for reasons we don't understand, we're both known to have ridden in from Crazy Horse Creek. My truck and trailer are parked there. Are yours?"

"Yeah, they are." I finished wrapping his arm with Vet Wrap and looked around for a suitable stick for a short splint.

"So, anyone who was halfway observant could know that we both planned to ride back out that way. Now that we're upset, it's a likely bet we'll head out. If this person is after one of us, wouldn't their likeliest move be to wait and sabotage us on the trail to Crazy Horse Creek?"

"It makes sense." I had an appropriate stick; I began ripping strips off Blue's bloody shirt.

He watched me blandly; the torbugesic seemed to be doing its job.

"So, they won't be prepared for us to ride to Bridgeport. And it's a shorter ride," he said.

"What's the most direct route?" I held his arm gently in place as I fashioned a rudimentary splint and sling to support his humerus bone.

"Over the bridge that's now gone." He winced as I wrapped the arm to the stick. "Otherwise we have to ride through Kerrick Meadow and down Buckeye Canyon. Right by Benson Lake."

"So you think we should go that way?" I tightened the sling.

"Yeah, I do. How much of that turbo stuff do you have, anyway?"

"About six more doses like the one you just had."

"We ought to make it, then." He looked over at the horses and stood up. "Let's go."

"Now? It's dark."

"Did you want to wait around here for whoever shot at us to come back?"

"I guess not." I stared at him in the dim light. "How bad's the trail going to be? It's not going to help us much if we escape being shot only to fall off a cliff in the dark."

"I agree. But the trail's not too bad—at least as far as Benson. And the moon will be up in another hour. If we start now,

174

we can make Benson Lake by midnight and then maybe stop and sleep awhile.''

"All right,'' I said dubiously. What he was telling me made sense, and I didn't have any better ideas. Nor did I want to abandon Blue to his fate, or for that matter, go my own way to deal with a lunatic in the backcountry all by myself. No, I definitely wanted to stick with Blue, now that I was sure he wasn't a villain. And Blue seemed pretty clear on what he wanted to do.

He started toward the horses, a little stiffly, but looking a lot better than before the torbugesic. I watched him untie them with his left hand. The little freckled dog ran up to him and wagged her tail.

He turned to me. "I might need help with this.''

"That's what I figured.'' I took the pack horse's lead rope. "I'll hold her.''

Blue got his left foot in the stirrup, while I steadied the dun horse by the bridle reins. Gripping the saddle horn with his left hand, and protecting his right arm as well as he could, he swung his right leg over the saddle; I could see by his face that it cost him. When he was settled I handed the lead rope to him and went to get my own horses.

Roey gave an excited yip as I mounted, and dashed over to her new canine friend, wagging her tail wildly. The dogs were ready to roll.

I wasn't so sure about Blue. He'd dealt with being doctored, and he seemed determined to move on, but just getting aboard his horse had been difficult, I knew. He sat crookedly in his saddle, reins in his left hand, lead rope dallied around the saddle horn, head down.

"Let's go,'' he said quietly. Turning his saddle horse he headed back toward the trail.

"Do you know where we're going?'' I fell in behind him.

"Pretty much. We leave this little meadow where the trail

forks and the sign says Kerrick Meadow that way."

I remembered the fork and the sign.

"Then the trail goes down into Cherry Creek Canyon and out the other side. Benson Lake is just before we get to Kerrick Meadow."

We were riding through the near-dark; I saw Blue rein his horse left at the trail fork and followed him. My horses seemed to be moving confidently, undisturbed by the lack of light. I was worried, though.

"I'm not sure I like this riding in the dark," I said.

"No one can see to shoot us in the dark," came back Blue's reply.

They would have a hard time setting snares in the dark, too, I added to myself. And I knew perfectly well that horses have much better night vision than people. Still, I wished the moon would rise.

We were riding through level, fairly open country; the trail was mostly dirt. At the moment, the darkness did not present much threat. As far as I was concerned, it would be an entirely different deal when we were descending into Cherry Creek Canyon.

We rode. Blue's pack horse had a flaxen tail; the pale straw-yellow color showed up well in the semi-dark. I fixed my eyes on her tail, and tried to trust that Gunner would see and deal with the footing.

We rode. There was a glow on the eastern horizon; the moon would rise soon. Dusk had definitely verged into night; stars showed as pinpricks in the blue-black sky.

Steadily the glow intensified. I watched the mare's tail glow whiter in the silvery light. We rode out of a small grove of trees, and the moon was visible above the rim of Cherry Creek Canyon. A gibbous moon, big enough to shed some useful light.

The trail began descending through granite; I was torn between fear and awe.

Cherry Creek Canyon was a sight. Moonlight reflected on the tumbled granite slabs and scattered scree. Ridges stretched out in the distance, impossibly rich with light and shadow, intricate and mysterious as a Chinese wood-block print. All black, silver, and gray, and yet each nuance, each shade seemed to have meaning.

I stared. Moonglow lit a granite world; trees were black silhouettes. I forgot my fear, I forgot the sniper. The great canyon glowed, as it did every moonlit night. Shadows of pine boughs laid bars across the path.

This is always here, I thought. Eternally present. Always, in myriad forms, the natural world sends its message of beauty blooming; we so seldom hear it or see it. I felt almost thankful that danger had driven me into this canyon by moonlight.

Blue's voice broke the spell. "How are you doing?"

"Okay. How about you?"

"I'm hanging in there."

"Good. This is really something, isn't it?" The moment the words were out of my mouth, I regretted them. How inane could you get? That's the trouble with things like beauty and truth. They don't translate into words.

Blue seemed to understand, though. I heard his voice come floating back. "It sure is."

I sighed and looked out over the endless vistas of silver granite under the three-quarter moon and thought how lucky I was. I'd survived so far, and now I was here. Things could be worse.

Three hours later, I wasn't so sure. We'd traversed Cherry Creek Canyon and were traveling through some rocky country to the east. Blue had assured me that the cutoff trail to Benson would appear any minute—but so far it wasn't appearing.

I was tired, the horses were tired, the dogs were tired. Blue and I had quit talking. We just rode.

I could only guess at how much pain the man ahead of me might be in. He said nothing. I could see how crookedly he slouched in his saddle, though, his whole body curved protectively around his right arm.

Suddenly he pulled his horse up. I saw him look down, saw him rein the horse to the right. In a minute, I knew why. The small wooden Forest Service sign indicating the cutoff trail was plain in the moonlight. We were on our way to Benson Lake.

I didn't ask how far it was; I just followed the pack mare's flaxen tail. On and on, down and down—the trail descending into a dense forest where the moonlight came in shafts. The trail wound between trees, crossed a creek, then followed its banks. More trees.

And then, without warning, the forest fell away. The trail led into a small meadow with the stream running through it and beyond . . . my God. Beyond stretched a half-mile crescent of shining white sand, ringing dark water. The moon lay a silver path down the middle of the water, bright as a fairy tale.

Blue pulled up and I rode alongside him. He turned his head to meet my eyes.

"So what do you think of Benson Lake?" he said.

TWENTY-ONE

We made camp on the beach. What camp we made, anyway. It was mostly a matter of unsaddling and unpacking the horses and putting them on run lines in the meadow. After that, both Blue and I threw our sleeping bags down on the sand.

"Do you want another shot of torbugesic?" I asked him. "It might help you sleep."

"Okay." He sat down on a fallen tree.

I got a syringe, needle, and the drug out of my saddlebags and filled the syringe by the light of the moon. Blue rolled the sleeve back on his left arm. His forearm was pale in the moonlight, the skin cool to the touch and yet warm, too, as I rolled it with the tips of my fingers.

How can skin be cool and warm at the same time, I thought distractedly as I found the vein and injected the shot. I held his arm with my left hand; I could feel the long bones and hard muscles cradled in my palm.

When I was done, we both waited. After a minute, Blue looked up at me and smiled. "That's better," he said.

I smiled back. "Good. Do you want something to eat?"

He shrugged his good shoulder. "I don't know. We'd better not build a fire."

"You think someone's followed us?"

"I don't know. If they have, they're pretty good. I haven't noticed anything, have you?"

"No."

"But lighting a fire would be stupid," he said. "Anyway, I'm so damn tired. I just want to go to sleep."

"How about a granola bar?" I had a couple of these stashed in my saddlebags for just such an emergency.

He shrugged again.

"Have one. You'll feel better in the morning."

"All right." He took the foil-wrapped bar I gave him and began munching steadily, as if eating it were a chore he had to complete.

I did the same. The granola bar didn't have much taste except sweetness, but I knew I should eat. As far as I could remember, I hadn't eaten a thing since the granola bar I'd had early this morning. It seemed like a lifetime ago.

When we were done chomping, Blue began taking off his boots. Or he tried to, anyway. Pulling off cowboy boots using just your left hand isn't easy. Especially when you're right-handed.

I watched him for a minute. He kept struggling.

"Let me help," I said.

"All right."

Taking hold of the heel of each boot in turn, I pulled them off his feet. It was an oddly intimate gesture and reminded me suddenly of the boyfriend I'd had in college.

I looked at Blue and our eyes met. His looked surprised, as near as I could tell in the moonlight.

"There," I said. "Good night."

"Thank you, ma'am." He got stiffly to his feet and walked over to his sleeping bag.

I unlaced my packer boots, which were a good deal easier to get off than Blue's traditionally styled cowboy boots, and crawled into my sleeping bag with relief. Roey curled up next to my body and I rubbed her head for a while.

Glancing over, I could see a small white shape curled up next to Blue Winter. Freckles slept with him, then, just as Roey did with me.

As if he could feel my eyes on him, I heard his voice come out of the night. "See you in the morning, Stormy. Thanks for everything."

"Right." I smiled to myself. By my reckoning, this was really a sweet man. What did he have to thank me for? A bullet in the arm, and the abrupt end of his planned vacation?

Or could this whole thing be about him? Was I the one who had been in the wrong place at the wrong time? Had the booby-trapped trail been prepared for Blue, and I happened to ride down it first?

And if so, my mind asked, did Blue really know what was going on here, and was he hiding it from me? Was that why he was so sure which way he wanted to ride out? Perhaps he knew just who the pursuit was, and where they were coming from.

On and on my mind went, inventing new and more compli-cated scenarios every moment. Just shut up, I told myself. Roey snuggled up to me.

My instincts said that Blue Winter was all right. If there were things he wasn't telling me, so be it. I was going to trust him and see where it got me. It was a cinch I didn't know what was going on, anyway, and I needed help. More than that, I wanted company.

The motionless shape in the sleeping bag ten feet away might not seem to be doing much for me, but he dispelled the frightening emptiness of the night in an amazing way. For a second I imagined myself lying here alone, not knowing who might be out in the dark, stalking me. I shook my head abruptly. No thanks.

Snuggling deeper into my bag, I tried to fall asleep. Maybe it had all been some isolated craziness, as I had first thought. Maybe that loony from Wilma Lake was camped along the trail to Cherry Creek Canyon. Maybe we had left the whole thing behind us. On that comforting thought I fell asleep.

I awoke to sunshine. On my face, on the aspen in the meadow, on the white sand of the beach. Turning my head away from the light, I closed my eyes. It was comfortable here in the sleeping bag, curled into the forgiving sand. I didn't want to get up.

I could see the horses looking impatient out on their run lines; they'd eaten all the grass within reach. Reluctantly I struggled out of my bag and pulled my boots on.

Glancing over at Blue's prostrate form, I ascertained that he was still asleep and decided to let him be. I walked out into the meadow, Roey following me. Freckles stayed with her master, though she flattened her ears and wagged her tail when I looked at her.

Gunner and Plumber nickered when I approached them; Blue's two horses followed suit. I studied the situation for a moment. Then I untied Gunner, an easygoing horse who could be trusted to get along with the others and stay out of trouble. Plumber was a little feistier, apt to pick fights with other horses.

Moving Plumber along the picket line so that he could reach more grass, I approached Blue's two horses. The small sorrel mare pinned her ears. The big dun gelding regarded me with wide, alert eyes. I moved the gelding down the line and retied him, then walked cautiously toward the mare. In general, I mistrusted cranky mares. I'd been kicked good and hard by a few of these.

This mare made a ferocious face at me, but when I took hold of her lead rope her ears came up and she made no attempt to bite or kick. I retied her where she could reach a new patch of grass and left all four horses happily munching.

Walking back to camp, I turned to watch the livestock grazing, their red, brown, and gold coats bright in the sunshine. It was a peaceful sight; yesterday's adventure seemed like a bad dream.

A little breeze rustled through the aspen trees that dotted the meadow, and I smiled. I loved aspens. Of all the mountain trees, they were my favorites. Always flickering, always talking, their green and silver leaves a glittering kaleidoscope against the sky.

"Pretty, isn't it?" came a voice from behind me.

Blue was awake. I turned to look at him, and beyond him at the white sand beach and the water of the lake—bright blue-green in the morning light.

"It's great," I said. "How do you feel?"

"I hurt." He smiled briefly.

I studied him. "Do you want me to give you another shot? I've got five doses left."

Blue lay on his back, staring up at the sky. "What's the plan?" he said, after a moment.

I stared back at him. "We ride out, I guess."

"The horses need to eat."

"I know," I agreed. "So do we."

"We'll spend a few hours here, then."

"Yeah, I guess so."

"Better give me some codeine, and save the shots for when we travel."

"All right." I got the small vial of codeine tablets out of my saddlebag. Six tablets—stashed for emergencies.

"This is going to make you drowsy," I said.

He gave me half a smile. "I better stay in bed."

"You do that," I said, as he swallowed a tablet. "Do you think we can risk a fire?"

We both glanced around. The rocky walls that ringed Benson Lake on all sides were quiet in the sunlight, the little meadow and the beach empty except for us. It all looked perfectly safe. Snipers seemed ridiculous.

"Sure, why not? They can see us in the daylight, if they're looking. A fire won't change anything."

"Okay. I'll make coffee."

Once the fire was made and the coffeepot was on, I poured some dog food for Roey. The little freckled dog wagged her tail and looked at me in a shy and ingratiating way. I laughed out loud.

"Can I feed her, too?" I asked Blue.

"Sure. There's some dog food in my pack."

"Okay." I got the dog food and poured some on the ground. "Here, Freckles," I said.

She walked up to me and lifted her head for a pat, which I gave her, then dipped her whiskered muzzle to the food. I laughed again.

"What are you laughing at?" Blue asked me.

"Your dog."

"Poor Freckles. Everybody thinks she's funny-looking."

"It's the blue eyes. Or maybe that terrier muzzle. I don't know. She's pretty cute. Do you want me to turn your horses loose?"

"You can turn the gelding loose if you want. He won't fight with the other horses and he won't leave the mare."

"Okay. What are their names?" I smiled. I had a thing about that. I always liked to know the names of the horses I handled.

"The gelding's Dunny," Blue said.

It figured. Cowboys often called horses by their colors. Bays

were Bay, sorrels Sorrelly, buckskins Bucky, blacks Blacky . . .
et cetera. Naturally the big dun horse was Dunny.

"I call the mare Little Witch," Blue went on.

I laughed again. "That fits."

He smiled over at me. "She just likes to act cross. She's
really pretty sweet. She's just a three-year-old."

I grinned at him. "I used to ride a horse like that. He pinned
his ears all the time, and acted like he wanted to eat you, but
he'd do anything for you." This was Burt, Lonny's head horse.

"Yeah. This filly's like that. I owned her mother, and I've
raised this one since she was born. She acts ornery, but she's
not, really. She's been easy to train. Better not turn her loose,
through. The geldings might fight."

I nodded. In my experience this was true. Mares were a problem, even if they were sweet-tempered themselves. All the
geldings fell in love with them and fought for their favors. It
didn't seem to matter that the relationship was necessarily going to be platonic; the geldings got pretty damn devoted. This
was a major nuisance and one of the reasons I refused to own
a mare.

I turned Dunny loose and watched as he sniffed noses with
Gunner. No squeals, no strikes. Gunner pinned his ears in a
mild way, stating that he intended to be dominant, and Dunny
moved off submissively and began eating grass. No problem.

I walked back to camp and poured coffee. Blue propped himself against a log and took the cup I handed him. Sitting down
on a rock, I took the first hot sip.

Our eyes met. He smiled. "Ahh," he said.

"It sure tastes good," I agreed.

I stretched my back, feeling the warmth of the sun through
my tank top. Sipped some more coffee and stared at the lake.

"There's an island right in the middle," I said.

"Yeah. I swam out there once. It's pretty big for an island
in a Sierra lake. Almost half an acre, I'd say. Mostly rocks.

There's a couple of trees and a little flat spot where it looks like somebody camped once.''

"That must have been interesting." I could see a couple of pines and a rocky outcropping from where I sat. Looked like it would be a decent swim. If this were still a vacation, I'd be thinking of swimming out there in the afternoon.

My eyes went back to the man beside me. He raised his coffee cup to his lips with his left hand; I could see the faint wince of pain at the movement. Sitting here in the sunshine, everything seemed peaceful and relaxing, but there was no getting around it, Blue had been shot.

We needed to get him to a doctor, and more than that, we needed to get out of the backcountry, on the chance that whoever had shot him was after us. But I still sat, feeling the sun on my back, idly watching my companion.

He raised his cup again and I saw the long muscles in his arm tighten; the light sparkled on the red-gold hairs of his forearm as on fine copper wires. I allowed the thought to cross my mind: This was really an attractive man.

For a moment I stopped to wonder what attraction is composed of, anyway. Would another woman think Blue Winter was attractive? I didn't know. All I knew was that his long, lean body, red-gold hair and quiet gray eyes were speaking to my physical self in a constant, powerful way.

Then I shrugged. He probably had a girlfriend. I had a boyfriend. For all I knew, he didn't find me physically attractive at all. Not to mention, his mind was hardly likely to be on such matters, not with a bullet in his arm.

"How about a granola bar for breakfast?" I asked.

"All right." He said it without enthusiasm.

"I know. But it's quick and we should probably get organized to go. How long a ride is it to Bridgeport?"

"A solid eight hours."

"We'd better leave in an hour or so."

"You're right."

We regarded each other morosely. Packing up seemed like a big chore. Better than getting shot, though.

I handed Blue two granola bars. "Eat these," I said. "You'll feel better."

"Okay."

We munched; I watched the horses graze. The dogs snoozed in the sunshine; the remains of my morning fire flickered. It was all so damn tranquil.

"I'd like to have a quick wash before we pack up to go," I said, as I stood up.

"Go right ahead." Blue looked rueful. "I'd like one, too, but I don't think I can manage it." He smiled up at me. "I don't think I'm going to be much help saddling and packing the horses, either."

"That's okay. I can do it. Is there anything you want before I go down to the lake?"

"No. I'll be fine."

"Okay." I took my boots off, got a towel and some soap, and started off across the sand. Benson Lake glittered ahead of me; the beach was warm and soft under my feet. I stared up at the towering rock walls that surrounded the water. This was really a unique spot.

The lake sat in the bottom of what was more or less a thimble. The canyon we'd ridden down was the only way in, the half mile of beach with the small meadow beyond it the only level ground along the shoreline. By the looks of it, it would be absolutely impossible to ride around this lake, and damn difficult to walk.

I was nearing the water; it was an odd feeling to be standing on a white sand beach lapped with little waves in the middle of the Sierras. Granite cliffs glowed in the sunshine. Suddenly, to my amazement, I heard a coyote howl. The sound echoed off the rocks and seemed to float upward—sweet, eerie, melodious—uncanny in the bright light of morning.

I stood still. Another coyote answered the first, and then another. The cliffs carried the sound. Many voices now, as the howls rose to a long keening and then a crescendo of sharp *ki-yi-yi*'s, bouncing off the walls, seeming to come from all directions.

Mesmerized, I stood like a statue, as the strange serenade filled the bowl of Benson Lake. I had never heard coyotes sing like this in broad daylight. What could it mean? Perhaps there was a den in these rocks.

The sound died. One last voice rose in a solitary, mournful howl. Then all was quiet. After a minute I walked forward and stepped into the lake.

Icy water lapped my ankle; I jerked my foot sharply out and whistled. This lake was cold. For a minute I rethought my bathing plans. Maybe I'd just stay dirty.

You'll feel better if you wash, I told myself. You've got a long ride ahead of you. But I damn well wasn't going swimming.

I splashed water on my face and hands, washed my armpits briefly, and brushed my teeth. Then I toweled off, feeling a little cleaner and a lot wider awake.

I could see Gunner and Dunny, a little ways down the beach, drinking out of the lake. I needed to take Plumber and Little Witch down for a drink before I packed them, I reminded myself.

Gunner lifted his head, ears up, staring out over the lake. Suddenly with a snort, he whirled and ran, Dunny following him. For a second they thundered toward me along the beach, running free, manes and tails flying, a poster come to life. I watched them with a wide grin as they swerved off across the sand and galloped back to the meadow and their companions. Those two were feeling fresh enough to travel, anyway.

Making my own, much slower, way back to camp, I untied Plumber and the mare and led them down to the lake, taking care to keep them well separated so they didn't fuss. No use getting a horse kicked if I could help it.

Bringing them back, I tied them to trees near the gear and caught Gunner and Dunny. Blue watched me without a word. It didn't look like he'd moved all morning. I was beginning to worry about how he would deal with the traveling. Maybe another shot would do the trick.

The brightness seemed to have gone out of the morning; as I brushed the two saddle horses and put pads and blankets on their backs, I could see a haze in the air.

I heaved the saddles up and cinched them lightly, tied the saddlebags in place, and looked at Blue. He sat on the other side of the fire pit, half propped against his log, staring out across the meadow. I could smell the acrid tang of wood smoke, mingling with the clear, piney mountain smell. Camp smells of wood smoke, always.

I started to brush Plumber and looked back at Blue. His face had a fixed expression. I turned around to look where he was looking. For a second I saw nothing, just the meadow under the hazy sky. Just the smell of smoke.

Then I got it.

"My God," I said. "There's a fire."

TWENTY-TWO

U p the canyon," Blue affirmed. I couldn't read either his expression or his tone.

"Jesus, what do we do?"

"It depends," he said.

Smoke was growing thicker in the air every moment; panic grew inside of me.

"Depends on what?" I knew my voice was shrill.

"Get the binoculars out of my saddlebag."

I got them and went to his side. He raised them to his eyes with his good hand and pointed them up the canyon. There was a long moment of silence, then he lowered them.

"See for yourself."

I looked. For a second everything was a blur; I adjusted the spacing—instant sharpness. It didn't tell me much. Heavy clouds of smoke billowing into the air at the head of the canyon, that was it.

"So what do you see?" I demanded.

"The fire's in the canyon and the wind's blowing this way," he said.

I looked at the aspen trees in the meadow. Sure enough, the ever-present Sierra wind pulled their feathery tops in the direction of the lake.

"So the fire will burn toward us," I said.

"That's right."

"So, what do we do?" I could hear my voice rising.

"We've got a couple of choices," he said. "I don't think riding up the canyon is a good one; fires are unpredictable, and that wind is rising. We could get ourselves in real trouble."

I listened to him, trying to keep my chattering nerves on hold.

"We could wait it out, on the beach," he said. His laconic tone was getting to me.

"Is that going to work?" I demanded.

"Probably."

I stared at him. His face was quiet and he seemed in no hurry to do anything.

"What are our other options, in your opinion?" I asked him.

"I guess the safest thing we could do is hike around the lake to the far end. It's all rock; the fire won't get there. We'd be perfectly safe."

"And leave the horses here?"

"We can't take them around the lake; it's impossible. I've hiked down to the far end before." He gave me a brief smile. "You'd probably have to leave me, too. I don't think I could make it with this arm."

I looked at him, then looked out over the lake; smoke haze, gray as fog, filled the air of the bowl. Without a word, I walked to Gunner and got the torbugesic and the syringe out of my saddlebags.

"I'm giving you a shot," I said to Blue.

191

"All right." He rolled his sleeve back. "You want to try hiking, then?"

I met his eyes. "And leave the horses?"

"We'd have to."

"Is that what you want to do?" I asked him.

"No. I'd wait it out on the beach, and stay with them."

"Would we be okay, do you think? On the beach. Holding the horses." I injected the shot into his vein.

"Probably. Depends on the wind. And how panicked the horses got. I'm not sure we could hold them."

I watched for the slight relaxation of his facial muscles, heard the tiny sigh as the drug kicked in. Then I looked up the canyon. Smoke billowed fiercely; the haze in the air was getting thicker every minute.

I looked back out over the lake. Then I looked at Blue.

"How about we swim to the island?" I said.

His eyes moved sharply to mine and I could feel the quick calculations in his head. "We could," he said. "Swim the horses, you mean."

"Yeah. And the dogs."

"We could do it. There's a sort of rocky beach on the far side. And there's room to camp once we get there."

"We'd be safe," I said.

"If we made it."

"They can swim that far. So can we. So can the dogs."

Blue got slowly and stiffly to his feet. "That's true," he said. "I once scared up a fawn on the shore of this lake. It could only have been a few days old. It swam out to the island and made it. I watched."

I looked back up the canyon. Heavy clouds of smoke seemed to pour toward us; the fire was definitely moving our way.

"Let's do it," I said. "We can't just stand here talking. Can you handle it, with your arm?"

"Sure. I grew up on a lake. I could swim out there with one arm, if I had to."

"What about the horses? How should we take them, do you think?"

Our four equines stood quietly, unperturbed. The fire wasn't yet close enough to alarm them. Smoke in the air didn't register as a threat.

"We'll ride the saddle horses and lead the pack horses. We'd better leave the packs and the gear on the beach. Those loads would make it tough on the horses to swim."

"Okay." I started hauling my pack bags toward the lake. "Should we leave the saddles on?" I said over my shoulder.

Blue took hold of one of his own pack bags with his good arm and dragged it after me. "The saddles should be fine," he grunted.

Even as I toted my gear, my mind dithered. Was I doing the right thing here? What was the best choice, for me, for my animals? For Blue, as far as that went. He seemed oddly detached about the danger we were in; I could only assume that the pain in his arm was overriding all other worries.

Try as I might, I could think of no better plan. I knew little or nothing about wildfires and how they behaved. The notion of standing on the beach while flames torched the forest in front of me did not appeal to me one little bit. I had read that big fires sucked up oxygen in incredible ways; I had heard how unpredictable they could be. I knew horses were terrified of fires. I wanted away from this one.

Dragging the rest of my pack gear down to the lake, I asked Blue, "Can you get on your horse?"

"I think so. You might have to help me."

He was towing his second pack bag; I forbore to tell him that I could do it.

When the gear was in a pile on the beach, we went back to

the horses. I could see an occasional flash of orangy flame through the smoke; it scared me.

"Come on," I urged Blue. "Let's go."

The dogs wagged their tails as we untied the horses. They didn't know we were in danger; they thought we were moving on in the normal way.

Let's go, let's go, the words rattled in my brain. Blue stared at Dunny as if the effort of getting on him was too much. How in the hell was he going to swim across the lake if he had to?

I stepped to his side and bent over, lacing my two hands together in a cup. "I'll give you a leg up."

Blue didn't say anything, but obediently lifted his left leg and set his toe into the step I'd created. Like everyone who's spent time with horses, he knew about getting a leg up.

"One, two, three," I said. I lifted, he pulled with his left arm and swung his right leg over Dunny's back. Thank God the gelding stood still. Blue was on, looking a little unsteady, but there.

I handed him Little Witch's lead rope and climbed on Gunner. We both called our dogs and headed off across the beach. I coughed. The smoke grew thicker every moment.

"Have you ever swum your horses before?" Blue asked.

"No. Not these. I used to swim the horse I had when I was a teenager, though. Bareback in the San Lorenzo River."

Blue smiled—a motion that came and went in an instant. "Then you know never to get in front of a swimming horse. They'll try to climb on you."

"Yeah," I said.

"They reach out in front of themselves with their front feet," he went on, "but they don't reach behind. You're perfectly safe right behind your horse. In fact, if he's having trouble swimming, it's best to slip off the back and hang on to his tail."

"Can't all horses swim?" I asked.

"Not necessarily. I had a big palomino gelding when I was

a kid who couldn't. I went camping with some friends by a lake and we all decided to swim our horses. This horse went in just fine; the lake was one of those with a shore that shelved down and then dropped off. This horse stepped off that drop and went straight to the bottom.''

"You're kidding."

"Nope. Down he went all the way underwater. Me, too. The waters just closed over my head; I didn't know what would happen."

"So, what did happen?''

"He went all the way to the bottom and then shot straight up and out of the water, like a dolphin. Then down to the bottom and then straight up again. It was a wild ride, I can tell you.''

"Great. Jeez, I hope neither one of my horses do that.''

Blue laughed. "They probably won't. I never knew another one that did. Just don't let go of your horse, whatever you do. Because if you're swimming out there and he sees you, he's going to figure you're something he could stand on.''

"Great.''

We were on the shore now. Fire behind us, water before us. I looked back over my shoulder. Smoke was gray everywhere. A fine dusting of ash covered my arms and Gunner's mane. I coughed again.

Digging into my saddlebag, I found the gun and got it out. "Heel,'' I said firmly to Roey. Then I looked at Blue. "Are you ready?''

"I'm ready.'' He tipped his fedora down a little further over his eyes.

I clucked to Gunner and kicked his ribs and he stepped into the lake. He waded to his knees with no resistance, Plumber following. Roey followed Plumber, looking nervous.

Gunner moved forward; my boots were in the water. It was cold, damn cold. We were committed now.

Deeper and deeper. Icy water over my thighs. I could feel the horse begin to grow weightless, to float. Water to my waist, water all around me. I held the gun over my head with my left hand and clung to Gunner's mane and the reins with my right. I barely felt the cold, so much adrenaline was pumping in me.

Gunner swam; I could feel the long strokes of his legs under me, see his head in front of me, nose determinedly lifted out of the water. I could only guess at his expression.

I looked back. Plumber swam, head up, eyes wide, nostrils flaring. Roey paddled behind him.

Next to me, Blue clung to the swimming Dunny. I looked over my shoulder; Freckles was still on the shore, dashing back and forth and uttering frantic yips.

"Your dog!" I yelled to Blue.

He turned and called. We both watched the little dog race back and forth, back and forth, crying.

"Come on, Freckles. Here, girl," Blue called again, his voice calm.

I looked at the billowing smoke filling the sky and felt anything but calm.

"Will she come?" I asked him.

"She doesn't like to swim. But she'll come."

Once again he called her; I could see her put both front feet in the water, hesitate, and then plunge forward. Then she was swimming, a ways behind us, but following. We were all afloat.

I looked ahead. The island seemed a long way away. But it was clearly visible with its trees and clumps of rocks. I guided Gunner straight toward it, prayed he'd make it.

I looked back at Plumber and Roey. Freckles was just visible, a tiny white dot in the water. Beyond that was the sand of the beach, a pale crescent beneath an angry blanket of roiling smoke. I could see an occasional flash of flame as trees in the little wood beside the lake torched alight.

Once again, I glanced at Blue. His face was steady and impassive, his eyes straight ahead. I couldn't imagine a man who was any calmer under pressure than this one.

The island was closer now, but I thought Gunner was tiring. He seemed to struggle more to keep his nose up; his swimming felt more frantic.

"How does my horse look?" I called anxiously to Blue.

His eyes moved to Gunner. "He's doing okay," he said. "We'll get to the island. Don't worry."

I let my feet slip out of the stirrups and my legs float to the surface, clinging to Gunner by his mane.

"Don't let go," Blue warned.

"I won't."

The island was distinctly closer. We'll make it, I told myself. "Come on, boy," I urged Gunner.

I doubt he heard me. The splashing hooves and the now-audible roar of the fire drowned out all but yells.

"The beach is on the far side," Blue shouted.

I could see only rocks, steep and precipitous, but I obediently steered Gunner to the left, following Blue's lead. In a moment, a small shelving, pebbly bank came into view. Must be what he meant.

Aiming for the so-called beach, I prayed silently that we would make it, we would all be okay. The two dogs still followed, Freckles swimming steadily at the rear.

The beach was close now. Suddenly I could feel Gunner's hooves touching bottom, the lift of his body under me as he picked up his own weight again. I reached my legs down his sides and clung with my knees and calves as he heaved himself out of the water, as anxious to be on solid ground as I was.

I could see Dunny scrambling ashore next to me, the two pack horses following in our wake. I looked back just as Roey made a landing; a minute later Freckles touched ground, looking scared, but all in one piece.

Suddenly Gunner shook himself, a vigorous, rattling motion

197

that made me gasp and grab his mane. I could feel Blue looking at me.

When I met his eyes, he smiled. "I hate it when they do that," he said. "I once fell off a horse when I was a little kid because he shook like that. I've never forgotten."

"Uh-huh." I said it absently; I was staring back at the fire. The little forest by the meadow was alight and burning, by the look of it. It was hard to tell because of the smoke.

I turned back to Blue. He was slowly lowering himself off Dunny, protecting his right arm as much as possible. Despite the pain he was undoubtedly in, not to mention our current predicament, his face remained detached. I was beginning to wonder if there was anything that could rattle this guy.

Dismounting, I looked around for a place to tie my horses. Choices were few. Half a dozen small pines formed a grove near the pebbly beach. Beside them was a fire ring—which looked as if it had only been used once or twice. As for feed, there were enough scrubby tufts of grass to give each horse a few mouthfuls, that was it.

Thanking God they'd filled up this morning, I tied Gunner and Plumber to the pines and walked over to a large rock that faced back toward the beach and our former campsite.

I sat down, soaking wet and beginning to shiver. Smoke filled the air, thick and smoggy as L.A. on a bad day. I couldn't even see the mountains that ringed the lake. All the beauty of the Sierras disappeared in an ugly haze.

Roey sat down next to me and I hugged her wet body to my side, feeling forlorn.

Oppressive and ominous, the smoke made me claustrophobic, even though I supposed we were perfectly safe here. But I was trapped, stuck on an island in the middle of Benson Lake, a long day's ride from any help.

Not for the first time, I wondered what in the hell I was doing here. Smoke seemed to press down on me like a gigantic hand. Life had never seemed grimmer. Some vacation.

TWENTY-THREE

Blue came and sat beside me. Seeming to guess at my thoughts, he put his good arm around my shoulders. "We'll be okay," he said.

"Will we?" I knew I sounded pathetic.

"Sure we will. We'll spend the night out here. By tomorrow that fire will have spent itself. The meadow's too wet to burn anyway. We'll swim back across, let the horses eat, and have a look around, see what's what."

"See what's what?" I asked him.

He turned his head away. "Find the best route out, I guess," he said noncommittally.

"What do you mean?"

He looked back at me for a long second, as if weighing what to say.

"What are you thinking?" I demanded.

More silence on Blue's part.

"Come on."

"Do you think this fire just happened by accident?" he said at last.

I gazed at the shore of Benson Lake, almost hidden now by a heavy curtain of smoke.

"Do you think it was set deliberately?" I asked him.

"I wonder. It's too early in the year and we're too high up for a fire to be very likely. There hasn't been any lightning. If it was a runaway campfire, where were they camped? There aren't any good campsites in that canyon."

"Oh."

More silence while I took this in, wondering how it all fit into the complex and disjointed sequence of current events.

"You think whoever shot at us and booby-trapped the trail tracked us here and set that fire, hoping to kill us," I said at last. "You think whoever it is is after us specifically. Or you. Or me specifically."

Blue considered this statement. "Yes, I guess I do. That fire is just too unlikely."

"I see." He still had his arm around me, and I leaned into him as the breeze riffled sharply across the lake, causing me to shiver. "Do you have any ideas who's after us, or which one of us they're after?"

Silence again. I waited. I was learning that this man didn't care for ill-considered replies.

"No, I guess not," he said finally.

"You're wondering about something, though."

"Well, it's also a question of who *could* have done it. Who's in the mountains right now. Who has a reason to know where either one of us is."

"Dan Jacobi," I said. "But why?"

I could feel his body shrug. "I don't know. Like you said, he's not going to kill me over a horse."

"And he's got no reason at all to kill me."

We were both quiet. I stared through the smoke haze glumly.

This whole deal was a miserable, surreal farce. What possible reason could Dan Jacobi have to stalk either one of us through the mountains?

And then I remembered the dead man in Deadman Meadow. Once again, he'd slipped my mind, a seemingly unimportant detail in this cascade of unlikely catastrophes. But surely he was the wild card—the unexplained and unexpected event that might have precipitated the chain. But how and why?

I looked over at Blue's remote face. I was growing used to his expression—reserved, aloof, still. It no longer connoted un-friendliness to me. But I still wasn't sure where I was permitted to tread.

"Bill Evans killed himself the night before you rode in," I said. "Maybe that was the trigger." I hesitated. "Ted said you used to live with Bill's wife."

Silence and smoke in the air. I coughed. Blue let his arm drop from around me. I could feel my shirt drying rapidly in the breeze.

"Is there anything about Bill Evans or his ex that could be causing . . . all this?" I waved a hand at the smoke-filled sky.

As I expected, a long pause. Then, "I wouldn't know what it would be."

"Whatever happened to her? Ted said her name, but I can't remember it."

"Katie." Blue smiled quietly. "Ted spent a little time with her, too. I bet he didn't mention that."

"No. He sure didn't."

"Katie was on the rebound, I guess. She wanted away from Bill and his drinking. I should have known better. I ran into her up at Crazy Horse Creek—it must be three summers ago. She was a pretty thing."

"Ted told me she lived with you awhile and then went back to Bill," I said diffidently.

More quiet. I was beginning to think Blue wouldn't reply to

this sally when he seemed to rouse himself. "She left me; I don't think she stayed with me longer than six months. She got bored of me, I guess. I don't make a lot of money, unlike her veterinarian husband. I couldn't keep her entertained."

"So she went back to Bill."

"I don't think she had any idea where else to go. She left him again pretty fast. And that time she spent a little while with Ted."

"You're right about Ted not mentioning that." But somehow I wasn't surprised. If Katie was "a pretty thing," it would have been like Ted to try and get her into bed.

"Did Bill Evans know about Katie and Ted?" I asked Blue.

"He must have. Everybody knew. But by all accounts, he didn't hold it against Ted the way he did against me. I didn't know the man, but a couple of guys told me he'd threatened to come kill me."

Well. If Bill Evans were only alive, we'd have a motive. But he wasn't. Once again, I wondered what Bill and Ted had really had words about the night before Bill shot himself. Had they talked about Katie? Was that why Ted had been so anxious to know what Bill had said to me?

Or . . . and then a very bad thought struck me. I held it in my mind, turning it this way and that, almost afraid to speak it out loud.

The silence grew and Blue turned his head to face me. "What are you thinking?" he asked.

I still didn't want to say it.

"Come on. We need to pool our resources here."

I stared at his face, but I wasn't seeing him. "I heard that Ted threw Bill out of the bar the night before Bill shot himself," I said. "And Ted was really anxious to find out what Bill said to me before he died. What if . . ." I could hardly bring myself to say it. It was ridiculous, I told myself.

"Go on," Blue said.

"What if they were fighting about Katie? What if . . ." Another thought, more fantastic than the last, struck me. "Whatever happened to Katie?" I asked him.

"I don't know. She disappeared. I never heard where she went to."

"She just disappeared, huh?"

Blue stared at me. "What are you thinking?" he said again.

"I don't like to say it," I told him. "It sounds ridiculous and I can't believe it myself."

"Go ahead."

I coughed and brushed ashes off my arm. "It's just that Ted was so anxious to know what Bill said."

"Wait a minute," Blue interrupted. "What do you mean, 'what Bill said'?"

"Oh. I guess you don't know. I found Bill Evans out in Deadman Meadow. He'd shot himself in the chest, but he was still alive. He told me he wanted to die . . . stuff like that. By the time Lonny and Ted and the rest of them got there, he was unconscious, and he died on the way to the hospital."

"So you're the only one who knows what he said."

We looked at each other.

"Yeah," I said. "And Ted was really anxious to find out what it was. And he'd gotten in a fight with Bill the night before. I keep wondering if it could be possible that they fought about Katie, say. And," I looked over at him, "I know this sounds unbelievable, but what if Ted shot Bill?"

"Why would he?"

"Over Katie."

"But she's long gone."

"I know. Where did she go? What if Ted, say, killed her, for reasons that we don't know, and Bill found out about it. Maybe Bill threatened to turn Ted in."

Blue took this all in and shook his head. "Then why didn't Bill Evans tell you that Ted shot him?"

"I don't know. Covering up for some reason. But the thing is," I looked at Blue again, "Ted's in the mountains, too. Right now."

"He is?"

"Yes, he is. Dan Jacobi told me. Looking for a crippled mule. At least that's what he said. But there's a way that Ted, unlike Dan, could know which way I'm going. Lonny knew, and I'm sure he would have told Ted if Ted asked."

Blue looked out over the lake and appeared to ponder.

I watched him and another thought came. Insidious as smoke, doubt crept into my mind once again. The motive I'd assigned to Ted could be Blue's motive, too. What if Blue had killed Katie, and killed Bill Evans because he found out? Suddenly I did not want to be stuck on this island with this man.

I stood and he looked up at me. His eyes, for all their stillness, had an earnest quality to them, reminding me of a young boy anxious to do the right thing. I simply had a hard time thinking evil of him.

And again, I told myself, why would Bill Evans cover up for Blue Winter, or for that matter, for Ted Reiter or anyone else? Knowing he was dying, or believing so, anyway, why on earth would he shield his murderer? It didn't make sense.

Surely Bill Evans had shot himself, just as he said. I only wished I knew why. I had the stubborn conviction that his suicide and my current predicament were somehow connected, but I sure as hell didn't know how.

"I'm going to unsaddle the horses," I told Blue.

"All right."

He remained seated as I took the gear off the saddle horses and turned Dunny loose. I left the others tied up, more out of a disinclination to deal with the confusion of four loose horses in such a small space than for any other reason.

"I'll let them all loose one at a time, so they can have a bite and get a drink," I offered.

"That's fine." Blue remained seated, staring in the direction of the beach, not that the beach was visible anymore. Heavy smoke obscured everything but the lake immediately surrounding us. Fortunately we were far enough away from the fire that no large sparks carried our way. Just a steady dusting of ash.

I began gathering firewood, more out of a need for something to do than any real reason. By my reckoning it was now mid-afternoon. If we were spending the night here, we might as well have a fire.

We wouldn't be having much to eat. I had a few more granola bars and some hard candy in my saddlebags. That was it. That and the gun, my veterinary and medical kits, my rain gear, my map, a water bottle, and one EZ Boot. I wondered what Blue had in his.

What else did I have? In my pockets were the waterproof container of matches, my knife, and the little flashlight, which probably wouldn't work after its soaking. Camp was going to be pretty sparse tonight.

Blue still sat and stared; I had no idea what was going through his mind. Belatedly it occurred to me that his arm might be starting to ache again; the shot would be wearing off. I had hoped we would get out today. At this rate, I would run out of shots to give him.

"How about a codeine tablet?" I asked him.

"I think I'd rather have a drink." He turned his head my way and smiled.

"Sounds good. Where are we gonna get it?"

"Out of my saddlebags."

I walked over and picked them up and brought them to him. He fished a tequila bottle out of the right-hand bag with his good arm.

"Tequila?" I said.

"My favorite. Care for a drink?" He produced a lime and a salt shaker out of the saddlebag.

I laughed. "Not yet. You go right ahead." I hesitated. The island was small enough that privacy would be difficult. "I'd like to get these wet jeans off and hang them up so they dry before dark, if you don't mind."

"I don't mind at all." Blue tipped the tequila bottle back and took a long swallow.

"Okay." It was easier to say than do, though. I felt uncomfortable undressing in front of a stranger. But my heavy jeans were damp and clammy. What the hell.

I walked around a rock, sat down and took off my boots, then stepped out of my jeans. My underwear was more discreet than most bikinis, I told myself. Plain red cotton underwear— no lace, no thong.

Draping my jeans, long-sleeved shirt, and socks over a rock to dry, I walked down to the shore of the island wearing my tank top and panties. I sat on a log and wrapped my arms around my knees. Blue could see me from where he was, but at least I wasn't right in his face.

I stared out at the pall of smoke and thought about the things we'd said. Nothing really connected, and yet I sensed the connection was there, somewhere.

Two hours later, the sun was starting to lower itself toward the western ridge, and I was no closer to an answer. I'd turned each horse loose to pick at grass for a while and get a drink, then tied them each back up. The pickings were pretty slim on this little rock outcropping. The horses would be hungry in the morning.

Us, too. My jeans and shirt were reasonably dry and I put them back on. Dug around in my saddlebags for the last couple of granola bars.

Blue lay on his back, head propped on the seat of his saddle, hat tipped over his eyes. I had no idea how much tequila he'd consumed.

"Hungry?" I asked.

"A little." He didn't move.

"We've got a couple of granola bars."

"Oh boy."

"Better than nothing. Did you save any tequila for me?"

"Yes, ma'am, I sure did." Blue pushed his hat back and sat up, very slowly and stiffly. "How about another shot of that torbu stuff?" he asked.

"We've got three more left," I said.

"I'd better have one."

"Okay." I got the syringe and torbugesic out of my saddle-bags and filled the shot. Blue rolled his sleeve back.

Once again I took hold of his forearm and felt for the vein. His skin was freckled with red-gold flecks. My eyes moved to his face. Mustache, eyelashes—all that fiery shade.

Blue raised his eyes to meet my gaze as I injected the shot. For a long moment we stared at each other. What in the world did I look like, I wondered. Best not to think about it.

Once again I saw the tiny relaxation of Blue's facial muscles, the curve of his mouth into the start of a smile. Torbugesic was doing its job.

"Thanks, Florence," Blue said.

"Any time. Feel better?"

"Yes, ma'am. How about we get a fire going before the sun goes down and then I'll make you a drink before dinner."

"Before my granola bar, you mean." I smiled at him.

"Right." Blue got to his feet and smiled back down at me. "Let's build a fire," he said.

TWENTY-FOUR

I put everything on hold. All my suspicions, all my ideas, all my worries. I didn't think about them. Instead, I drank tequila.

I will admit that initially the thought crossed my mind: Is this wise? But it went away after a couple of shots. As if we had made an agreement, Blue and I tacitly avoided all mention of the fire, of Bill Evans, of saboteurs and snipers. We talked of horses and dogs and our lives back in Santa Cruz County.

The fire flickered; darkness hid the smoky sky. Orange glows along the shore of Benson Lake marked smoldering trees. Our dogs lay close to us, and we all moved closer to the campfire as the night grew colder.

I took another small swig of tequila and a squeeze of lime. "So just what do you do for a living?" I asked Blue.

"I'm a greenhouse manager and a plant breeder. I grow roses."

"Roses?" I'm not sure why I was surprised.

"Roses, you know. Old garden roses."

"Really." I stared at the fire. "I like old-fashioned roses."

"I work for Brewer's Roses, in Watsonville," Blue said. "We've got a display garden you can come look at, if you're interested."

"I'll do that." Inwardly I was trying to put it all together, paint a mental picture of the man beside me. He seemed to be such an interesting juxtaposition of contrasts. Team roper, solitary mountain man, plant breeder. I wouldn't have thought it a likely combination, but there you are. Like his hat, which somehow managed to connote both a cowboy hat and a sophisticated fedora straight out of a forties movie, Blue Winter was hard to categorize.

He was quiet now, seeming content to stare at the fire and take occasional sips from the bottle. I liked the way his face looked in the firelight, still and intense at the same time. I liked his strong chin and the shape of his mouth.

Reaching for the bottle, I took another sip. The tequila was going to my head; I could feel it. I wasn't sure I cared. I wanted to touch Blue Winter's skin.

Roey pressed against me and curled up a little more comfortably. I looked down at her and thought of Lonny. Lonny playing with my puppy. What about Lonny?

I should be loyal to Lonny, as Lonny was, I believed, loyal to me. Nothing that had happened, including my frustration with Lonny or this unexpected proximity to Blue, was a good reason for cheating on my boyfriend.

Even supposing this man had any interest in me. Snap out of it, Gail, I told myself firmly. Quit being an idiot. And no more tequila.

I sat up a little straighter, feeling uncomfortable with myself. I needed to break this strange mood.

"So what's your real name, if you don't mind me asking?" I said.

Blue smiled at the fire. "I don't mind. Robert. When I was a kid, they called me Rob."

"And you got named Blue in Australia."

"That's right. I traveled for a while when I was in my twenties. How about you? Have you done any traveling?"

I shook my head. "No. I'm kind of ashamed to admit it, but I've never been out of California, except for going up to Tahoe. I was born and raised in Santa Cruz County, and my parents died when I was in my last year of high school. I spent my twenties putting myself through college and veterinary school, and then I went into practice."

That was a nice, short, neat summary of my life, I reflected. No pathos, no mention of what a struggle it had all been. No, I hadn't had time or money for traveling. It was only recently that I'd started to feel financially secure.

"So, where do you live?" I asked Blue, wanting to keep the conversation going.

"On the rose farm." He smiled at me. "In a trailer. One of the reasons Katie didn't care for me, I think. It isn't too up-scale."

I took that in. "And you keep your horses there, too?"

"That's right. It suits me," he said quietly. "I'm not ambitious. I don't need a lot of money, or a big house. I like where I live."

It was the most personally revealing statement he'd made yet, and I added another facet to my mental image. No doubt about it, this man interested me.

Too much, I told myself. Too much. I stood up.

"I think it's time for me to get some sleep. I'm going to drag the saddle pads over near the fire. I'll bring you a few."

"Thanks." Blue remained sitting; I was glad he seemed willing to accept my help when it came to small chores. He needed to conserve his strength for the ride out.

I started to lay the pads near the fire; as I walked by Blue he reached up and brushed my arm. "My rain jacket's in my saddlebags," he said. "We could lay it over us for a blanket."

Us? What did he have in mind?

My thought must have shown on my face. Blue smiled at me. "We'll be warmer if we lie next to each other."

"Uh-huh." I got our respective rain gear out of the saddle-bags and brought it over.

Blue patted the pads next to him. "Just lie down here and put the raincoats over us. I'll keep you warm."

I regarded him steadily. "What do you want?" I asked.

"To keep you warm." He met my eyes. "I know you have a boyfriend."

"And you?" I found I really wanted to know the answer to this question.

"No one. I'm a solitary wanderer." He smiled again, but I had the impression the smile concealed some sadness.

I sat on the pads next to him and then lowered myself down on my side. Leaning my head on my hand, I looked at the fire, feeling unsure and uncomfortable. What did I want here?

I could feel him moving, laying raincoats over the two of us with his good arm. "Just relax, Stormy," he said. "I won't bite. Put your head down."

So enjoined, I rested my head on a saddle blanket, which smelled strongly of horse, and closed my eyes. Very gently his hand touched my back, caressing me in long strokes, as one might pet a cat. In another minute he turned, and I felt the warmth of his long, strong back pressed against mine.

"Good night, Stormy," he said.

"Good night."

I wasn't sure if I was disappointed or relieved. Both, I guess. I lay there and listened to Blue Winter breathe and restrained myself forcibly from rolling over and putting my arms around him.

Leave it be, I told myself. If this is meant to happen, it'll happen in its own time, and when it's right.

211

So I lay against his back, with the fire's warmth on my face, and waited. Some time later, I fell asleep.

Waking up wasn't easy. Not just because of the tequila, though I'm sure it was a factor. Dawn was faint in the sky when I opened my eyes. Immediately I shut them again. I didn't want to wake up.

My head hurt, and the day loomed in front of me like an insurmountable mountain. Besides, it was cold. The fire had gone out during the night.

Blue lay on his back next to me, with his good arm thrown across me like a blanket. I snuggled into the warmth of his body, forgetting all possible reservations. At least he was warm.

Still asleep, too, or so it appeared. He breathed gently and quietly and molded his body against mine.

I wondered what the day would bring, and had an even stronger inclination to keep my eyes shut. Why couldn't I just lie here next to this man, content with the feel of his long, strong body and the peaceful sense I had of him?

But my mind, the incessant chatterer, wouldn't let me alone. The horses are hungry, it said. And what about that fire? Who set it; who's out there? And what are you going to do?

Damned if I knew. Maybe Blue had an idea.

"Are you awake?" I asked.

"No." Blue didn't open his eyes or move.

I started to get up, and felt his arm pinning me down. "Just lie here," he said. "Just for a minute."

I subsided, and looked over at him. Slowly, very slowly, he turned his head so we were face to face. Then he opened his eyes and looked into mine.

"I was wondering if you'd care to give me a kiss," he said. "Just one. Just a token."

Despite everything, I had to smile. I leaned toward him so our lips touched; damn, I'd wanted to do this. He kissed me as gently as he'd touched me last night, and yet firmly, too, with a sense of something more, waiting.

When our lips parted, I kissed him again, with longing and curiosity. It felt good.

This time Blue smiled when I moved away. "That was nice," he said.

"Uh-huh." Now is not the time, I told myself. "We'd better get up and get going," I said out loud.

Blue moved slightly and winced. "You'd better give me another shot of that stuff."

I hesitated. "There's only two doses left."

"I know. But if I'm going to get up and get on that horse, I need something. I can always take codeine to keep going. With any luck, we'll get out to Bridgeport today."

"With any luck." I echoed his words. With luck, and no snipers. But I kept that last bit to myself. What was the point of saying it? We both knew.

"So, do you have a plan?" I asked him as I began filling the syringe.

"Sort of." He gazed up at the sky as I injected the shot. "If the smoke's cleared enough, I thought I'd try to get an idea through the binoculars where they're camped."

"You think they're out there, then?"

"Sure. They must wonder what happened to us. That smoke was too thick yesterday for them to see us swim out to the island. At a guess, they're camped at this end of Kerrick Meadow, which is right about there." He pointed a finger in the general direction of the trail that led up the canyon. I could see nothing.

"We really can't get out of here without riding up that canyon," he went on, "and they must know that. What they might not know is that there's a little plateau about halfway up the canyon which will give us a good view of their camp, if they're where I think they are."

213

"Then what?" I asked.

"Then we make a plan. If we're careful, we can get the advantage on them. Or him. Whoever it is."

We were both quiet. "All right," I said. "Do you figure we'll just shoot whoever it is?"

"I don't know," Blue said. "We'll have to see what's what."

"All right." This didn't sound like a hell of a plan to me, but I acknowledged that it was impossible to know what to do until we understood the situation. We would just have to play it by ear.

Slowly, with numb fingers, I began assembling the gear and saddling the horses. Everybody was impatient, moving about, tossing their heads, stomping their feet. They were hungry.

I was clumsy and short-tempered. Gunner stepped away from me for the third time and I whacked him hard with the end of the lead rope. "Dammit, stand still!"

I could feel Blue's eyes on me, but he said nothing.

Eventually the saddles and what little gear we had was aboard the horses. Blue got stiffly to his feet, and with my help, climbed on Dunny. The sun wasn't yet showing over the eastern ridge when we stood facing the cold water of the lake.

Once again I got my pistol out of the saddlebag. Holding it in my left hand, I gripped the reins and a chunk of Gunner's mane in my right. My heart pounded steadily as the horses waded in. I knew how icy it would feel. I was scared and excited and just plain shivering with cold, all at once.

My feet were brushing the surface of the water now; cold wetness crept up my calves and my thighs, which were tingling with shock. I clung to Gunner's mane and fixed my eyes on the white beach. I just had to hang on till we got there.

Gunner was swimming now; I looked back to see Plumber swimming, too, Roey just behind him. Blue and his two horses were afloat, and Freckles, I was glad to see, had gone right in this time. Maybe she was getting used to swimming.

Once again I looked ahead. To the beach, to the eastern ridge, with the sun about to peek over. Some faint smoke haze still hung in the sky, but nothing like yesterday. I looked over at Blue on the swimming Dunny, his hat tipped forward over his eyes. For just a moment, I saw it all as a picture—cowboys, horses, and dogs, swimming a lake at dawn, under a pale, metallic sky. Something out of a Charles Russell painting.

Then it was back to the present. Freezing cold water lapping at my waist and the horse swimming underneath me, the beach still a long ways off.

We would make it, I told myself. We'd all swum across successfully once before.

Slowly, we drew closer to the beach. I could see the meadow clearly now. It looked empty, and the grass was still green, although some of the aspen were scorched. The forest was pretty black.

We probably would have been okay on the beach, I thought. But the island had felt a lot safer. If only I could get out of this frigging icy water, I'd think we made the right choice.

My legs had gone from tingling to numb to a slow, steady ache. I wondered exactly how cold Benson Lake was.

The beach was close now. I could see our packs on the shore. Not burnt, thank God, or disturbed. There would be dry clothes and food in those packs.

What seemed an eternity, but was probably only a minute or so later, the horses scrambled up on the beach. I heaved a deep sigh of relief and climbed off Gunner.

Then it was back to work—unsaddling the horses and turning them loose to graze, unpacking the packs and searching for food and dry clothes. Feeling considerably less shy, I stepped behind a bush and stripped down to my clammy skin, not particularly worried about whether Blue watched or not. I was too damn cold.

215

Dry clothes felt good. I stepped back out into the open to see Blue sitting on a log. His shirt was off, but he still wore his dripping jeans and boots.

Belatedly it occurred to me that he might be having a hard time getting them off.

"Do you need help?" I asked.

"I guess so." He sounded sheepish.

"I can help," I said.

"If you could just help me get my boots off," he said.

"Sure."

I bent to the task for the second time, aware as I did so how silly I must appear. The left boot came free; I set it on the ground and looked up at Blue. He was smiling.

I shook my head at him. "So you like having a valet?"

"I don't mind at all. You make a pretty cute valet."

I smiled. In general, I'm not crazy about being called cute, but somehow when Blue said it, I kind of liked it.

I pulled off the right boot, set it on the ground, and straightened up. "So what's the plan?"

"The plan is, I put on some dry clothes and we walk up the canyon with the binoculars and see who, if anyone, is camped at the end of Kerrick Meadow."

"Should we leave the horses here?"

"I think so. They need to eat, and they're hungry enough not to wander. If you want to string a run line and put the mare on it, we can be sure they'll stay put."

"Okay." I agreed with Blue. Tying Little Witch up would safeguard us against losing the horses in the event something startled them. After spending several days together, our four equines considered themselves a herd, and the geldings would certainly be unwilling to leave the mare.

I strung a picket line and put Little Witch on it, making sure she could reach plenty of grass. By the time I was done, Blue had changed into dry clothes. Like me, he wore nylon and rubber sandals suitable for walking or swimming. I smiled again.

"You don't look much like a cowboy in those," I said.

He glanced down at his feet, which were as long and slender as his hands, and pretty much snow-white. "I don't know," he said. "Cowboys all have white feet."

"True enough."

We grinned at each other companionably. Despite the problems ahead, I had a faintly euphoric feeling—perhaps the successful swim, perhaps just this man's presence.

Blue seemed to feel the same. Swinging his binoculars by the strap, he gestured at the canyon.

"Lead on," he said.

I led. We walked up the trail, out of the meadow, through the blackened forest, avoiding smoldering tree skeletons. The fire was pretty much out, except for the occasional stump. Soon we were clear of the forest and headed up the canyon. Vegetation diminished.

Blue stopped. "Here's where this fire was set." He pointed to various spots. "Here and here and here and here. It looks to me like whoever it was had a hard time getting it going."

"Whoever it was." I said it softly and Blue looked my way. "Come on," I said. "Let's go."

Reaching down, I touched the butt of my gun. It sat in its holster on my belt and made me feel safer. What good it would actually do me if whoever it was appeared, I didn't know, but it sure was better than nothing.

Blue led me off the trail and up a side canyon. We were scrambling through the rocks now, but I felt better as soon as we got off the main trail. Whoever it was would have no reason to be up here.

Up and up we went. My hands and nose were cold, but in

217

general, the exercise was keeping me warm. Shafts of early sunlight lit the granite here and there. Blue picked our way slowly, trying to protect his arm.

Suddenly and without preamble we stepped into a pocket meadow high on the canyon's side. I could see Benson Lake below us in its thimble-like hollow. Blue stopped, took a deep breath, and raised the binoculars to his eyes.

I looked where he pointed them, on the opposite ridge, where the main canyon topped out. I could see a flat spot and some trees, that was it.

For a moment Blue was quiet, staring, his face as unreadable as ever. He adjusted the binoculars, moved them slightly. A more pronounced stillness seemed to come over his features.

''There he is,'' he said quietly.

TWENTY-FIVE

W ho is it?''

"See for yourself." Blue handed me the binoculars.

I looked where he pointed and saw only a blur. Fiddling with the adjustment blurred things more rather than less. Suddenly pine trees swam into focus. I saw a tent. And then I saw a man.

Dan Jacobi. Engaged in the prosaic task of building a fire.

I lowered the binoculars. "Do you really think he did all this?"

"Who else?" Blue said. "I don't believe it's a coincidence he's camped here."

I picked up the binoculars again and scanned. No sign of Steve or Jim. I could see a couple of horses picketed in the meadow. Dan continued to crouch over the fire.

Once again I put the binoculars down. "But why?"

I was trying to put it all together in my mind. The snares along the trail, the shooting, the fire. I could picture blond Steve doing those things. Suddenly it bothered me that I couldn't see Steve.

"Let's get back to the horses," I said.

"All right." Blue seemed as eager as I to see the stock.

We scrambled down the canyon as fast as he could do it, the dogs trotting happily with us. They were glad we'd gone for a walk.

Once we were on the main trail, I kept my eyes open while thoughts sailed in and out of my brain like kites.

"Do we have to ride by them to get out?" I asked Blue.

"Yes. Unless you want to head back toward Crazy Horse Creek. But that's more than three days' ride. And Bridgeport's about eight hours away. But we have to go through Kerrick Meadow."

"What's the trail like on the other side?"

"Right as you come out of the meadow there's a tough spot. It's called The Roughs. It's tricky, but it's short. After that it's all easy riding down Buckeye Canyon to town."

"Are there any really dangerous spots in The Roughs?" I asked him.

"There's a place called Dead Horse Corner. It's not that bad if you stay to the inside. But the rock slopes out and down, and it's slickrock. You can see the bones of a horse or two down below."

"That ought to work," I said.

"What do you mean?" Blue stopped in his tracks.

"Come on," I said. "I'll tell you while I'm packing up to go."

We were in the meadow now; despite my racing heart, I took a moment's comfort in the sight of our placidly grazing horses, their backs shiny in the early sunlight. But I kept moving.

I caught horses and began saddling and packing. Blue helped me as much as he could. And while I packed, I talked.

I told Blue about the snares along the trail to Cherry Creek Canyon, told him in detail this time. Particularly about the slicker.

"Could you," I asked him, "rig a horse-spooker like that?"

"Sure. I used to make snares for rabbits when I was a kid. I know how to carve the trigger."

I nodded in satisfaction. "And we've got a raincoat and some twine."

"So, what do you want to do, Gail?" Blue stared at me, holding a bridle in his good hand.

"Trap them with their own trap," I said. "It looks like they're barely awake; their horses are still out in the meadow. They know we have to ride by them to get out, so they figure they're sitting pretty. They're not afraid of us."

"True enough." Blue sounded puzzled.

"So, let's say we go galloping right through their camp, flat out. We'd catch them by surprise, wouldn't you think?"

"Sure."

"So, what do you think they'd do?"

"Saddle the horses and go after us, I guess," Blue said.

"That's what I think, too. But they'll be a ways behind us. And if we can get up into The Roughs and rig a horse-spooker at Dead Horse Corner, we might catch them by surprise again."

Blue took this in and then grinned. "You want to set them up?"

"That's right. Look at it this way; if they're innocent, they won't chase us, and if they do chase us, they're the ones who've been trying to kill us."

Blue's grin grew wider. "How many bullets do you have left?"

"Four," I said.

"All right."

Neither of us extrapolated on this. The horses were packed and saddled.

"Let's get you on," I told Blue. "We don't have any time to waste. I want to catch them while they're still in the sack."

Once again we went through the ritual of boosting Blue onto

Dunny. Then, pack horses and dogs in tow, we headed out of the meadow.

My heart was really thumping now. Like a rope horse about to make a run, I could feel adrenaline surging into my system. Fight or flight—the old message. Live or die.

I knew that I could be killed. They had shot at us once; they could shoot again. There was no knowing. My heart pounded furiously.

I thought of the horses, and the dogs. We would all have to take our chances. I prayed that we'd survive, that we'd all come out unscathed.

We were out of the meadow now, on rock, climbing the trail that led up the canyon. Blue was in the lead; once again I followed Little Witch's flaxen tail.

On and on, up and up. Past the marker that pointed to Benson Lake, back on the main trail, up toward Kerrick Meadow. Not too far now, by my reckoning.

Blue pulled his horse up at a flat spot. I rode alongside him.

"That's Ranchero Creek," he said, indicating a small, clear stream to our right. "When we round the next bend, we'll be in the lower end of Kerrick Meadow. They're camped to the right of the trail, along the creek, where the meadow narrows."

We both stared at the trail ahead. Innocuous in the morning sunlight, it looked pleasant and inviting. Level trail, leading to a meadow. With an enemy guarding it.

"Should we start moving here, or when we round the corner?" I asked Blue.

"Let's kick the horses up to a trot here," he said in even tones, as though he'd been thinking about it. "That way we'll all have some momentum going. As soon as we round that bend we'll see their camp. Beyond that the trail runs on level ground through the meadow for at least a mile. We can cover the whole thing at the lope. Then there's another mile uphill through forest before we hit The Roughs."

"Okay," I said. "Are you ready?"

"I'm ready."

Both of us clucked to our horses and leaned forward in our saddles. Gunner picked up the trot easily. I dallied the lead rope around the saddle horn and pulled Plumber out of the walk and into the trot.

"Heel," I told Roey, probably unnecessarily. She was following right in Plumber's wake.

The bend was coming up; I clucked again as I saw Dunny and Little Witch break into a lope. The pine trees rushed by me as Gunner picked up the gait.

Then we were around the turn, the meadow ahead of us. My eyes shot to the right. Tents, still quiet. No sign of humans. I kicked Gunner in the ribs.

Hooves pounded, saddles squeaked. We thundered down the trail past the campsite. A horse neighed out in the meadow and Plumber answered shrilly back. A man's voice, loud and surprised, "What the fuck?" Steve's voice.

Motion around the tents, I thought, but I kept my eyes straight ahead. My body rocked to the rhythm of Gunner's long stride; I could feel Plumber galloping alongside, leading like a well-trained dog on a leash.

We were past their camp. More neighs from horses in the meadow. Yells behind us. Then the sharp crack of a shot. I ducked lower over Gunner's neck, my heart pounding.

Gunner galloped on without a check, as did Plumber. I could see Blue and his horses and dog. I looked back over my shoulder. Roey was there.

There was a man standing in front of the tents. Steve. He pointed a pistol at us and shot again. I ducked and hustled my horse, but I knew we were out of pistol range. Thank God, he didn't have a rifle.

In another minute we would be out of sight of their camp. Kerrick Meadow opened up around us, green and sunny. We raced headlong down the trail, horses and dogs and all.

At a guess, Dan and crew would now be scrambling to catch horses and saddle up. We would have at least ten minutes' head start on them. We needed to use it.

Moving at the high lope, Kerrick Meadow sped by. Sharp, silvery, saw-toothed peaks rose on the skyline; we were on the eastern side of the Sierras now, everything steeper and more abrupt. The meadow was a green plateau in a vertically thrusting rock landscape.

Gunner stretched out eagerly underneath me, trying to stay ahead of Plumber. The competitive instinct seems to be bone-deep; horses don't need to be taught to race.

Even though I knew the hunters were behind us somewhere, my heart lifted at the rhythm of the gait and the wind on my face. To be galloping across a sunny mountain meadow in a charging pack of horses and dogs—some atavistic gene, some ancestral hunting instinct, spoke to me in an exhilarating voice.

On we galloped, the trail following the creek, more or less. Level and sandy, it wound in gentle serpentine curves through the grass, leading us toward a forested ridge.

Gradually the land began to rise. We drew closer to the ridge. Gunner was tiring. I could see the damp sweat on his neck, feel his inclination to slow. I let him drop to the trot.

Plumber fell in behind him. Blue looked back and checked Dunny. "We'll be in The Roughs in about a mile," he yelled.

"Let's see if we can cover it at the long trot," I called back.

"All right."

Blue's two horses lined out along the trail; I followed Little Witch. The dogs were staying with us, but their tongues were hanging out.

Trees around us now, but the ground was still sandy. Growing steeper all the time, with occasional rocky outcroppings.

Off to our left, the little creek poured over one such spur, cascading in a white waterfall to a good-sized pool with a beach beside it.

"Wow," I said out loud. Now there was a campsite. I earmarked it for a return journey.

If I survived this one. We kept trotting through the woods; the trail growing progressively steeper. Occasionally I looked back over my shoulder, but there was no one there.

I didn't see how there could be. Even if Dan and crew were willing to ride bareback, which I doubted, they would still have to catch and mount their horses. At the very least, we had to be five minutes ahead of them.

The trail was getting rocky. Over a small ridge and then down into deep forest. Loam and ferns under the trees—a mix of cottonwoods and pines.

The trail crossed the creek, and Blue stopped to let the horses drink. I did the same. Only half a minute, then we tugged their heads up and moved on.

The trail rose rapidly out of the woods, ascending toward a dramatically steep granite ridge. In a minute or two we were on a ledge where the route had clearly been dynamited.

Blue led at the walk. "We're in The Roughs now," he called back over his shoulder.

Up and up, steeper and steeper, rock all around us. My heart, which had slowed down, pounded faster.

I could see a sharp notch above us, looking like the spot where the trail topped the ridge.

"So where's this Dead Horse Corner?" I yelled to Blue.

"Just over the top," he said. "You'll see."

I concentrated on helping Gunner pick his way. This bit of trail was as steep and tricky as any I'd been on yet. The horses seemed to be handling it, though.

We were nearing the notch; I watched Dunny scramble a little as Blue was silhouetted on the skyline. Then they were over, Little Witch following smoothly.

The V-shaped notch was tricky for sure, slanted rock on both sides. Gunner and Plumber negotiated their way up it and we stepped through the gap.

I looked up, for a second, away from the trail, and gasped. Before us, a steep cliff and then a long canyon winding off into the misty distance, into the high desert of Nevada. We had crossed the mountains.

Twenty feet below the pass, Blue pulled his horses off the trail into a small level hollow. I rode alongside him.

"That corner is just ahead," he said. "What I think we need to do is have you hide the horses and the dogs while I set the trap."

"All right," I said.

Blue dismounted awkwardly and tied Dunny and Little Witch to pine trees.

"Just follow the trail," he said briefly. "Be careful and stay to the inside of the bad corner. Not too far, and you'll come to a grove of willows. You could tie your horses and dog in there and then come back for mine."

"All right," I said again. I didn't ask him any questions; there wasn't time. If we were to get this done, I had to trust that we would both do our parts.

I rode Gunner out of the hollow and headed down the trail, Plumber and Roey following me. Sure enough, immediately ahead was a straight drop down to the creek, many feet below. The trail had been blasted into the cliff, and to the inside, where the rock was rough, it looked perfectly safe. But as Blue had said, the trail sloped out and down; I could see how dangerous it would be to get caught on the outside.

Hurry, hurry. The voice in my head said we would run out of time. I hushed it. Tried to sit relaxed in my saddle. Let Gunner and Plumber pick their way over the rock slowly and carefully. Not a footfall slipped. I kept my eyes averted from the drop.

Now we were around the corner, negotiating our way down the slope. Some loose rock, much rough trail. No place for hurrying, though hurry, hurry said my mind.

It seemed like forever until we were in the willow grove. I found a place and tied the horses, got twine from the saddlebags and tied Roey, too. I could hear her whining after me as I jogged back up the trail.

I was gasping for breath as I got back to Dead Horse Corner. Blue's voice came from up above. "I'm getting this thing rigged. I've got the trigger carved now. When you come back, keep your eye on the trail, so you don't trip the trap. And bring the gun back with you."

"All right," I panted.

Clambering up the last stretch, I forced myself to slow to a walk as I approached Blue's horses. Hurry, hurry. They would be coming.

I gave a moment's thought to raising Blue's stirrups to fit me, but rejected the notion. I untied Dunny and climbed on, my feet dangling freely, praying he would be as gentle and trustworthy as he had appeared. Not to mention surefooted.

Leading Little Witch, I called to Freckles, who was lying obediently with the horses. She looked at me doubtfully, but she came.

Off we went, to the incessant ticking of the timer in my head. By my reckoning, they might be here in five more minutes. Hurry, hurry.

I took a deep breath. Purposefully relaxed all my muscles. Tried to send Dunny a positive, confident message. He felt entirely different from Gunner. Taller, wider, and much heavier-moving. Like riding a draft horse.

He picked his way over the rock with the same care, though, and I could feel his intelligence and willingness in his body. We rounded Dead Horse Corner and Freckles looked up toward where I knew Blue was.

227

"Come on, girl," I encouraged her and she followed the horses, looking back over her shoulder.

Now we were going down, drawing closer to the willows. Dunny stumbled once in the scree, bringing my heart rate sky-high, but he recovered and kept going.

I could hear Plumber's shrill nicker as we approached the spot where the horses were tied. I rode Dunny into the willows and found a place near my two horses. Working carefully and methodically, trying not to fumble or waste motion, I tied Dunny and Little Witch up, found another piece of twine in my saddlebag, and tied Freckles. Then I got the gun.

One more glance over the horses and dogs to make sure everybody looked safe, and I was running again, holstered gun clutched in my hand. Hurry, hurry.

Back to Dead Horse Corner. I stopped abruptly. I could see nothing on the trail, but Blue had said to be careful.

In a second I heard his voice. "Come on up here, Gail, I need your help."

"All right."

"Climb up here," he said. "Just to your right. The trip line's about ten feet ahead of you, across the trail. I rigged it with fishing line."

I couldn't see it. Obediently I clambered up a cleft in the rock; in a minute I could see Blue, though he was completely hidden from the trail.

He gestured back over his right shoulder with his chin. "Take that sapling and bend it down to the ground as far as you can."

I could see the sapling he meant. I pulled it downward with all my strength. I could hear the small sounds of Blue working behind me, a muttered "damn."

Then, "All right, you can let go of it—real gently."

I eased the pressure off the tree. It stayed bent. Blue gave a small grunt of satisfaction, then pointed to a flat rock. "If we sit here, we get a good view of the trail. They won't be able to see us." He looked at the gun, still clutched in my left hand. "We'll have the advantage."

"So you think we should shoot them?" I said evenly.

"We can't count on the trap working, and we definitely can't count on it taking out all three of them," Blue said.

"Do you think they'll all come?"

"They might."

I looked at him. "There are four bullets left. I don't shoot all that well. Do you want the pistol?"

"I'm righthanded." Blue said. "You've probably got a better chance. But I'll take it if you want."

Thoughts spun through my brain. Useless, disconnected. I didn't want to kill anyone. It was my gun, my responsibility. I didn't want them to kill me or Blue. I didn't want our horses and dogs abandoned up here.

That last thought decided me. "I'll carry the gun," I said. "But I'm really not a very good shot. And I haven't practiced in years."

"I'll help you." Blue crouched behind the rock and indicated a place for me next to him. "Rest the barrel on this rock so it stays steady," he said. "Sight down it, until you're aiming at the spot by that pine sapling next to the trail. Imagine there's a man there. Aim for the middle of his body. Okay?"

"I don't know," I said.

"It'll be okay. I'll tell you when to fire." Blue's voice was calm.

I was far from calm. My heart thumped steadily and my hands were shaking. I rested the barrel of the pistol on the rock and took a deep breath. Hold it together, Gail.

We waited. Nothing but quiet and the small sounds of the mountains. Wind in the pines, the distant murmur of the creek far below. We're ready, I thought. Blue turned his head sharply.

"I heard a voice," he said.

Ready or not, they were coming.

TWENTY-SIX

I couldn't see them, but I could hear them. Or rather, I could hear Steve.

His light tenor voice, carrying through the rocks to our hiding place. "Those stupid bastards can't be far ahead, Uncle Dan."

Uncle Dan? I wondered for a second if it was a Godfather-like term of respect, or if Steve was really Dan's nephew. Then my mind snapped back to the present.

They were coming up the slope. They would appear in the notch soon.

"What's the plan here?" I whispered to Blue.

He looked over at me. "Take them out, I guess."

We stared at each other.

"We can't count on being able to hide from them, or get away from them," he said quietly. "Just remember what I told you about aiming the gun. I'll tell you when to fire."

I didn't say anything. I simply could not believe the mess I was in. People were hunting us through the mountains, trying to kill us, for no reason that I knew. And I was trying to kill them in return. Believe it or not, Gail, I urged myself, just keep your mind on the job. Focus.

I narrowed my vision to the spot where the trail appeared through the notch. Waited.

Steve's voice again. "Once we get through these rocks, there's a big valley. We'll catch them there. We can move a lot faster than they can with those pack horses."

A low reply. I couldn't hear the words, but I recognized the deeper baritone of Dan Jacobi's voice.

And then Steve appeared in the notch. Riding a sorrel horse, wearing a straw cowboy hat, pistol prominent on his belt. The sorrel slipped and scrambled a little in the V-shaped cleft, and Steve cursed him.

"You dumb son of a bitch. Keep your feet under you." He gave the horse a sharp jab with his spur.

The sorrel lunged forward, slipping again, but managed to stay upright.

"Stupid bastard." Steve jabbed the horse one more time.

Now the big gray gelding was silhouetted in the gap—Dan Jacobi, following Steve. My heart pounded. Steve was coming toward us, toward the trap, toward Dead Horse Corner. On they came, looking ahead, down Buckeye Canyon.

"I can't see them." Steve sounded disappointed.

I could feel Blue's body tense next to me. Almost there. Steve would never see the fishing line.

The sorrel horse took another step. And things started happening so fast I couldn't follow them. With a *woosh*, the pine sapling cut loose and Blue's raincoat flew into the face of the sorrel.

The animal shied violently; his foot came down on the steep, sloping slickrock, he slipped, came up, scrambled, slipped

231

again. Steve yelled, a short, startled bark of anger and fear.

Then the horse was down, his hooves crashing and clashing, fighting for purchase as he slid over the bank.

"Shit!" Steve was off, struggling to get away from the frantic horse, and the horse was going over.

Whump. Whump. Whump.

I gasped at the sound, horrible beyond belief, of the horse's heavy body hitting and falling and hitting and falling again.

"Damn." Dan Jacobi's voice. The gray horse had spooked back and slipped—all this registered in the periphery of my vision—gone down, and got up. Dan Jacob was off, lying on the ground. The gray horse trotted away, going toward our horses, apparently unharmed.

Steve stood, his hand on the butt of his pistol; Dan Jacobi lay by the trail. I could see no sign of Jim.

Steve looked around, his face and body rigid.

"Those bastards," he said furiously to Dan.

Dan said nothing.

Steve was scanning the rocks above the trail. He drew his gun. He walked toward us.

My heart thudded. He understood the horse-spooker trap; he had rigged one himself. He was looking for our hiding place.

The gun trembled as I did. Blue put his left hand over the barrel and looked me in the eye. His lips formed the word. "Wait."

I waited, resting the pistol on the rock, sighting down the barrel, watching Steve walk in our direction.

Closer he came, and closer. I took a deep breath.

Blue's hand moved to my wrist; his eyes cautioned me.

Steve was twenty feet away now, looking up in the rocks. He stared at the sapling.

"You bastards," he said again. And pointed his pistol and fired.

Crack! The shot was aimed in our general direction, but I didn't think he could see us.

He took another step forward and pointed the gun right at us.

"Now," Blue said urgently.

I pulled the trigger.

Ka-boom. The .357 went off in a deep-voiced explosion. Echoes bounced, my hand jerked back. For a second I saw Steve's face—amazed, furious—as the force of the bullet shoved him backward. He fell, rolled, and went over the bank, leaving only the rattle of falling scree behind him.

I looked at Blue. His face registered nothing. He watched the cliff where Steve had disappeared.

I looked over to where Dan Jacobi lay on the ground. He, too, watched the spot where Steve had fallen.

It seemed for a moment that we all held our breath. No noise, nothing. Just the sound of the creek in the canyon.

Dan's face turned in our direction. "I haven't got a gun," he said clearly. "I think my leg's broken."

Blue and I glanced at each other. "What do you think?" I whispered.

"Be careful," he said.

"Put both your hands where I can see them," I called to Dan, training the pistol on his body.

Slowly he raised both empty hands in the air.

"Where's Jim?" I yelled.

"Back in camp."

Once again, Blue and I looked at each other. "Let's go," I said. "Let's get out of here."

He took this in and stood up. Slowly we clambered back down to the trail. I didn't look at the cliff, tried not to think about Steve or the horse. I kept my eyes on Dan, kept the pistol pointed at him.

He lay on the ground, hands raised. He neither moved nor spoke until we stood on the trail.

"Don't leave me here," he said evenly.

I stared at him. By the angle at which it lay, I could see that his leg was broken—a compound fracture, probably. I knew the kind of pain he would be in. His face was quiet; his eyes watched us.

I felt no sympathy for him. I felt no anger either. I felt detached. There he lay in front of me, suffering, and I felt no more pity than a rabbit who is suddenly empowered to kill the bobcat. Let him suffer, I thought.

Dan showed no sign of the pain. His face stayed quiet, composed even. A little tightness in the way he held his mouth, that was all.

He met my eyes. "Help me," he said.

"Why?" I pointed the gun at his face. "Why did you do all this?"

For a long moment those hard, dark eyes looked right at the end of the gun. "I can show you," he said at last.

His hand moved and my own hand jerked in response.

"I don't have a gun," he said again, holding still. "I want to get something out of my pocket."

I stared at him. "If you pull a gun, I will kill you," I said steadily.

"I know that. I don't have a gun. Can I show you?"

I wavered. What in the hell? "Move very slow," I warned him.

His hand went slowly to the pocket of his shirt. He unbuttoned the flap, reached in, fumbled a minute, brought his hand out, fist closed.

"See," he said. And he opened his hand.

For a moment I didn't understand what I was seeing. Small, shiny pieces of glass, little clear stones that glittered in the sunlight. I peered forward, keeping the pistol on Dan's face.

They were jewels, I realized. Loose, not set. Cut, faceted gemstones, clear and shiny, green in color. Emeralds? If they were emeralds, they looked strangely pale and washed out, there in the palm of Dan's hand, in the clear, pure Sierra sunlight. Like chips of glass, lacking any of the green fire in their hearts that the word emerald brings to mind.

"Green fire," I said out loud.

"That's right." Dan looked mildly pleased. "I knew you'd see it, sooner or later. One way or another."

My mind was adding things now, coming up with a new equation. "Green fire in their bellies," I said. "That's what Bill Evans meant."

Dan nodded ever so slightly. I looked over at Blue, who was watching us silently.

"That's what all this was about. I heard Bill Evans say 'green fire in their bellies.' I never thought twice about it. I thought he was talking about colic. But he meant horses with smuggled emeralds in their guts. That's why they colicked, probably."

"That's right," Dan Jacobi said. "We brought Peruvian Pasos in from South America. Juan used a balling gun to give them the emeralds down at the other end. Sometimes they colicked; a couple of them died. Bill was my vet. He knew all about what we were doing; it was impossible to hide it from him when he was dealing with the colicked horses. I gave him a cut, but he was never happy about it."

"When he said 'green fire,' he meant the smuggled emeralds," I said again, still taking it all in.

Dan watched me quietly.

"But I had no idea what it meant," I said. "I never would have guessed."

Dan nodded slightly. "In the end you would have repeated it to someone, though. And 'green fire' has a real specific meaning to anyone in the trade. Those cops were already asking me questions about my relationship with Bill. They've been trying to catch me for years.''

"They knew you were smuggling emeralds?''

For a brief second Dan almost smiled. "Nah. They thought I was smuggling cocaine. Every time I'd bring in a load of horses from South America they were worried. They even brought their sniffing dogs out to my place once. But there wasn't anything to sniff. These don't smell.'' He rolled the stones in his palm.

I stared at the shiny bits. "You didn't smuggle cocaine?'' I asked him, curious despite everything.

"Nah,'' he said again. "I don't like the business. And I don't care for the people you have to deal with. These,'' he rolled the jewels again, "you deal with a different bunch. A better class of crooks.'' His lips twitched.

I stared at him. "You were crazy to try to kill me,'' I said at last. "It was an off chance that I'd ever repeat that phrase or anyone would ever understand what it meant. You're in a lot worse trouble now.''

"You're right.'' For a second Dan glanced at the cliff. "Steve convinced me we could get rid of you and no one would ever know. Just a minor problem solved.''

"That rockfall,'' my mind was jumping back, "that was what he tried first, didn't he?''

Dan wouldn't meet my eyes. "I just wanted to talk to you, find out how much you knew,'' he said finally. "I got Ted to take me to your camp. But I made the mistake of telling Steve. He's worked for me since he was a kid. He's my sister's son. She never could deal with him. He knew all about the jewel business; he handled the horses at this end and got a cut. He wanted to get rid of you.''

Dan looked into my face again. "I'm not a killer,'' he said. "I'm a horse trader. And I'm not above smuggling a few emeralds. But I've never killed anyone in my life. Steve just left camp one morning and said he was going to take care of my problem. I let him go.''

236

"You knew," I said. "You knew what he meant to do."

"Maybe," he conceded. "But I didn't ask him. When he didn't get it done the first time, he got more determined. And when he came back the second time, he said we had to kill both of you because you would figure out who was after you."

"So you set the fire." I said.

"Steve did." Dan shook his head, almost imperceptibly.

"You could have stopped him." Suddenly I was angry. I turned toward Blue. "Let's go," I said. "Let the son of a bitch lie."

"Take me with you." Dan said it quietly; it was as close to begging as he would get.

I ignored him and spoke to Blue. "We can't. We'd never get him on a horse with that leg. And I don't trust him."

Blue looked at Dan, then at me. "What do you want to do?" he asked me.

"Leave him here. We'll send the paramedics, and the sheriffs, after him when we get to Bridgeport."

Blue watched Dan, who stared at us, saying nothing. "Let's give him a shot of that stuff," Blue said.

"We've only got one shot left. Don't you think you might want it?"

Blue twitched his right shoulder and winced. "Give it to him. I'll take a codeine. Give him what's left of the codeine, too."

I was quiet. I looked at Blue, then looked at Dan. A dozen thoughts came into my mind. I looked at Blue again. "All right. If that's what you want. I'll go get the stuff. You hold the gun on him. I don't trust him."

When I returned, Blue was leaning against a rock, the pistol idly pointed in Dan's direction. Both men were quiet.

I approached Dan, holding the syringe in my hand. "Keep the gun on him," I said to Blue.

To Dan I said, "If you do one thing that even vaguely alarms me I will tell him to shoot you. Believe me. You owe this painkiller to Blue, not me."

237

Dan nodded slightly. He set the handful of emeralds on the ground beside him. "Take these," he said.

I felt slightly sick. The pale green stones gleamed against the rough gray granite. Little bits of glass—oddly out of place.

"I don't want them," I said. "You?" I looked at Blue.

"Not me."

"Give me your arm," I told Dan. I injected the shot as quickly and competently as I knew how, closing my mind to everything but doing a job. "Keep your emeralds," I said when I was done.

He picked one up and looked at it. "Pretty things," he said. "Must be the gypsy in me. Steve was like that, too. He loved them."

Automatically, it seemed, we all looked at the cliff. I didn't want to think about it.

I tossed the codeine vial at Dan. "Keep what's left of these. Codeine," I said briefly. I set a water bottle on the ground near him. "We'll send the paramedics after you. Just remember one thing. I am going to tell the sheriffs in Bridgeport every single thing you told me as soon as we get there. There isn't going to be any reason to go after me anymore. The cops will know everything I know."

"I understand." Dan showed no more sign of the relief of his pain than he had of the pain itself.

"All right?" I asked Blue.

Without a word, he turned and walked down the trail, pistol in his good hand.

We untied the dogs and the horses, and I helped him on Dunny, stowing the pistol back in my saddlebag. For a second we both looked in the direction where Dan lay.

"It's all right," Blue said. "Come on. Let's go."

I turned toward the man on the lion-colored horse and followed him, not looking back.

TWENTY-SEVEN

We rode into Bridgeport that day. Through The Roughs and down Buckeye Canyon, right to the main street of the little town. Bridgeport sits where the sharp spires of the eastern Sierra Nevada meet the plains of the high desert, as dramatically beautiful a spot as you'll find. It seemed surreal to be there on such strange business.

It was surreal enough just to be in the midst of civilization again. We clopped down the road in the late afternoon, and I stared at houses and cars as if I'd never seen them before.

Blue guided us to the Bridgeport Inn, which actually had a hitching rail in its dirt parking lot. We tied the horses up, and the dogs. The four horses stood quietly, heads down, close to each other, back feet cocked. The dogs lay down, side by side.

Blue looked at me and caught my weary expression. He smiled. "Can I buy you a drink?" he said.

"I guess so." I gave him a weak smile in return, thinking of investigations, and probably, inquests.

We walked toward the Bridgeport Inn; I stumbled, climbing

the wooden steps, and Blue took my elbow with his one good arm.

So it ended. In a bar in Bridgeport, appropriately enough. Blue Winter and I sat side by side on bar stools in the Bridgeport Inn, having called sheriffs, paramedics . . . et cetera. They were coming, they said; we would wait.

I stared at our reflections in the mirror behind the bar. My dark brown hair waved in messy rivulets around my dirt-smudged face; Blue's fedora was dusty and limp. Even his red-gold curls looked limp.

The dead man in Deadman Meadow had brought another dead man in his wake. He lay at the bottom of The Roughs, waiting. As Dan Jacobi lay waiting.

As for me, I sat by the side of this tall, red-headed stranger and wondered what I was here for. Perhaps I was waiting, too. Waiting for the change that would unmake my life.

I should call Lonny, I thought. But he seemed distant, unconnected to my present reality. Trouble was, I wasn't even sure what that reality was. Something had shifted during the last few days, and I had a sense that the change was only just beginning. Who knew where it would end?

I met Blue's eyes in the mirror. He looked at me, then down at his margarita. Raising the glass in his left hand, he turned his head and met my eyes directly.

''Here's to you,'' he said.

I raised my own margarita and clinked it gently against his glass. ''Here's to us,'' I said.